CRITICAL ACCLAIM FOR
AMANDA FILIPACCHI'S DEBUT NOVEL

"The voice, language, and style of *Nude Men* has a lilting quality that is at once charming and enticing—[with] a quirky, inquisitive tone . . . Filipacchi is sure to provide delight with [this novel] and those future books that lurk in her head, waiting to be written."　　　　　　　　　　　—Tama Janowitz, *Elle*

"Filipacchi is fearsomely witty. . . . [Read] *Nude Men*, [and] you [will] be swept up in that rare comodity—a truly clever first novel, one that makes *you* feel clever as you read it."　　　　　　　　　　　—Elizabeth Deveraux, *The Village Voice*

"An enchanting fable, a sobering tale of a young person's initiation into an adult reality both alluring and necessarily compromised, *Nude Men* offers the reader the exhilarating pleasure of watching a writer discover herself."
　　　　　　　　　　　—*Chicago Sunday Tribune*

"*Nude Men* is more than a little bit fantastic. . . . Filipacchi's [writing] is truly funny, [and] she has the self-mocking, well-chosen arrows of John Fante; I look forward to more writing with that directness."　　　　—Wendy Gabriel, *Paper*

"Witty and unpredictable to the end, *Nude Men* is a quirky tale of twisted morals."
　　　　　　　　　　　—*Vogue*

"This is one of the most bizarre, challenging novels I've ever read. It's also one of the best. . . . *Nude Men* is, by turns, shocking, funny, moving, perverse and very, very clever."　　　　　　　　　　　—*British New Woman*

"*Nude Men* is everything you don't expect it to be—hilarious, full of plot surprises, and completely original."　　　　　　　—Louis Malle

"Even at its most twisted . . . *Nude Men* somehow has the charm of a fairy tale."
　　　　　　　　　　　—Phoebe Hoban, *New York Magazine*

"With a hint of Angela Carter's magical realism, and the spiraling, freefall feel of *Alice in Wonderland*, *Nude Men* is a peculiar piece of writing from a young, aspiring author. So how come Britain can't produce young writers as fresh and inventive as Amanda Filipacchi?"　　　　　　—*The Face*

"Filipacchi's novel of manners . . . is a sly look at contemporary sexual politics and mores."　　　　　　　　　　—*Vanity Fair*

PENGUIN BOOKS

NUDE MEN

Amanda Filipacchi was born in Paris in 1967 and moved to America when she was seventeen. She went to Hamilton College, and got her M.F.A. from the Columbia Writing Program. This is her first novel. She lives in Manhattan and is working on her next book.

nude

Penguin Books

Amanda Filipacchi

m   e   n

PENGUIN BOOKS
Published by the Penguin Group
Penguin Books USA Inc., 375 Hudson Street, New York, New York 10014, U.S.A.
Penguin Books Ltd, 27 Wrights Lane, London W8 5TZ, England
Penguin Books Australia Ltd, Ringwood, Victoria, Australia
Penguin Books Canada Ltd, 10 Alcorn Avenue, Toronto, Ontario, Canada M4V 3B2
Penguin Books (N.Z.) Ltd, 182–190 Wairau Road, Auckland 10, New Zealand

Penguin Books Ltd, Registered Offices: Harmondsworth, Middlesex, England

First published in the United States of America by Viking Penguin,
a division of Penguin Books USA Inc., 1993
Published in Penguin Books 1994

3   5   7   9   10   8   6   4   2

PUBLISHER'S NOTE

This is a work of fiction. Names, characters, places, and incidents either are the product of the author's imagination or are used fictitiously, and any resemblance to actual persons, living or dead, events, or locales is entirely coincidental.

Grateful acknowledgment is made for permission to reprint excerpts from "Tonight" and "I Feel Pretty" from *West Side Story*, music by Leonard Bernstein, lyrics by Stephen Sondheim. Copyright © 1957 (renewed) Leonard Bernstein and Stephen Sondheim. Jalni Publications, Inc., U.S. and Canada; G. Schirmer, Inc., worldwide print rights and publisher for the rest of the world. International copyright secured. All rights reserved. Used by permission.

THE LIBRARY OF CONGRESS HAS CATALOGUED THE HARDCOVER AS FOLLOWS:
Filipacchi, Amanda.
Nude men/Amanda Filipacchi.
p.   cm.
ISBN 0-670-84785-2 (hc)
ISBN 0 14 01.7892 9 (pbk.)
I. Title.
PS3556.I428N83   1993
813´.54—dc20   92–32338

Printed in the United States of America
Set in Bodoni
Designed by Michael Ian Kaye

For my parents, Sondra and Daniel

O thou, that from eleven to ninety

reign'st in mortal bosoms . . .

—Palamon's speech to Venus,
Two Noble Kinsmen,
attributed to William Shakespeare

acknowledgments

*F*or their advice and enthusiasm, I am very grateful to Sondra Peterson, Nan Graham, Melanie Jackson, and Alice Quinn.

I would also like to thank Courtney Hodell, Giancarlo Bonacina, Hal Fessenden, Edmond Levy, Frederic Tuten, Richard Locke, Robert Towers, Peter J. Smith, Michael Kaye, and all my other friends.

Et surtout Minou.

I am a man without many pleasures in life, a man whose few pleasures are small, but a man whose small pleasures are very important to him. One of them is eating. One reading. Another reading while eating.

I work at *Screen*, a magazine on movies and celebrities, here in Manhattan. For lunch I go to a little coffee shop that is farther away than the other standard lunch places. It is also more expensive, less good, and less exciting, but it has one tremendous advantage. No one I know goes there.

Recently I discovered another coffee shop. It is even farther away, but the lighting is better for my reading. And no one I know goes there even less. Or more. Or whatever. You know what I mean.

This morning was exhausting at work. I sense that I will get one of my headaches this afternoon. I am hungry for food and literature. As I leave the office building for lunch, I try to decide if I have the strength to walk the extra distance to my new, well-lit coffee shop or if I will settle for the closer one with inferior lighting. I opt for light. After such a morning, I deserve to have a perfect, intensely pleasurable meal. On top of it, I want to see very clearly what will happen to Lily Bart in *The House of Mirth*.

The restaurant is called Grandma Julie's, and it's as cozy as its name. I'm sure everyone feels a little embarrassed walking into a place called Grandma anything, but once you're inside . . . the warmth, the neatness, the sheer professionalism, make you forget your shame.

Today the place is full. I ask the waitress how long it will take to get a table. She says two minutes. I wait, thinking my lunch might not be ruined if I truly get a table in two minutes. A woman enters the coffee shop and waits in line behind me. She's in her late thirties and looks perfectly nice, normal. Two minutes later, the waitress tells me there's a table.

The woman behind me touches me and asks, "Are you alone?"

"Yes," I say.

"Would you mind if we shared the table?"

I visualize my lunch spent sitting in front of a stranger. It would be hell. Her eyes would be resting on me while I read. She might even want to talk: "What are you reading? Do you work around here? It's unusually cold today, but they say it'll get warmer by evening. There's so much noise in this place. I asked for tuna salad, not egg salad. I can't eat this, I have high cholesterol."

My first impulse is to mumble, "It doesn't matter," and rush out the door to my old coffee shop.

What I do answer, very distinctly, but with a slight grimace to soften the blow, is "I'd rather not."

The woman and the waitress stare at me with more surprise than I expected. I try to think of a justification for my response and come up with "I . . . *have* to eat alone. But you go ahead if you want." I gesture toward the empty table.

"No, no, you go ahead," she says, touching my arm with more familiarity than I like.

I sit down, making sure my back is turned to the woman I have just rejected so that she won't be able to observe me. She has ruined my lunch. Even though I'm alone, I won't be able to concentrate on my novel because I feel like a villain. I have never done anything like this before in my life. I eat my grilled cheese sandwich, unable to read, furious, not making eye contact with anyone. How dare the woman do that! I order Jell-O to cheer me up.

I glance furtively at the customers around the room. I'm curious to know where the woman ended up. I look at the people seated at the counter. They all have their backs to me except for one, at the end. She is turned in my direction, her legs are crossed, her elbow is resting on the counter, and she is looking at me fixedly, with a slight smile. At first I think she is my rejected woman, but when I look again I see that she clearly is not. This woman is beautiful, sexy, late twenties. She has a very thick upper lip, which gives her a pouting, capricious look, an air I simply adore in women. Like the actress Isabelle Adjani, my fantasy woman.

She seems like the feminine type, the romantic type, the Sleeping Beauty type, blond hair, the type my girlfriend would perversely say looks jaded because she happens to have a charming face and laugh lines on either side of her mouth.

I am not absolutely certain that she is looking at me. I don't have terrifically good eyesight, so although I was able to notice her plump upper lip, I might be mistaken as to where her pupils are directed. She could be staring out the window next to which I am sitting. Or she could be looking at the businessman at the table in front of me, or at the secretary behind me.

I decide to take a risk anyway. I don't know why. It's not like me. Perhaps because after having bluntly rejected a woman for the first time in my life, I need to bluntly accept one too. I gather every ounce of courage in my body and smile at her, sort of unconsciously sticking out my upper lip so we have something in common.

She pays her bill and walks over to me. Her stomach softly hits the edge of my table as she slides into the opposite seat, making my three cubes of green Jell-O jiggle.

I am racking my brain for something to say, when she says, "I like your mouth."

"The feeling is mutual," I answer with a James Bond tone. I am amazed at the good fortune that made her mention my mouth, giving me the opportunity to come up with this ultimately seductive answer, which surpasses any I have ever heard in movies.

To my great chagrin, she seems annoyed by my response. "I didn't mean it that way," she says. "I study people's features, and your mouth is simply aesthetically satisfactory."

"The feeling is mutual," I want to repeat, but don't dare. "Thank you," I say instead.

With my spoon I scoop up a big green cube of Jell-O, but it

jiggles so much from the shaking of my hand that, halfway to my mouth, it plops back down into the dish.

"You should have cut it in two," says the woman. "It's too big."

I try to figure out if there's an erotic insinuation in that comment, but I'm not sure.

"Yes, I should have," I say, and put down my spoon.

For the first time since she sat down, she smiles. She points to the book lying next to my elbow and asks, "What are you reading?"

"*The House of Mirth*."

"Is it good?"

"Yes, it's great. Have you read it?"

She shakes her head and asks, "Do you work around here?"

"Yes, not too far away. Do you?"

"Sort of. What work do you do?" she asks.

"I'm afraid it's not very interesting. I work at *Screen* magazine. I'm a fact checker."

"I know *Screen*. I've bought it a few times. It's a lot of fun."

"Thank you. I guess that's what I should say. What work do *you* do?"

"I'm a painter."

"Ah! How nice. Is your work exhibited anywhere right now?"

"Yes." She pauses. "I work at home."

"That must be the best place for a painter to work," I say, feeling a little confused by her sudden switch of subject. "What type of painting do you do?"

"People. I paint people."

"I love people. I mean, paintings of people. Are they abstract?"

N u d e   M e n

"No. Well, everything is abstract in a way, isn't it? But no, my people are not strictly abstract."

"So, you paint people. That's why you said you study people's features. It's because you paint them."

"Yes, that's why," she says.

"What types of people do you paint?"

"I don't really paint 'types,' unless you call men a type. I paint men."

"What types of men?"

"I don't really paint 'types' of men, unless being naked is a type. Is a naked man a type of man? Some types of men are almost never naked. Then there are the others, who are also a type, the type who are *not* almost never naked. Which type are you?"

I stare at the transparent greenness swaying almost imperceptibly between us. I wonder if there's an erotic insinuation in her question.

"Such a thing is hard to know," I answer. "I never figured it out myself. Is your work exhibited anywhere, or did I ask you that already?"

"My work is exhibited in *Playgirl* magazine. Toward the back of the magazine. I get two pieces shown. Sometimes only one, spread over two pages. My work has been appearing for six years."

I plunge my spoon into a cubical section of my green gelatin dessert and lift it to my mouth. "So, you paint nude men," I say, squishing the sweet greenness between my tongue and palate.

"Yes. And I like your mouth, so I was wondering if . . . you'd like to pose for me."

I grin at her, hoping there's no gelatin stuck between my teeth.

"I'm flattered, but one's mouth is not a very good representation of one's naked body."

"A mouth is a very good representation. There are clues and signs in a mouth. Will you do it?"

She gives me that pouting, capricious look, making her upper lip flare out more than ever. Her resemblance to Isabelle Adjani in *The Story of Adele H.* is striking. I melt. There is nothing I would not do for the owner of that upper lip at this point. I'm usually very shy, but this woman seems like such a good catch for me, and I'm so attracted to her, that I think I will agree to pose for her. At least I can get into her apartment, and then, at the last minute, if I become chicken, I can always change my mind about posing.

"You want me to pose nude for you?" I ask.

"Yes I do. I spotted you from all the way over there, remember?" She points to the counter. "I'll pay you thirty dollars an hour, if it's okay with you. That's the standard price. But if you want more, we can discuss it."

I cringe at her words. I don't want to have a professional relationship with her, just a romantic one. I should have accepted right away, before she brought up money.

"I would love to pose for you," I say.

"I know. I'm glad," she answers. Her voice is soft, and her face delicate and serene. Her hands reach inside her bag.

"When are you available?" she asks, handing me her card.

"Anytime. When are you?"

"How about Saturday at six p.m.?"

"Perfect," I say, delighted at the late hour she chose.

"Could I have your card?"

I jump up in my seat, tap my pockets, and say, "I don't have one with me right now, but here, this'll do just as well, if you don't mind." I write my name, address, and phone number on the paper napkin under my Jell-O dish. I hand her the napkin, which she takes between her thumb and forefinger, pinkie lifted. I think I detect slight snobbery, but I'm not sure.

She reads it aloud: "Mister Jeremy Acidophilus." She added the "mister." She keeps staring at my name on the napkin, looking puzzled, and I know what's coming next. She says, "Acidophilus, as in the yogurt culture?"

Here we go. One of the big dramas of my life. "Yes, the yogurt culture," I reply.

"Is there a story behind that?"

Although the truthful answer would be "None that I know of," I decide instead, perhaps because I'm slightly masochistic, to say: "When my father was a young man, he saw the word on a yogurt container and thought it sounded very intelligent and interesting. He made it his name." This is a lie I made up a few years ago but never had the guts to use on anyone. The most daring thing I ever do, sometimes, when people ask me my name, is to adopt a James Bond tone and reply "Acidophilus. Jeremy Acidophilus." The truth about my name is that there is no anecdote about it, not even a rumor. Some people are named Bazooka, others are named Fender; why should some not be named Acidophilus?

She folds the napkin in four, looking at me with a tiny smile. Mocking? Perhaps. Playful? More likely. She slips the napkin in her purse and gets up, hitting the edge of the table with her stomach again, a little harder this time. The two and a half cubes of gelatin dessert dance in unison.

"Well, Mister Active Yogurt Culture, Mister Friendly Bacteria, it's been a pleasure meeting you," she says, shaking my hand with small, hard fingers that are nevertheless not rough.

She walks toward the door. I don't turn around to watch her go out. I'm not the type to stare at a woman's backside; not that I don't want to, but I'm afraid someone might see me do it. At the last minute, however, I do look back and I see it, just before it disappears behind the door. It's nice, small but not too, with a clearly defined pit, or slit, or whatever you call it, that I can see through the fabric of her skirt. I heard recently that some women undergo cosmetic surgery to have the cheeks of their backside spread farther apart. Supposedly it makes a nicer outline, nicer definition. I can imagine how that might be, though it seems a little too finicky. Anyway, I'm glad to report that my new woman will never need that surgery.

I stare at my two and a half cubes of green with satisfaction. I do not eat them.

That was a very pleasant encounter indeed. I look around the room very bluntly. No meek sweeps of the head, no furtiveness. Large, broad sweeps of the head. Where is my rejected woman? I feel eternally grateful to her. If it hadn't been for her, I would never have felt the need, nor had the courage, to return my new woman's smile. I would have accused my eyesight of fooling me. I would have buried my nose in my book, even held up my book as a shield against the charm of the plump upper lip.

I pay my bill, get up, and look at all the faces as I walk toward the door. I would like to find her, smile and nod my head as I pass her. She is not there. I leave Grandma Julie's. I think I will walk the extra distance in the future. Who knows, I might even share my table with a stranger.

chapter two

I go back to the office, holding my briefcase in one hand and my Jell-O spoon in the other. I would have taken a cube of Jell-O as a souvenir if it had been practical, but it obviously was not, so I decided to steal the spoon. Walking down the street holding that stainless-steel spoon firmly in my hand makes me feel like Dumbo the elephant, clutching his feather and flying.

My magic Jell-O feather carries me straight to a newsstand. I spot *Playgirl* magazine, whip it open to the second-to-last page, and find myself confronted with a pretty painting of a pretty naked man, the type of man I imagine could make me gay if I could be made gay. It is signed by Lady Henrietta. At least she told me the truth about painting nude men. As for what she truly wants to do with me, that is a separate question entirely. It seems that one way or the other, I can only be flattered. If she wants to paint me, I am flattered that she finds me attractive enough. If she just wants to sleep with me, I am even more flattered. I buy the magazine.

As I walk back to the office, I am conscious of my naked body under my clothes. I feel the fabric rubbing against my skin, everywhere. I am aware of general nakedness in the world, of people's bodies rubbing against their clothes. I feel sexy. But then I get frightened by a memory: the memory of what my body looked like, just this morning, in the mirror. Maybe it wasn't so bad. Perhaps the mirror fooled me with an unflattering optical illusion. I want to rip off my clothes, stand in front of a shop window, and examine my reflection to see if I made a mistake by agreeing to pose for the painter of nude men. I do not rip off my clothes. All I do, as I walk, is peek out of the corner of my eye to catch my image in a window. All I catch, reflected in a shoe store, is the shine of my spoon traveling stiffly by my side.

But seriously now, why the hell did this woman come and talk to me? Maybe she's eccentric, a little extravagant. Maybe she picks up strangers off the streets all the time to do God knows what. A madwoman. Maybe she's just bold and unashamed to walk up to prospective models and frankly state her interest. No matter what, the fact is that I am now obsessed with my body, its adequacy or lack of it.

By now you are probably dying to know what I look like. And the moment you find out, you'll start comparing your physical appearance to mine, to judge if you, also, have a chance of one day being accosted by a creature equal in loveliness to the one who approached me at lunch.

Let me spare you the trouble, for now, of having to make these degrading comparisons, and simply tell you that yes, you do have a chance, and no, I am not willing to describe my beauty or lack of it right now, other than to tell you that I'm not fat.

Arriving at my office, I sit at my desk in semidarkness, staring blankly at the fat, round doorknob, and slowly I start puffing out my cheeks, digging my chin into my neck, creating a tiny, puny, double chin, spreading my ten fingers apart, lifting my arms away from my body, opening my thighs, and filling my stomach with air. Oh, and I also lower my eyelids, because the fat around my eyes would prevent me from opening them completely. Now there is good reason for me to be nervous about posing nude.

I debloat: I suck in my cheeks, stretch out my neck, empty my stomach, lower my arms, open my eyes, and close my thighs and fingers. Now there is not good reason for me to be nervous about posing nude.

I bloat up again. Now there is.

I debloat. Now there's not.

Amusing.

Now there is. Now there's not.

I am bold this afternoon. I do things I would not normally dare do, like spin my chair around to my computer and type: "I am *not* fat. If I were fat, there would be a reason for me to be nervous about posing nude. I am *not* fat. I am nottttttttttt."

I stare at my words on the screen without blinking. The lines become blurry. I am in a trance, wallowing in thoughts about Lady Henrietta and about the wonderful fact that I'm not fat. You may be starting to suspect that perhaps I used to be fat.

No. The reason I'm so happy I'm not fat is that I've got to try to be happy about *something*, and I don't have many things to be happy about. I could just as easily be getting excited about the wonderful fact that I am not bald, or that I have two arms.

I am awakened from my daydream by Annie, the twenty-six-year-old editorial assistant, who's married. She says to me, "Charlotte's on the phone."

My girlfriend, Charlotte, calls me every day at work. I told her not to call me. Not every day. Not even every week. It's embarrassing. She does it anyway. Now Annie, and everyone else, knows I have a girlfriend named Charlotte who calls me every day at work.

I pick up the phone and hear her granular, cottage cheese voice. "I was wondering what you'd like for dinner tonight, darling."

"Cottage cheese," I mumble absentmindedly.

"What?"

"Oh! What would I like for dinner? I'll have to work late this evening. And then there's some work I have to do at home. I'm simply exhausted. I don't think I'll be able to see you tonight. You understand, don't you?"

"That's too bad. I was thinking we could have an especially nice evening."

Cottage cheese, cottage cheese.

She's talking about sex. She uses it as a bribe, always, when I'm not enthusiastic about seeing her.

"Oh, now I feel especially sorry that I can't see you," I say. "But we'll do it another night."

"You mean tomorrow night, right?"

"Of course that's what I mean."

"Okay. Goodbye, wooshy mushy."

"Goodbye, twinkle face," I whisper, not wanting Annie to hear me.

"Have good dreams, I'll talk to you later, I love you." She makes a big noisy kiss.

"Me too, me too too."

I hang up the phone and go to my boss, the head researcher, hoping he has some fact checking for me to do.

"No, I don't have anything right now," he says. "But maybe Annie has some filing for you."

Of course, as usual, maybe Annie has some filing for me. I am twenty-nine years old, I am a fact checker, and maybe Annie has some filing for me. A fact checker is what I am. I'm not a filer, I'm not an editorial assistant. I'm a little better than that, which is normal because I paid my dues for many years, I worked my way up. I'm a fact checker, hoping to be a writer. I would like to be a journalist, a writer of magazine articles, an interviewer. The glamorous people I would write articles about would then know me, be my friends, and perhaps even marry me.

Three years ago, when I started my fact checking job at this magazine, I let my superiors know that it would please me greatly to write little articles once in a while. Sure, they said. The only thing they've given me so far is a small, unimportant story on the little boy who played in *Willy Wonka and the Chocolate Factory*. That was a year ago. Since then, nothing. The other fact checkers, and even the editorial assistants, get to write articles all the time. I, on the other hand, file. For hours at a time, I file. They give me mountains of it. Sometimes, when I'm filing, I almost cry. I get tears of rage in my eyes. Why, I wonder, must I do this? Why am I the only one? They know I want to write. How many times must I tell them?

I walk toward Annie and stop in front of her desk. "Hi, Annie. Is there any filing?"

"When there's filing, it's on the file cabinets as usual, Jeremy," she says without looking up.

Condescending! People at work are often condescending to me, especially the lowly editorial assistants. I should not pretend I don't know why, just as I should not pretend I don't know why I don't get articles to write. It's because I am mushy. I am a mushy man. I reek of mushiness and meekness. People at work have always been condescending to me. They talk to me with excessive self-confidence. When they're in a group, talking together, and I pass by, one of them might say very loudly, "Hi, Jeremy!"

"Oh, hi," I answer cheerfully, pretending I am a normal person who did not notice the mocking loudness of the greeting. Then I think that perhaps they mock me because I don't say hi to them often enough.

I try to think of new ways to act, ways that might make people respect me more. For example, one day I came in and talked very loudly to everyone.

I said, "Hi, Annie!" very loudly, and then I went to John, the head researcher, and said, "Hi, John! Do you have fact checking for me today?" Very loudly.

I did not notice any increase in their respect for me.

Another day I tested a new technique, which was to not pretend I liked them, to not pretend I liked my job, and to not pretend I was in a fine mood. I even decided to not hide any anger I might have.

"Hi, Jeremy," Annie said.

"Yeah, hi," I answered. I sat at my desk, took my time, ate a banana, and slowly made my way to the head researcher's office. "I'm here," I said glumly.

"Hi, Jeremy," said the head researcher. "I don't have any fact checking right now, but maybe Annie has some filing for you."

I left his office without answering, went back to my desk, ate another banana, and said to Annie, "Any filing?"

"Yes, actually there's quite a lot of it today. I put it on the file cabinets."

Another time I tested the technique of being extremely nice to everyone.

"Hi, Annie," I said sweetly, happily, tenderly. "How are you?"

"Okay."

"If there's any work you need help with, just tell me and I'll give you a hand."

"No thanks. There's just the filing on the file cabinets."

"Sure, I'll do that, but first I have to go ask John if there's any fact checking he might need help with."

"Hi, John," I said. "How are you today?"

"Fine, thanks, Jeremy."

"I hope you're not too overloaded with work. Is there any fact checking or anything else I can help you with?"

"No, thanks," he answered, not really paying attention because he was working at his computer. "Everything's under control. Ask Annie for some filing."

I am not a mean person. I have never been mean to any of these people. I get a feeling of helplessness, of having tried everything and failed. I get tears of rage. I am exasperated, desperate, bitter. I am a bitter lemon. A mushy bitter lemon. Half-rotten. I want to go to extremes. I want to say things that have never been surpassed in cruelty or offensiveness. I want to revel in the viciousness of it. But I have no viciousness to revel in.

I go to the file cabinets, the monsters. There is a mountain of clipped articles on top. Some articles are only a sentence long, one inch by one inch, so you can imagine how many separate articles can be contained in one small mountain.

The file cabinets consist of thirteen huge drawers, nine of which are filled with celebrity files, two with film and TV show files, one with gossip columns, and one with miscellaneous. In the nine celebrity drawers you get Marilyn Monroe, Sylvester Stallone, Princess Di and children . . . In other words, all actors, all musical groups, and all royalty, some boxers, some directors, and some models, one or two best-selling writers, and Bush and family and Clinton and family.

In the miscellaneous drawer you get tons and tons of un-alphabetized miscellaneous, such as celebrity fragrances, celebrities in the slammer (or at least arrested), births, deaths, marriages, divorces, couples, celebrity causes, deaths while filming, Aspen, Oscars, music awards, Emmys, etc. The files are mostly labeled with my handwriting, because, of course, I am mostly the one who files around here.

I feel strong this afternoon. I feel ready for a few hours of mountain climbing. Even though the mountain of clippings ends way over my head, I feel taller than it. After all, in my pants pocket I have my stainless-steel spoon, which will serve as my stainless-steel mountain-climbing spike and later will become my stainless-steel Dumbo feather, to help me fly off the stinking mountain and into the arms of my painter of nude men.

I take the first small clipping from the top of the mountain. The name of the celebrity is highlighted in yellow for my convenience, so that I don't have to spend one or two extra seconds figuring out who the article is about. Thank you, Annie, or whoever was responsible this time, for the thoughtful gesture. The highlighted name here is Madonna. The *M* drawer is one of the more pleasant ones, at a comfortable height that requires no bending. The Madonna file is large, packed full, messy, over-flowing with clippings. It's hard to squeeze the tiny newcomer in. I manage.

I am happy, happy, happy. Go lucky, go go lucky. Why shouldn't I be? Two hours have passed, and I got fewer paper cuts than usual. Only one per hour. I am now holding an article on Brooke Shields. I read it, as I always do when I come across an article on her. She used to be the most beautiful woman I had ever seen. That's before she gained weight. But *I* haven't gained weight. I'm not fat.

I'm annoyed at myself. It annoys me that everyone, including me, assumes that no one wants to be fat. People take this for granted, which I find offensive and unfair. What counts in life is to have enough energy to work and file. The rest doesn't really matter. Fat, not fat, bald, not bald, old, young, man, woman, fact checker, writer, filer, what does it all matter? In the long run, the differences make no difference. I must remember that. The differences make no difference. That's what I believe, no matter what proof to the contrary you may ever find.

I keep filing, looking at my watch every five minutes. The time passes so slowly. I force myself to stop looking at my watch for what seems like a considerable length of time, hoping I'll get a nice surprise. Forty minutes must have passed. I look, and only fifteen have gone by.

The skin around my nails is raw, bleeding, from my always having to squeeze my fingers into overstuffed files. Good. Good punishment. Punishment for what? I'm not sure. Perhaps just for being myself. Bleed more. Here, squeeze your fingers into Michelle Pfeiffer. She's a tight one. Rip a little more skin off. Good.

At ten minutes to six, I go to the men's room. My hands are

black from the newspaper ink. I need to wash them many times to get all the ink off. The head researcher walks in and enters a stall. When he comes out, I'm still standing there, washing my hands.

He stands at the sink next to mine, washes his hands, and says, "It's all that newsprint, isn't it, Jeremy? It's hard to get off."

chapter *three*

*H*eat. What is heat?
Every day, when I walk home from work, I wonder if there will
be heat in my apartment. Today is no exception. As I walk down
the street, I forget about Lady Henrietta, my naked body, everything except whether I will find symptoms of heat in my apartment. To tell you the truth, I don't really know what to expect
or to look for, because I don't really know what heat is. I have
lived twenty-nine years and never learned exactly what it was.
I must admit I never bothered to look it up in the dictionary,
but really, one would think that by now I would have picked up

scraps of definition here and there. If the heat doesn't come soon, I will take my cat to the vet. I tricked you.

"God, that woman looks like she's in heat," is just about all I've ever heard about heat. I suspect heat has to do with vigorous energy, lust for life. The women referred to with those words seem more alive and happy than us poor folks who don't have our heat. Their eyes twinkle and their hair whips the air. But I might be completely wrong; these characteristics may be purely coincidental.

On my way home, there's a pet store I always look into. I like to check if any of the kittens displayed in the window are more beautiful than my cat, Minou, a blue-cream Persian. None ever is. My cat has long gray fur with a cream throat, and a beautifully mushed-in face.

Today the pet store window is filled exclusively with Himalayans, those vulgar cats who have the Persian's long hair combined with the Siamese's markings. They are so dull, always the same, like clones. Disappointed by the lack of competition, I don't even bother to stop.

I suddenly notice a woman running in my direction, so I start running toward her, because when a woman runs in your direction, there is one chance in a hundred (or a thousand, or a million) that she spotted you from afar, was stunned by your looks, decided then and there that you were the man of her life, and took it into her head to throw herself into your arms. Wouldn't it be a shame not to reciprocate her enthusiasm from the very beginning? I think it would be a shame. So even though today has been a pretty good day, romancewise, and there is no reason for me to be that desperate, I am now running toward the woman out of habit, holding my arms slightly open so that if she is running *to* me, I will be running to her as well, and we will throw ourselves into each other's arms, and it will all be extremely romantic. On the other hand, my arms are not open enough for it to necessarily mean anything or to embarrass me in case she happens to be running to someone behind me, or to no one in particular, which is usually the case. Rather, *always* the case.

At home, Minou is sitting in a corner of the apartment. That's unusual for her; she usually runs to greet me at the door. I hang up my coat, drink some orange juice, go to the bathroom.

How's the weather outside? asks Minou from her corner.

Fine. Why are you sitting in that corner? I ask.

Cause I like it. Did you see any cats more beautiful than I in the pet store window?

No. Only vulgar Himalayans. Are you feeling okay? I've never seen you sit in that corner before, I say, thinking that perhaps this is the first symptom of her heat.

I'm feeling fine. What's that spoon you're holding?

I look at my hand, startled. Before leaving the office, I had taken my spoon out of my pants pocket and held her in my hand all the way home, even while running with open arms toward the running woman, but I had forgotten to put her down when I drank my orange juice and went to the bathroom.

Incidentally, you may be wondering why my cat is talking to me. Let me assure you that our conversation is probably not really taking place. I'm virtually certain that it's only in my head that we're talking, but sometimes I'm more certain than at other times. I realize it does not seem quite normal that I spend so much time conversing with my cat (and I confess that I do indeed spend a lot of time doing it), but I can't help it.

I am able to read all her expressions distinctly, unmistakably. Each of her gestures is translated by me into specific sentences whose subtlest intonation I can make out. Her words ooze out of her every strand of fur so unambiguously that even human beings cannot make themselves so well understood to me. What is most captivating and enslaving is that her language is specific. When she says, I want some heavy cream, I am not unclear as to how, precisely, she expressed herself. She did not say: I would love to have some heavy cream, or: Please, I haven't had heavy cream in a long time. No, she said, I want some heavy cream. She seems to speak to me so clearly that I can't very well not answer her, can I? It would be rude.

I believe that most of the time I don't talk to her out loud. I usually "think" to her, but I must admit I did catch myself a couple of times actually speaking to her in a clear voice, as though to a human friend.

I do try to control myself. Often by not looking at her. But even when my back is turned to her, I can usually still "hear" her. She's a very expressive cat. So magnetic. I suppose that explains it.

I have a feeling she'd stop talking to me if my life ever became satisfactory.

What's that spoon you're holding, Jeremy? repeats Minou.

I had Jell-O for lunch. This is my Jell-O spoon. Aren't you even going to leave your corner to say hello to me?

I said hello.

First of all, no, you did not say hello, you asked me how the weather was. Second of all, I want one of your usual warm welcomes, I say, walking toward her.

No, she says, cringing farther into the corner.

No? I stop a foot away from her.

Please, Jeremy, I do not want to be touched today. I'm not in the mood.

(Could this be her heat?) Nouniou, are you upset about something, I ask her, using one of my many pet names for her, variations of "Minou," which come to me naturally when I feel particularly affectionate toward her: Ninou, Nounou, Niouniou, Nounette, Nouni, Nounina, my Ninoute. I crouch down in front of her.

Ah! Not so close. Move back, she says.

At that moment, the explanation of her behavior comes to me through my nostrils. Oh, Minou. I pick her up, lift her tail, and look at her backside. Her long, beautiful butt hair is covered in poop.

Let me down, she says, wriggling her back legs.

It's the heavy cream I gave you as a treat for breakfast that gave you diarrhea, isn't it?

No, it is not the heavy cream. I like the heavy cream. You must continue giving me the heavy cream. It is fate that gave me diarrhea.

This time I'm going to cut off your butt hair. I keep saying I'll do it, but I never do, and then this always happens.

I don't want you to cut off my butt hair. It'll be embarrassing to have a bald butt.

I won't shave it off, I'll only trim it. It's either that or no more heavy cream.

I *want* the heavy cream.

I know you do.

I feel her tense up, because she knows what comes next: the bath.

Jeremy, she says, I was thinking. Perhaps today we don't need to do what we usually do at this point.

I'm sorry, but we do. Believe me, it pisses me off at least as much as you. It's a total drag.

No, no, no, let me finish. I was thinking that we could just let it dry, and then I'll clean it myself.

No, that's disgusting. I'm not going to let you clean it yourself; you could get sick.

No I couldn't. How do you think animals in nature do it?

Animals in nature do not have long hair like yours. You are not a natural animal, you are an artificial one, created by humans. You have been bred.

She looks at me with a traumatized expression, even though she knew these facts already. I feel sorry for her. To make her feel better, I add, You have pure blood. You are a Persian. I carry her to the bathroom sink.

I am warning you, Jeremy: If you turn on that water I will never forgive you.

Relax. We've done this many times before, and you know it never hurts you.

I am warning you, Jeremy, do not turn on the water. I am warning you, do not—do not—do not . . . Ahhh! she shrieks.

I have just turned on the water.

During the bath, she doesn't say much. She just swears at me occasionally. Her body is stiff and trembling. She hates the blow dryer almost more than the water; I don't know why. The bath and the drying take two hours. Afterward she's much calmer and holds no grudge against me.

She says, Howr war your dar atr wokr?

I've told you a hundred times not to purr while you're talking. I can't understand a word you're saying.

How was your day at work? she repeats.

Interesting.

Tell me aboutr itr, she says, unable to rid herself completely of her purring.

I met a woman at lunch who's a painter. She wants me to pose for her. I'll go see her Saturday. Stop talking now and just purr, please.

She obeys me. I pick her up and press her head against my ear to hear the loud purring, which is so soothing to me. I raise her a little higher and press the side of her stomach against my ear. I hold her this way a long time, drinking in the murmur, absorbing the affection. She smells good too, which is why, when I finally step out of the bathroom, the contrast in smell hits me more forcefully than ever. The smell comes from my disgusting apartment. I usually don't notice its filthiness, out of habit, but right now I do. The odor is floating around the room, probably coming from the rotting, moldy, shriveled-up, empty half melon on a tray on the floor near the TV. There is nothing, in terms of rotting food, that gives as strong a smell as melon. I look at the floor and see that there are also shrunken avocado skins, remainders of frozen dinners, piles of dirty plates, empty yogurt containers, and Kleenexes: used, dirty tissues sprinkled over everything. But nothing quite matches the rotting melon.

My apartment has always been this way. About once a year, I decide to clean everything. It takes me at least a week, and the neatness lasts two weeks at the most. But on the whole I love adding to the messiness. I revel in it. When I want to get to my radiator to turn the heat on or off, I have to walk over piles of magazines, and when I do, I sometimes hear something break under my feet. I don't even bother to look under the magazine to see what it was. Probably a cassette box. Or maybe something more valuable.

I am like this in other aspects of my life as well. Like with my body. I trash my body. I don't do one grain of exercise. Ever. When I go to the supermarket, I walk through the aisles, picking up everything that will make me feel the sickest, make me the ugliest, and kill me the quickest, like bacon, Oreos, eggs, butter, ice cream, potato chips; I rack my brain to come up with even more evil things to buy. And after I have finished gorging myself on the poison, I look under my nails, and I see the brown of the chocolate, the orange of the barbecue-flavored potato chips, and their salt, and their grease, and I think: *Good, now I really feel like a bum.*

Recently I have tried to figure out why I am this way, and I have come up with an answer that seems logical. The answer is that being this way allows me to have the following thoughts: No wonder my life sucks: I am like a bum. No wonder my social life sucks and I barely know anyone. It's because my apartment is too gross for me to invite anyone over. No wonder not too many people like me: I have a white, skinny, unhealthy, flabby body that turns people off. Not only that, but the food I eat is so lacking in nutrition that I never have any energy to do anything, and I'm always blacking out and feeling as though I'm going to faint. Half dead.

The few times I tried to shape up in every way, I became more depressed than ever, because there was no reason anymore for my life to be horrible, and yet it was.

I get undressed and look at myself in the mirror. I'm not the type of man who can look at himself naked in a mirror, be startled, and say, "I haven't looked at myself in so long that my reflection is a shock to me. I hadn't realized that I had grown so old, or fat, or thin, or whatever."

I know very well what I look like, but now I'm looking at myself through *her* eyes, the eyes of the painter of nude men. I look like a worm. Like a louse. Like a . . . What are those worms that crawl on dead bodies? A . . . maggot. Yeah, that's what I look like. Jeremy the maggot. I have a pale, weak, flabby, thin but at the same time chubby body. I'm frightened about posing.

I tell myself to see fat. See fat in the mirror. I see it. Enormous stomach, butt, and thighs, crawling with stretch marks. See fat. You are not fat.

I am of average height, average weight. My eyes are the color of shit. My hair is the color of shit. You know, the average. My face is the most average face in the world. You forget it the moment you see it.

Can work be done in four days on this maggot body of mine? We are Tuesday today. Can an improvement be made by Saturday, 6:00 p.m.? A tan. I could get a tan. I could build muscles. I could go on a diet. I could take steroids. I could . . . That's all I could do. No, there's one more thing. I go to my bedroom.

I have a little ivory elephant, which I keep on my night table in a gray felt pouch. If there's ever something I want very badly, I take out the little white elephant, hold it tight in my hand, and make a wish on it. This may sound retarded, and I agree completely: it is, if you don't know the details.

Unlike normal people, I never got over my childhood obsession with magic. And I have a very good reason for that. When I was eleven, something happened to me that should never happen to children because it can mess up their minds forever.

That summer, at the beach, I found an ivory elephant in the sand. A gold loop stuck out of its back. It was a pendant. I was rather pleased.

I sat on a sandy hill and decided I would test the white elephant for magic powers, something I did about twenty times a day, with any object I happened to come across, perhaps because my mother was not religious and I was not brought up religiously. In fact, I was gently discouraged from getting interested in religion. I recall asking her, when I was nine, whether I could start attending Sunday school with my friends. She answered, "What would you prefer, to attend Sunday school or get a guitar?" I said a guitar, of course, but was a bit disappointed nevertheless. I was never even baptized, but I'm not complaining; I like it that way. However, I suppose most people crave belief in the supernatural in one form or another. Personally, I prefer to believe in little objects rather than in a big blurry thing. It's more original, if nothing else.

Despite their originality, my experiments never worked, so I went about testing the objects mechanically, without any real hope, which is how I proceeded that day, sitting on the sandy hill. I wanted to get this compulsive chore over with, so I held the elephant in my right fist and thought to it halfheartedly: If you are magic, I make a wish that when I put my hand in the sand, there will be a quarter.

I wearily put my left hand in the sand, at my side, and there was a quarter. I raised it to my face and stared at it, while a hurricane of chills coursed through my body. And the thought I kept repeating to myself, was: I *knew* magic existed! I *knew* it. You *see*, I was *right*, I knew it all along.

And then I thought: This is incredible. I will not tell anyone. I will not make another wish right away. I must think, first, what to do, how to go about it. I don't want to ruin it.

I was not able to wait more than ten minutes before making another wish, to test it again. I don't remember what my second wish was, but it did not come true, and neither did any wish after that. I also wished on the quarter, on the chance the elephant had transferred its powers to it. But it had not. For a few months I kept both the quarter and the elephant sacredly, and then I neglected the quarter. I don't know what became of it, but I never lost the elephant. Could you imagine losing such a thing!

So that explains my long-term psychological damage. The coincidence of finding a quarter under the sand on a beach, right where you put your fingers after having made a wish to find one, that coincidence is so enormous, how can it not mess you up?

The result is that after all these years, I still keep my little white elephant on my night table and often make wishes on it before I go to sleep. These elephant wishes never come true, except maybe one in fifty, by coincidence, and those are the easy general wishes. Sometimes I wish on other curious objects that happen to strike my fancy, hoping I might find another source of magic, but those wishes don't come more true than the elephant ones.

Right now, sitting on my bed, I take the elephant out of its gray felt pouch, hold it tight in my fist, close my eyes, and think: If you are magic, I make a wish that Lady Henrietta finds me good-looking when I pose for her. In fact, I want her to find me the most beautiful man she has ever seen, and I want her to fall in love with me, if she hasn't already.

I breathe deeply, squeeze the elephant, and add: Please.

I open my eyes, and methodically put the elephant back in its pouch.

Making wishes on the elephant is emotionally dangerous, because inevitably one's hopes rise abnormally high, unhealthily high, and when the wish does not come true, one's high hopes get crushed more painfully than if one had not asked for the help of supernatural powers. Therefore, one should always try to make the wish casually and forget about it instantly after making it, which is what I try to do now.

I make an appointment in a tanning salon for eight o'clock

that night. In the meantime, I do push-ups, sit-ups, and stretches, and I invent many other types of movements and exercises. People say that God helps those who help themselves. In my case, I suppose I should say the elephant helps those who help themselves. I will make it, I tell myself, while I'm sweating, hurting, pushing myself to the limit and beyond. I have never hurt myself so much. This is a new me, a me who can hurt himself, who can endure any pain to achieve a goal, the goal of love, the love of Lady Henrietta, the painter of nude men. I decide to exercise, diet, and tan every evening until Saturday. I'll even have sex with Charlotte if she wants. It'll be additional exercise.

"**C**an you come for dinner at seven-thirty tonight, honey?" Charlotte asks me on the phone the following day at work.

"No, actually, I can only come later. I have a lot of work to do again tonight. Is nine o'clock okay?" (My tanning session is scheduled for seven-thirty.)

"Well, if that's the earliest, I guess it's okay. Please wear a tie."

"Why?"

"Because you know how much I like it."

"And you know how much I hate it."

"Just this once. Tonight is special."

"Why?"

"It's a surprise."

"Aren't you going to ask me what I want for dinner?" I am hoping she isn't planning a rich meal that will ruin my diet.

"No."

"Why not?"

"Because tonight is a surprise."

"I can't eat anything heavy. I've been having stomach trouble recently. One of your light, healthy dinners would be just fine."

"Oh." She sounds disappointed. "Well, this won't be too extravagant."

Before leaving my apartment to go to Charlotte's, after my exercises and tanning session, I remember that she wanted me to wear a tie. I stand at the door, hesitating. I hate the fact that she likes ties and imposes her taste on me. It just reinforces the side of her personality that I can't bear. If she likes ties, she should get involved with a banker or a lawyer. No, I will not put on a tie. It pisses me off too much.

Charlotte's table is set for two. There are lit candles and flowers in the middle.

"It looks nice," I say, as always, when I enter her apartment.

She is wearing light makeup, which makes her features stand out in a pleasant way. She sort of has a tree-trunk figure. Her waist doesn't curve in very much, and her breasts don't curve out very much, but it could be worse. She could be fat. *I* could be fat. I am not fat.

She is wearing a proper green dress that falls exactly one inch below her knees, pearls, and sensible shoes: pumps with a one-inch heel.

Charlotte has the peculiar habit of never looking up. She always holds her head bent down and peeks up at you from under her eyebrows. Perhaps she does this to give herself a femme fatale look, the look of a seductress, or perhaps one day something fell in her eye when she looked up. I don't know. I just know that I tested her once to see how extreme this quirk of hers was. I asked her to look up at the clouds, and she didn't. I asked her a second time, and she changed the subject. I never asked her why she has this habit, because honestly I don't really care. Nothing concerning Charlotte interests me very much. Nevertheless, it's a useful quirk to know and to keep in mind, for if I ever need to hide something from her, I will nail it to the ceiling.

Charlotte greets me with a smile, but when she sees my absent tie, her smile fades.

"You're not wearing a tie," she says.

"No, I didn't feel like it. Sorry. Maybe next time."

"But I asked you to," she nags.

"I really didn't feel like it. I've had a tough day. Please don't make a big deal about it."

"I had a tough day too, you know? But I made the effort to arrange a great evening. I made myself look nice. All I asked of you was to come eat my meal, enjoy the candlelight, and wear a tie. I didn't even ask you to stop on your way here to buy anything to contribute to the meal. Okay, forget it, let's pretend this didn't happen. Let's pretend you're wearing a tie. Would you like something to drink?" she asks, like a perfect hostess.

"No, thanks," I say.

"Oh, now you're mad."

"Nope."

She goes to the stove and says, "How was your day at the office, honey?"

I lie on my back on her bed, letting my legs dangle over the edge. "I spent the whole day filing. All seven hours."

"What a shame. Isn't there anything you can do about that?"

"I got nine paper cuts."

"Oh, sweetheart. I hope you disinfected them well. I have some rubbing alcohol in the bathroom closet above the sink. You should go and clean the cuts. Better safe than sorry," she says, turning the chicken over.

"It's okay," I say.

"Is there anything new in the celebrity world?" she asks.

I think for a moment. "Andy Rooney is in big trouble. He made a racist comment or something. I filed that one about twenty times."

"What else?"

I think some more. "Princess Stephanie had a fight with her dad about her bodyguard boyfriend. I forget his name. I filed that one only five times. The stolen shoes of Marla Maples I filed about twenty-five times. The new Brady Bunch show I must have filed fifteen times. The Liz Taylor party thirty times. The—"

"Do you want capers on the chicken or not?" interrupts Charlotte.

"Yes," I answer absently. I stare at the ceiling, thinking about my filing, and tears come to my eyes. I could talk to Charlotte about it. I could ask her what she thinks I could do or say at work that would make them stop giving me filing. Charlotte's a psychologist. But she's mushy, like I am. She's cottage cheese, I remind myself. She would give me a cottage cheese answer. I don't say anything. I am too depressed, too lonely. I make myself think of Lady Henrietta, the painter of nude men. Even thinking of her and of our meeting Saturday doesn't cheer me up anymore. I'm afraid, nervous, and anxious. Why did I agree to pose for her? It'll just bring me humiliation, probably even terrible embarrassment. Perhaps—I realize in horror—even rejection. When Lady Henrietta, the painter of nude men, sees me, Jeremy the maggot, naked, she might just totally refuse to paint me and say, "Sorry, I made a mistake. A mouth is not a good representation of a naked body. It does not have clues and signs. Sorry." What will I answer to that? Should I say, "Well, I'll let you paint my mouth if you want"?

I clasp my hand over my eyes.

"Is something wrong?" asks Charlotte.

I yank my hand away, startled. "It's the filing," I lie. "I hate the filing."

"Poor sweetheart. We must talk about that. We must think of something you can tell those monsters who are exploiting you. But right now supper is ready, so why don't you go wash your hands and come sit down like a good little boy."

"Yes, Mommy," I say, to please her.

I go sit down.

"You forgot to wash your hands," she says.

"No I didn't."

"Yes you did. You forgot to go to the bathroom and wash your hands. You got up from the bed and you came straight to the table and sat down. You must be a little dazed from all that filing, Jeremy. Now run along and wash your hands before the chicken gets cold."

"Charlotte, I did not forget to wash my hands. I didn't do it because I didn't feel like it."

"You can't eat without having washed your hands."

"Is that a new thing with you? You never talked about washing hands before."

"That's because I always thought you did it."

"Charlotte, I have a confession to make. I never wash my hands after I go to the bathroom."

She looks at me in silent amazement for a while and then slowly says, "That is totally gross."

"But I wash my hands after I file. Does that make up for it?"

"No. That is totally gross," she repeats.

"To please you, I will go wash my hands."

I get up and wash my hands. I come back and sit down. She is still standing there, staring down at the table.

"What's wrong?" I ask.

"It is totally gross, Jeremy. I'm not sure I'll be able to eat now."

"Relax," I say, tapping her elbow. "A little shit on your hands once in a while isn't the end of the world. It's healthy."

"It's abnormal. I'm worried about you, Jeremy," she says, shaking her head slowly.

"Oh well, let's eat," I say, trying to change the subject. "Come sit down, sweetheart. The chicken's getting cold."

She remains standing, still shaking her head.

"Are you okay?" I ask.

"No, not okay at all. I'm worried about you, Jeremy."

"Why? You think I have a psychological disorder?" I chuckle.

She stops shaking her head and stares at me without answering.

"What?" I say defensively, my mouth full of chicken. "You think I have a psychological disorder? Is that what you think?"

"Yes."

"Because I don't always wash my hands?"

"After going to the bathroom, Jeremy. It's a sign. It means something."

"Would you like me to leave? Perhaps I need to be punished to be cured. Would you like to spank me?" I say, smiling mischievously to relax her.

She looks at me sadly. "No punishment can cure you. You must find the strength within yourself."

"I'll work on it. In the meantime, I'll tell you what. Let's play

[37]   N u d e   M e n

pretend. Let's pretend I'm wearing that nice blue tie you like so much. I must be careful not to drip any grease on it, now mustn't I? And let's pretend I always wash my hands before and after going to the bathroom and that my paper cuts have been disinfected three times with alcohol. I even used the nailbrush. Look," I say, holding out my hands. "You can still see the redness around the nails."

She sits down and starts eating her chicken.

"It's very good," I say.

"Thank you," she replies.

After the chicken, she brings dessert, a big, rich lemon chocolate cake. It's something she hasn't made for me very often, because she says it's very difficult and complicated, but I must say that chocolate cake is the best I have ever eaten.

"Do you want to cut it, or do you want me to cut it?" she asks.

"It looks wonderful, but unfortunately I don't think it would be wise of me to have any of that cake tonight. I'm on a di—I have stomach troubles."

"You're on a diet? If you're on a diet, just say so. You don't have to pretend you're having stomach troubles. There's no reason to be ashamed. We all gain a little weight once in a while. And we must all go on a diet occasionally. Are you on a diet?"

"Yes."

"Well, have some cake and start your diet tomorrow."

"I started it yesterday."

"Make an interruption tonight, since I made this difficult cake just for you. Go back on your diet tomorrow."

"Actually, I do, also, have stomach trouble."

"Are you going to have some cake or not?"

I hesitate, realizing it may make a tremendous scene if I don't have a piece of cake, but then I decide no, I cannot break my commitment to the destruction of the maggot in me.

"I'm afraid I shouldn't," I say.

"Does that mean no?"

"Yes."

"You are so selfish. You ought to have your head examined."

"By you?"

She doesn't answer. We clear the table.

Charlotte rarely wants to have sex. I guess she's simply not a very sexual person. When we do do it, she just lies there stiffly. She must think that's the romantic way to do it, the Snow White-ish way, the feminine way.

So I suppose I'm a sexually frustrated guy. This evening we do not do it, which is just as well because I don't really feel like it anyway. I go home feeling depressed, empty.

That evening, my mother calls me, something she does about once a week. She's seventy-one years old and lives alone in Mount Kisco, in Westchester County. My father was twenty-eight years older than her. He died of old age when I was four. I guess she's lonely. She always asks me when I'm going to visit her. I go see her sometimes on weekends, and I bring my cat. She loves Minou and wants me to come every weekend so she can see us.

Unfortunately, she also enjoys paying me surprise visits in the city, once every couple of months. She says, "There is nothing healthier in the world than having your mother visit you by surprise once in a while."

Her last visit was two weeks ago. It unfolded in the usual manner, as follows:

My buzzer rings. I'm not expecting anybody.

"Who is it?" I ask in the intercom.

"It's me."

I recognize my mother's voice.

"Mom?"

"Yes, Jeremy, it's me."

"What are you doing here?"

"I'm visiting you."

"But you didn't call beforehand."

"You know I prefer it this way."

"I can't let you up. You should have called me. I'm sorry."

"Of course you will let me up. Open the door."

"No, I'm sorry, you should have called. I've told you this before. If you want, I'll come down, and we'll go and have coffee."

Are you kidding yourself, Jeremy? She is not interested in going out for coffee. Five more minutes of begging, and I have no choice but to let her up. Sometimes, while she's still begging downstairs, someone enters or leaves the building. Taking advantage of the open door, she enters and continues the begging in front of my apartment. Either way, I always end up letting her in, to my deep regret, because she lets out a loud scream when she sees the mess in my apartment.

While she climbs up the stairs, I scramble to clean the filthiest things in the room, which almost always turn out to be my cat's old vomited fur balls, lying in dried-out puddles of stomach fluid, like little orange sausages. There are usually about five of them, which I frantically pick up, sometimes even with my bare hands in the rush of it. I invariably miss one, which my mother invariably finds, and although I'm sure she knows exactly what it is, she goes down on her hands and knees, examines it from very close, and says, "What *is* that? It looks sad. Or dead. Is it a mouse? Oh, it must be your cat's poopy. But no, it has no smell." She then crawls over to the moldy, shriveled-up melon shells and shrunken avocado skins and, groaning, says, "Oh my God, I *can't* believe it, it stinks, it smells like the Antichrist. . . ." Etc.

Thank God the last visit happened two weeks ago, which means I should have about six weeks of peace before her next one.

When we talk on the phone, like tonight, she's usually bearable and sticks mainly to asking me when we'll see each other, although she does, naturally, lapse into a few criticisms of me and throws in some dull, nagging questions for free, like: "Have they promoted you yet?" "How's it going with the goody-goody?" (her pet name for Charlotte) "Have you cleaned your apartment?" But these are too negligible to dwell on.

The following day my muscles are hurting like hell. Good. The exercises are finally being felt. The maggot is dying. The Ugly Duckling is turning into a swan. But when I look in the mirror, Jeremy the maggot is still there. It doesn't matter, I tell myself. You may *think* that there are no changes, but that's where you're wrong. There are tremendous changes, changes your untrained eye may not detect but that the expert eye of a painter of nude men cannot fail to notice.

What's this bullshit, Jeremy, what's this bullshit? It doesn't matter. It does not matter. Just do the exercises and don't think.

And then I stop. I suddenly stop. I get a revelation. I realize that there is nothing in the world I can do between now and Saturday that will make a difference. And if I exercise too much I will have a very hard time posing, because my body will be in such pain.

I feel helpless and depressed. That night, I buy potato chips and take my cat to the tiny park near the river, three blocks from my apartment. In the park, I let Minou walk on the ground, on a leash. Then I put her on my lap and just sit there, on a bench. A man, slightly drunk, probably gay, and probably trying to pick me up, says, "Is that a little dog?"

"Yes," I say, not wanting to arouse his interest by saying it's a cat.

"What brand?" he asks.

I know perfectly well he means breed and is too drunk to know it.

"No brand," I say. "He's a street dog. A bastard."

"The best kind," says the man, and walks away.

Saturday afternoon I am taking a shower. It is three o'clock. At six I must be at Lady Henrietta's apartment. My buzzer rings.

"Who is it?" I ask.

"It's Tommy."

A minute later, he's up the stairs, walking through my door. I am dripping wet, with a towel around my waist. I haven't seen Tommy in a month, since before Christmas. He's half American, half French, and he went to spend the holidays with his extremely rich family in France. He's eighteen.

"I had a horrible Christmas" is the first thing he says.

"Why?" I ask.

"My sister is a witch."

"Witch as in bitch or as in fairy?"

"As in bitch."

"That's too bad."

Tommy is one of my only friends. And I wouldn't even call him a real friend, I don't think. We are not equals. He's way above me. I am certain the reason he likes me is that he thinks of me as his little curiosity.

We met in a cheese shop, where he started talking to me for no apparent reason. I was uncomfortable with him from the beginning. I felt he considered my choice of cheese dumb. I thought he was laughing, or snickering. In any case, he was smiling. I asked for some Brie. I said I wanted a piece that was very ripe. I pointed to the piece I wanted. It was plump, with the inside bulging out. And apparently Tommy found something funny in that. He started talking to me, saying this was the best cheese shop in the neighborhood, and such stuff. Then he asked me where I lived. But he's not gay. He's a playboy. Loves girls. Good-looking. He is very conscious of fashion and tries to dress in a manner considered cool, but he wears decorative pins on the crotch of his torn jeans, which is something I don't like. What does he think he has under there?: Something very special? One of the pins has a buffalo on it. Another one has a bicycle under the words "Put some fun between your legs." These little medals are like a crown for his dick.

He collapses on my bed and clasps his hands behind his head. "I like you, Jeremy," he says. "I like you a lot. You're very comfortable."

But he's not gay. He comes and talks to me when he has nothing better to do. He's one of the only people I allow in my repulsive apartment. Even when he makes a comment on the filth, I don't mind, because we come from two different planets, and his rare criticisms of my life have never hurt me.

I sit on a chair, still dripping wet, cold. He finally leaves.

It is 5:55 p.m. I arrive at her building. Her doorman rings her. When I step out of the elevator, the door to her apartment is wide open. I enter. There is no one in the large living room. There is an easel in the middle, with a big blank canvas, and tons of paint beside it. Behind the easel is a couch, covered with many pieces of long, colorful fabric. In a corner of the living room there is another couch, comfortable-looking, made out of parachute material, and next to that another couch, even more comfortable and luxurious, covered in beige suede. There are tables and curtains, thick curtains. The walls are covered with life-size paintings of beautiful nude men. I start getting more nervous, because I'm obviously nowhere near as beautiful as they are. On her coffee table there is a novel: *The Picture of Dorian Gray*, by Oscar Wilde. I've always meant to read it. Under the novel lies a large book of paintings: *Mirage*, by Boris Vallejo. Its cover has a painting of a beautiful naked woman with wings. I flip through the book and see many beautiful naked women. Some have wings, some have tails, some are half snakes, some are riding dragons, some are making love to naked devils, some are making love to naked men, some are making love to other naked women, some are warriors.

"Boris is the painter who has influenced me most," says Lady Henrietta, standing in a doorway.

"I can see the similarities," I say. "You both have a beautiful technique."

"Thank you. I call it the 'more beautiful than life' style."

"Indeed more beautiful than life."

I had almost expected her to come out in a satin dressing gown or something, but no, she's perfectly normally dressed.

"Please sit down," she says.

I sit on the couch, and she goes to the kitchen. She comes back a moment later with herb tea. I drink the tea and sit there, tense, knowing that any minute now I will have to take off my clothes. I am resting my elbow on the arm of the sofa, and I am resting one of my front teeth against the cap of my Bic pen, which I happen to be holding, I don't know why. I took it out of my pocket without thinking. I often do this when I'm tense. The tip of my tooth is lodged inside the little hole at the tip of the cap. The tooth is supporting the weight of my entire head. I guess it relieves tension because of the slight danger involved. The danger is that sometimes the pen slips and stabs your palate. And that's what happens to me now. My pen slips and stabs me right behind my front teeth. Blood is invading my mouth, gushing out. I lick it up and swallow it as quickly as possible. I don't want the blood to spread in front of my teeth and be visible to Lady Henrietta. If she sees my mouth suddenly full of blood, she'll think I'm weird. I make a mental note never to rest my tooth against my pen again.

"Would you please take off your clothes," she says.

Does she mean right now, right here? She gets up, walks over to a corner of the room, and pulls back a curtain, revealing a little changing room, exactly like a fitting room in a clothing store. I'm very nervous, but I don't want to seem like a chicken, so I walk to the fitting room and step inside. She pulls the curtain closed. There is an odd-looking mirror on the wall. It is very wide but very low. I can see myself only from the waist down. I undress. When I see the reflection of my naked stomach, penis, and legs, I want to change my mind. I feel very handicapped and awkward, not being able to see the top half of my body, so I lie down on the floor, on my side, to see myself full length one last time before revealing myself to Lady Henrietta.

"Are you okay in there?" she asks.

I did not realize my foot was sticking out from under the curtain. There is a space between the bottom of the curtain and the floor, and she is looking at me under the curtain, and I am looking at her, and she can see me lying down.

"Why are you on the floor?" she asks, very nicely. "Are you feeling okay?"

"I'm feeling fine," I say, still lapping up the blood and wishing she'd stop watching me. "I was looking at myself in your strange half mirror. Is there any reason why it is so low?"

"I'm sorry if it bothers you. I feel it relaxes men not to look at their top half. The top half is where they can see their anxiety. And it's not just in their face, it's in the position of their shoulders, the way their arms hang. It's bad for the nerves to see your own anxiety."

Well, maybe I'm strange and different from every other man, but personally, I believe it's my bottom half that makes me most nervous.

I decide I have no choice. I can't back out, no matter what.

I'm just about to emerge, when Lady Henrietta says, "Would it make you feel better if another model came and posed next to you?"

"No," I answer, and pull back the curtain.

I don't take my eyes off her as I step out, so I can see her reaction to my naked body. Will she look down? That is the question. Or will she keep her eyes on mine? She does look down, but so casually and rapidly that it makes me feel even less uncomfortable than if she had not looked down at all, which would have suggested she was using all her willpower to resist the temptation of looking at my thingy, which would have brought more attention to it. She acts perfectly normal, makes no strange expression, doesn't even raise an eyebrow, which surprises me a little but is great.

She leads me to the couch behind the easel and asks me to lie down in the most comfortable position I can find. I must say, she looks and acts very professional.

She starts painting, and she makes me talk about my life, and she talks about her life. I am amazed at how comfortable she is able to make me feel. I like her more and more because of it. Next to her is a tray of small marzipan pigs and rabbits, which she nibbles on while she paints. After an hour or so, she puts a big sheet over the canvas and says she is finished for today.

"Can I see it?" I ask.

"No," she answers. "Never until it is completely done and dry."

She tells me that I am a very good model and asks if I would mind coming over and posing again. I eagerly agree. We set a date.

"By the way," I say, "how should I call you? Lady Henrietta, or Henrietta, or Lady?"

"Henrietta is fine. Do you know why I call myself Lady Henrietta?"

"No."

"Have you ever read *The Picture of Dorian Gray*?"

"No."

"Well, you should. It's my bible. There is a character in there, Lord Henry, who is in a certain sense my god. I admire his philosophies of life. I decided to take the liberty of making myself the female version of his character. He is Lord Henry. I am Lady Henrietta."

I leave, on great terms with her and very happy and in love. The next appointment is in five days. The moment I step out of her building I run to the nearest bookstore and buy *The Picture of Dorian Gray*. I read it that evening, and I am puzzled. Lord Henry is not a particularly admirable character. Some might even call him mildly evil: a meek devil. His chief sin is manipulation for the sake of manipulation. I must admit that his ideas about life are amusing in their extreme cynicism, but I don't understand. I did not detect any similarities between Lord Henry and Lady Henrietta. Perhaps similarities will soon surface, in which case I will not be overly disappointed, because the evil in question is rather more like spice than like, let's say, poison or acid.

I suppose my elephant wish did not come true. I suppose I'm not the most beautiful man Henrietta has ever seen. Though maybe I am. She did nothing to indicate that I definitely was not. As for her falling in love with me, there's no way to tell if that part of my wish came true. It probably didn't. I must stay pessimistic, for my own good. Some people might even call it realistic, though that's not nice.

I don't go on a diet, as I did before, and I don't exercise. I think Lady Henrietta is great because she accepts me as I am. For five days, I'm so happy. But there's one thing that puzzles me. I know that no portrait of me could ever be in *Playgirl*. I am simply not good-looking enough. I wonder why she chose me and why she needs a portrait of me. I fantasize that maybe it's for her own pleasure. Maybe it's to keep for herself. But I doubt it.

I am a little ashamed to admit that since posing for Henrietta I have become very confident when I'm around my girlfriend, Charlotte, and neglectful, as though I have power now.

chapter *four*

The day of the second posing
arrives. I buy Lady Henrietta a potted lily of the valley, my
favorite flower. She likes it, smells it, and is very polite and
proper. I realize that I want to ask her out on a date. But I
have to wait a little while to see how things go.

Like the last time, she tells me to lie down in the most comfortable position I can find. She paints me while nibbling on
marzipan lions, and I feel great. I become even more self-
confident, and I continue talking about my life.

After fifteen minutes of posing, Henrietta shouts, "Sara!"

A moment later a tall little girl enters the living room. She has long blond braids and reminds me of a child heroine from a fairy tale, like Alice in Wonderland, or Gretel. She is so pretty, her skin is so flawless, and her features are so perfect, that she looks like a cartoon. She is wearing white knee socks and holding a Barbie doll. I can't quite determine her age. Her body is rather developed and looks inappropriate in her childish clothes, but her face is very young, very little-girlish.

She walks over to Henrietta and stands next to her, looking at me.

"What do you think of my new model?" Henrietta asks the little girl.

"Excellent," says the girl. "Where did you find him?"

"In a coffee shop, eating Jell-O."

"I've never seen a more extreme O.I.M."

"Thank you," says Henrietta. "Jeremy, this is my daughter, Sara. Sara, this is Jeremy."

I want to ask them what is an O.I.M., but due to the terribly awkward situation I'm in right now, my curiosity leaves me as quickly as it came. Sara walks over to me and extends her hand. I am so shocked that this little girl can see me naked, and that Henrietta has a daughter, and that the girl is approaching me, and that she wants me to touch her while I'm naked, that at first I don't move. I feel that any movement on my part would emphasize my nakedness. But the girl doesn't move either. She just stands there with her hand extended, so I finally shake it. I have a lump in my throat, the same sort of lump one gets while watching a sad movie and trying not to cry.

"Sara, I have a little problem here," says Henrietta. "I need your expert opinion. Jeremy is supposedly lying in the most comfortable position he could find, but it doesn't look quite right."

"You're right," says the little girl. "It's totally off. It looks very tight. And he lied to you. He's not in the most comfortable position he could find. In fact, he's not very comfortable at all."

I marvel at her perceptiveness. I am lying in a rather uncomfortable position, and I hadn't bothered to change it.

"Naughty, naughty, Jeremy," says Henrietta, shaking her paintbrush at me. "You are not comfortable. How do you expect me to do good work if you're fooling me? Do something about it, please, Sara."

Sara stands right in front of me and says, "Get up."

I get up. I have never, ever in my life been so conscious of my penis. The greatest wish I have right now is to be castrated and look like a doll, with no sexual organ, just smooth flesh.

Sara puts a pink sheet on the sofa, and then a black sheet, and she tells me to lie on it again, in the most comfortable position I can find. I obey her. She covers one of my legs with a corner of the pink sheet, and she says to her mother, "How's that?"

"You are a genius, my daughter. Thank you. Now run along and get ready for your dancing magic lesson."

"Please," says the girl, "I *really* don't want to go today. *Please*."

"Oh, come on, it's only twice a week."

"That's a *lot*. Don't say 'only.' That is so much a lot."

"But you're always in such a good mood afterward."

"That's because I know I have three entire wonderful days of peace before my next stupid dancing magic lesson."

"No excuses. Come on now," says Henrietta in a high-pitched, nanny, Mary Poppins voice.

Sara leaves, her cheeks and lips red and shiny, shooting dark-blue glances at her mother.

Henrietta says to me, "Sara has exquisite taste. She always

manages to find the perfect position for my models. And she knows precisely what props to use."

"You mean you always let her see naked men?"

"Of course."

"How old is she?"

"Eleven."

I decide to change the subject, not wanting to seem critical of her. We talk of pleasant things. After an hour, she tells me that the painting is finished, or at least that she can finish it without me. She says I can come and see it next Saturday, when it is completely done and dry. I feel sad, afraid that she intends our next meeting to be our last.

Then I remember I wanted to ask her what she's going to do with her painting of me.

"I know I'm not very good-looking," I say. "Why did you choose me?"

She smiles kindly, probably at my modesty, and says, "I have my perfect models, which I use for the magazine, and I have my imperfect models, which I use for artistic reasons. I find that painting imperfect models is a much more interesting and intel-ligent thing to do. It is a way of admitting the defects of life." She stops abruptly and then says, "I'm sorry. I just realized this may have been hurtful to you. I apologize."

"I wasn't hurt at all." This is not true. I was hurt. She chose me as an imperfect model. She chose me to be a representation of the defects of life. I am lying to her because I want her to keep talking, to say all the horrible things that are on her mind, so I'll know from the very beginning what she really thinks of me. I try to act relaxed and cheerful.

"Could I see portraits of your imperfect models?" I ask.

"Sure."

She leads me to the other end of her living room and takes paintings out of enormous cabinets. She leans them against the wall. Some are very funny. They are all much worse than I am, which depresses me.

"Do you think I look as bad as they do?" I ask glumly.

She smiles slightly and says, "No. I'm changing my style, moderating it, using more subtle subjects."

I feel better. I think this is a good time to ask her out. Even though she has a daughter (which doesn't change my feelings for her at all) and may also have a husband, she also may not, so I might as well try my luck. She doesn't *seem* to be living with anyone, but of course one can't be sure.

Before I came over today, I thought a lot about asking her out, so I know exactly what I'm going to say.

"Would you like to go and see a movie with me?" I ask.

"Ah! I'm glad you brought it up," she says. "I wanted to talk to you about that type of thing exactly."

I raise my eyebrows nervously and resist the urge to ask something that might sound stupid, such as "What type of thing?" So I remain quiet. I bet she's going to tell me that she doesn't date her models. Or on the other hand, maybe she feels I took too long to ask her out. In any case, if she accepts my invitation and wants me to choose the movie, I chose one already. It's Spanish, with English subtitles, about a toreador caught in a love triangle. Nice and intellectual. Nice and artsy. It's called *We Are the Taurus*.

She says, "One of the reasons I decided to speak to you that day, in the coffee shop, was that I wanted you to meet a friend of mine. I think you'll like her."

I don't understand what she's talking about. Does she want to match me up with someone other than herself?

"Her name is Laura," she continues. "She's performing to-night at Défense d'y Voir, a little club. We could have dinner there and go to a movie afterward."

"She's a singer or something?" I ask.

"No. A dancing magician."

I frown. "Like Sara's lesson?"

"Yes. Laura is Sara's instructor."

I wish I could ask, "What *is* a dancing magician, by the way?" But I don't allow myself to, because I'm afraid the answer might be too obvious, like: a magician who dances. I wonder if the little scenario that took place earlier between Henrietta and her daughter wasn't arranged solely for my benefit, to pique my curiosity or something, which it did. Maybe it was supposed to make me think: Wow, I am going to meet someone who does what Sara begs her mother not to make her do. It must be something awe-inspiringly unpleasant.

Later, in my apartment, while standing in front of the mirror and getting dressed for the evening, I realize I look just as maggoty as ever. I immediately try to push that negative, grossly inaccurate, grossly exaggerated, paranoiac thought out of my mind. Then I remember that the little girl called me an O.I.M., and I try to guess what those letters stand for: Obviously Imperfect Maggot, Ordinary Inbred Mosquito, Occasional Insect Murderer, Odiously Immortal Man. No, it must be something good, because Henrietta said thank you: Optimally Impressive Mannequin, Outrageously Inspiring Model, Our Incomparable Male, Obediently Indecent Meat. But the girl is the one who said it, and maybe she saw me as a threat: Old Intruding Molester.

I pick up Henrietta that evening at eight. I'm surprised she got so dressed up for me. I'm flattered. It makes me feel very self-confident, and I act a bit more familiar with her.

"You look great," I say.

Défense d'y Voir is an unusual little club, more of a restaurant, really, except that there's an open space among the tables for dancing, and a small stage at the end of the room. Henrietta explains to me that the restaurant's name is a French play on words that means "forbidden to see" or, when spelled differently, "ivory tusk."

Apart from the choices on the menu, it's casual in every way: the prices are reasonable, a few jeans are sprinkled here and there, and there's no coat check. Henrietta tells me that she will pay for us, that she's inviting me. I'm so surprised to hear her telling me this before we even start eating that I don't even bother to object. I'm also slightly mortified, but I force myself to forget about it instantly. The waiter comes to take our order.

Lady Henrietta says, "To begin, I would like the *petite croûte d'escargots et champignons sauvages.*"

I barely know any French, so I read the English translation of what I want: "And I'd like the pigeon salad with couscous and Xérès vinegar."

"And as a main course," says Henrietta, "I would like the *steak tartare pommes frites.*"

I say, "And I'd like the roulade and grilled legs of partridge with leeks on a bed of wild greens."

Lady Henrietta orders red wine for us.

I am curious to know when the dancing magician woman will come out, but I don't ask because I don't want to seem interested in this person, which I'm not. We eat. It is okay. I try to make her talk a little about her life. I don't want to say anything that might jeopardize our relationship or turn her off.

"Are there any other men in your life?" I ask gently.

"There are none," she says, sort of distractedly. This answer makes me so happy.

She's looking at the people around us a lot.

"How old are you?" I ask. Whether she's twenty or forty doesn't make any difference to me. I'm asking her because I want to know as much about her as possible, and I believe in directness.

"Thirty," she says.

"I'm twenty-nine. What about the *past* men in your life?"

"Oh, they were like anyone else's past men."

"Which is?"

"I went out with a few. They lasted a year at the most. It was fun while it lasted."

"Would you like to find a relationship that will last?"

"I'm sure I do."

"What do you mean, you're sure you do? Is that a way of saying you're not sure?"

"One of my traits is that I am usually not sure about anything."

"What about Sara's father?"

"What about him?"

"What became of him?"

"He died."

"Oh, I'm sorry."

I know I probably shouldn't ask "how." But what about "when"? Am I allowed to ask "when"?

"When?" I ask in a small voice.

"Ten years ago."

"I'm very sorry."

"Yeah, me too," she says, and looks around at the people, probably wanting me to drop the subject.

"How did it happen?"

She looks at me. "Flying accident."

"A plane crash?"

"No, hang gliding."

Am I allowed to ask, "Have *you* ever hang glided?" or would that be dragging out the unpleasant subject for too long?

"Have *you* ever hang glided?" I ask.

"No, it was never my cup of tea," she says, pushing the hair out of her face, probably desperate for me to shut up. She looks around at the people more eagerly than ever, and I decide to point it out to her.

"Are you studying subjects for your paintings?" I ask.

"How perceptive," she says, smiling, probably relieved that I dropped the subject. "Recently," she goes on, "I realized more clearly than ever that movement is an excellent thing to study for painting. Especially now, for my new, more moderate paintings. Everything is more subtle, so I have to start observing things that don't seem relevant for painting. Like voice, conversation, and intelligence."

I'm a teeny bit jealous that she looks at other people so much. Obsessively Infatuated Martyr.

"I like optical illusions," she adds.

I can't think of anything else to say, so even though I don't really care about the answer, I ask, "Where is the dancing magician?"

"She should be out soon. She's getting ready. It takes her a long time."

I wonder why she is smiling when she says this. The waiter comes to take our order for dessert.

Henrietta says, "I would like the *poires aux amandes sur une mousse de vin blanc.*"

I say, "I would like the homemade honey ice cream, please."

The background music suddenly stops, and a different music begins. It sounds rather Arabian.

A woman comes out on the stage, carrying a box full of objects. She puts it down in a corner. I guess this is Laura. She has not been announced, but since she starts dancing, it must be her. She is dressed rather normally (for living, that is, not dancing), wearing boots and a loose jacket, no special costume, except for a top hat, which looks out of place with the rest of her outfit. The hat is held on her head by an elastic under her chin, so that it won't fall off when she dances. She's not bad-looking, except that her mouth seems a bit deformed. She twirls and skips and raises her arms. I can tell right away that her dancing is very amateurish: the kind bankers might do, on the spur of the moment, in the privacy of their homes. The magic has not come yet. She bounces, taps her feet. She pulls a flower out of her boot and raises it triumphantly, leading me to believe with disbelief that this flower-out-of-boot business is to be considered a magic trick. I'm bewildered. She does a touch of tap dancing, a touch of belly dancing, a bit of moonwalk, a modest leap, and pulls a small toy rabbit from inside her jacket. Oddly Incompetent Magician. I'm astonished. She skips some more, jumps, spins, kicks up one leg, and takes a big white marble out of her mouth, which explains why her mouth looked deformed. She is much prettier now. She raises the shiny wet marble to the audience victoriously. It's appalling. I try hard not to grimace. She claps her hands, slaps her thighs, swings her arms, pivots on her heels, and from her other boot pulls out a stick, which I think is supposed to be a wand. She waves it wildly, at first like a lasso, then, more appropriately, in the manner of a witch. She turns her back to the audience for a few seconds, doing something we cannot see. She then faces us and (ta-da!), she is wearing glasses. Her grand flourish of a pose leads us to understand that she has just accomplished her fourth magic trick, unless the wand-out-of-boot was supposed to be one, in which case this would be the fifth. It's exhausting, trying to pinpoint her tricks; I must give her credit for that.

Not trusting my own judgment, though, I lean toward Henrietta and whisper, "I don't understand."

"There's nothing to understand," she whispers back.

"It's very unusual. Is she very successful?"

"No."

"Then how does she get hired?"

"Connections, first of all. The club belongs to a friend of her father's. Other than that, the way I see it is that the dancing compensates for the mediocrity of the magic."

"The dancing? But it's as . . . problematic as the magic."

"Well, the magic makes up for the lack of skill in the dancing."

"The overall effect is not unpleasant, though," I lie. "Lack of competence in magic and dance mix quite well."

For the first time, Henrietta laughs rather hard at my wit and looks at me with interest through her squinting eyes. I want to milk my witty idea, so I add, "That's what you have to look at: the whole." This does not make her redouble with laughter, but oh well.

Back onstage, Laura takes a tennis ball from the box, holds it in her hand, slowly turns her back to the audience, and when she faces us again, her hand is held out in front of her, gloriously empty. I feel like hiding under the table with embarrassment for her. She resumes her skipping, shakes her head, wriggles her shoulders, leaps, waves the wand. From the box she takes a little orange hard candy, wrapped in a conventional transparent wrapper. She unwraps the candy, pops it in her mouth, and presents her open empty hands to the audience, letting the wrapper flutter to the floor. It's heartrending. She rocks her head, undulates her hips, flutters her fingers, flaps the sides of her jacket like wings, curves her spine concave and convex, shuffles her feet, meanders, zigzags. She takes off her top hat, pulls out some sort of stuffed animal, raises it with a flourish. Ludicrous. I smile stiffly. She bends her legs, twists and wiggles her body as though she has ants in her pants, shakes her hair, crouches, stands up, and pulls a knife out of her sleeve. I think: Oh, good, maybe she'll do something traditional, like swallow it.

But no, she drops it in the box on the floor. She takes a handful of white powder from the box, vigorously extends her wand, as though casting a magic spell, and throws some of the white powder in the direction of the wand, which thankfully is not aimed at the audience. She casts many rotten powdery magic spells in various directions, like a proud witch. Suddenly, she bows, and all her hair falls forward, and it is rather pretty; she has nice hair.

People clap very softly. To clap with less enthusiasm would not be possible, but I am surprised they are clapping at all. A young man at a neighboring table claps with the tips of his two index fingers, to the amusement of his female companion. The performance lasted ten minutes at the most. Laura, the Obstinately Incompetent Magician, bows again and disappears backstage.

"How long has she been doing this?" I ask.

"A few months. Four or five, I think."

"How does she make a living?"

"Her family is rich. She doesn't do this show for the money, and she doesn't do it to become successful. She does it for the respectability."

"How does she figure she gets respectability from this?"

"It's work. It's more respectable than not working."

"Why did she choose this particular work?" I ask.

"She probably thought of it off the top of her head. She's a very easygoing person."

"Then why does she care about respectability?"

"She doesn't care about it passionately. It's simply more comfortable to be respected than not. She also gives lessons to children, which adds to the respectability, because it's additional work."

Henrietta stops talking, looks above my head, and smiles. I look above my head too. It's Laura. She joins us, and Henrietta makes the introductions. Laura smiles warmly and shakes my hand firmly, to indicate intelligence and strength of character.

"It was good tonight," says Henrietta to Laura.

"Oh, thanks. I was very nervous," replies Laura, glancing at me.

I feel I should say something. "You didn't look nervous," I say.

"Thanks, but I was," she answers, looking modest.

"How was the lesson this afternoon? Was Sara good?" asks Henrietta.

"She's very talented, but I can tell she doesn't practice enough."

Henrietta nods gravely.

Poor Sara. Poor little, little Sara, to have to endure these inane dancing magic lessons. I sympathize with her completely and utterly. *And to have to practice at home!* I can just imagine

Laura's wise words: "One does not take one's wand out of one's boot in that manner. One takes it out in *this* manner. . . . Make sure your back is completely turned to the audience before you put on the glasses. . . . Be sure your pose is very grand and flamboyant after each and every magic trick, or people might not realize you've just done a trick. People are not always very bright, especially when they're eating, so you have to help them understand that they have just been entertained."

Henrietta asks her friend if she has had dinner and whether she wants to order something. Laura says no, thanks, she's not hungry. They start talking about Laura's brother. Laura doesn't seem at all as dumb as her show might suggest. In person, she is extremely normal, and therefore my mind starts to drift, I can't concentrate. Normal people bore me, not because I feel superior but because I don't understand them or what they are saying. They make me feel like a child watching the news; I look at the pictures but think of other things.

I think of Henrietta and of the movie we will go to see soon, and should I do anything while we're watching it, like touch her and/or make astute comments about the editing, dialogue, or plot? No, of course not; I'm just raving in my head right now. I may be socially inept to a certain extent, but I'm not quite *that* bad.

A tall, blond, and extremely good-looking man comes to our table. He could be one of Henrietta's *Playgirl* models.

"Sorry I'm late," he says to Laura. "Did I miss your show?"

"Yes," she says pleasantly. "It doesn't matter."

He kisses both Laura and Henrietta on the cheek. Henrietta says to me, "Jeremy, this is Damon, my ex-model and Laura's brother. I have a *mad* crush on him."

I do have just enough sophistication, finesse, and knowing

what fork to use, to realize that she's joking, or she wouldn't say it right out.

"Damon," she says, "this is Jeremy, my present model."

She does not add that she has a mad crush on me, which means she might. Damon shakes my hand.

They talk, and I go back to watching the news. I blink with intelligence and laugh mechanically when they laugh. I am even able to appear bright and perky every time they address me, and to answer "I don't know" with shrewdness in my tone, astuteness in the pacing of my three words, and wisdom in my eyes.

Movie, movie, movie, I begin chanting in my head, while tears of boredom start running down my mind. Movie, movie, movie. Almost, almost, almost. Soon, soon, soon, soon. Move, move, move, move.

"Let's dance!" says Henrietta. A few people are dancing in the open area between the tables.

I dance with Henrietta. Laura dances with her brother. I spot a dollar bill on the floor, being trampled by people's feet. I point it out to Lady Henrietta. "Do you want to get it?" I scream at her over the music, which has grown louder.

"No, it's okay, but you go ahead," she says.

I shake my head.

I see a thread dangling from my shirt-sleeve button. I pull the thread out completely. The button detaches itself. I put it in my breast pocket. Lady Henrietta is watching me. I smile. Ornamentally Interesting Moron. Outstandingly Intelligent Mute.

We switch partners (not my idea, of course). I feel a little panicked, dancing with Laura. I keep getting the urge to take a Kleenex out of my pocket and raise it triumphantly, to be her worthy dance partner.

Finally, we are about to leave. Henrietta asks Laura if she'd like to join us for the movie. Laura accepts, to my great disappointment. It was supposed to be a private date, at least the movie was. Damon is invited, too, but says he already has plans, and adds, "unfortunately." Henrietta acts very disappointed, and I am suave enough to know she's not sincere; it's all fashionable flattery.

We see *We Are the Taurus*, the film about the toreador caught in the love triangle. I sit in the middle. Overwhelmingly Impressive Matador. Laura's hands are resting calmly on her lap. She's a relaxed, well-balanced person. Henrietta is sitting normally too. Halfway through the movie, I notice that she is not looking at the screen. She's looking at the head of the man sitting in front of her. Toward the end of the movie, she is sitting forward in her seat, looking very closely at his head.

"Are you okay?" I whisper in her ear.

She whispers back to me, "That man is an O.I.M."

"What's an O.I.M.?"

"An Optical Illusion Man."

Wow. So *that's* what I am. I'm an Optical Illusion Man! It sounds almost like the Invisible Man. Almost a superhero! "What does that mean?" I ask.

"It means he's almost something but not quite, or maybe he is and it's impossible to tell if he is or isn't. One second you think he is, and the next you are certain he isn't."

I look closely at the back of the man's head, to see what he almost is or isn't. I feel very intelligent and perceptive, because I notice right away what she means. The man almost has a bald spot. His hair is thinning in the middle of his head. One moment I think he does have the bald spot, and the next moment I think no, no, he definitely doesn't have it yet. It is a strange sensation, and it is the first time I have ever noticed an optical illusion in a person. I suddenly become anxious at the thought of what optical illusion Henrietta sees in me.

The movie ends. I have had trouble focusing my attention on it, as I'm sure you can imagine. Nevertheless, my vague impression makes me pretty confident that my choice is not something to be ashamed of. I believe that *We Are the Taurus* gave Henrietta a favorable opinion of my taste in films. Not much happened in the story, which I am again refined enough to know is always a plus. Additionally, the ending was unhappy, which I know is a *must* (a European trait and therefore excellent): The woman the toreador loved got pierced by the bull's horns, and the woman who loved him stopped loving him once her rival was dead. In his grief at the unfortunate perforation of his beloved (who by the way did not reciprocate his affection), he gave up his superstar career forever.

This ending, although appropriately somber, is, as you can judge, a tad too action-packed, which I can assure you made me glance at Henrietta apprehensively, even though I did have the excuse of never having seen the movie before. Still, insecure as I am, I do feel the need to reassure Henrietta of the soundness of my taste by making her aware that I am aware that the boo-boo in the ending is indeed a boo-boo. So when we get up, I tell her, "Not a bad film, but the ending was a bit much, wasn't it."

"Really? I sort of liked it," she replies, giving me gray hair over the sudden, budding, but thankfully still debatable realization that perhaps my taste is too good for my own good.

She walks over to the O.I.M. and starts talking to him. I am not close to her, so I can't hear what she's saying at first. Becoming indignant, I move closer.

She turns to Laura and me and says, "Good night, you two. Jeremy, I'll see you Saturday."

Ark! She's leaving me alone with Laura! Ark, berk, peu, spl, gerk. "Don't you want me to take you home?" I ask.

"No, thank you. This gentleman will take me home," she says.

The man is looking at her with big watery eyes. And his mouth is wet too, probably with lust.

She gives me an intimate smile and raises her eyebrows, sort of saying: I have just found my next model, I must paint him tonight, please don't spoil my inspiration.

I smile back at her, and she leaves the theater, accompanied by her O.I.M.

I turn to Laura. "Are you taking a cab home?" I ask.

"Yes, I think that's the easiest way."

We walk out. To avoid having to share a cab with her, I won't ask her if we live in the same direction. I hope she won't bring it up, and I hope a cab will be easy to find, so we don't have to make small talk.

As if by magic (the most magical thing of the evening, in fact), a taxi comes immediately and stops in front of us before we even raise our hands. Laura climbs in and is driven away. I hope I never have to see her again. I did not appreciate getting matched up, especially by the very person I am interested in.

When I get home, my cat, Minou, says, What is heat?

I look at her apprehensively, because I recently discovered that heat may have something to do with sex, and I don't know how to go about discussing that subject with my cat.

Where did you learn that word? I ask.

Someplace. What does it mean?

You know very well what it means. Heat is what comes out of the radiator.

Oh, Jeremy, spare me. What does "to be in heat" mean?

In the meantime, my girlfriend, Charlotte, has been saying that she wants to live with me. I don't have the strength or the interest to fight her, so I let her move into my apartment, but I ask her to keep her own apartment in case one of us ever wants a break.

I can imagine Charlotte as being the snoopy type, and I do own a few things that I would not like her to see: my boyhood diary, the *Playgirl* magazine containing Henrietta's painting, and a pair of handcuffs that I bought a while ago because I wanted to be a person who owned a pair of handcuffs. Being such an owner changes one's personality slightly, and for the better, I believe. It makes one more exciting, even if only in the subtlest way. When people see me, I want them to think: Now, this man has the personality of someone who owns a pair of handcuffs. He's an exciting person.

And my self-image changed a bit too. It became: Me, Jeremy, the owner of a pair of handcuffs.

I need to find a good place to hide these three things. After much deliberation, I decide to take advantage of Charlotte's habit of never looking up. I nail my belongings to the bathroom ceiling.

One isn't likely to be lying on one's back in the bathroom, unless one is taking a bath, but in that case the highest level Charlotte would look at is straight ahead at her feet.

The following Saturday I bring the little girl a bunch of white peonies, my second-favorite flower, thinking it will please Lady

Henrietta. It turns out that it pleases the little girl even more. She jumps around my neck gratefully, which makes me uncomfortable because she has seen me naked.

I ask Henrietta what happened with the O.I.M. she brought home the other night. She says she painted him but it's not finished yet, so she can't show it to anyone.

She shows me the painting of myself. I almost laugh at how much she changed me. She made me look like a very effeminate man, lying in a feminine pose. Then I am overcome with a feeling of awe. It is very well painted. It shows me lying on the couch, naked, on pink and black sheets, my arm behind my head, looking at the painter. The painting is full of optical illusions, especially in my expression and the way I hold myself. I look as if I'm almost happy, but I also look as if I'm anxious and very desperate. My body looks comfortable, relaxed, and even self-confident, but at the same time the facial expression indicates a wish for the body to be veiled, and indeed, it almost does seem that a barely perceptible veil covers me entirely, except for the eyes, like a Halloween ghost costume.

"It's very good," I say.

"I know," she says. "It is without doubt the best painting I've ever done. You were the best model."

"Was I an Optical Illusion Man?"

"Yes."

"Your daughter said I am the most extreme O.I.M. she has ever seen. Is that true?"

"Yes. I have never seen a more complete Optical Illusion Man than you."

"How am I an O.I.M.? What is it that I am almost but not quite?"

"You are almost ugly, but not quite. You are almost good-looking, but not quite. There is almost a tire of fat around your waist, but not quite. Your ribs almost stick out too much, but not quite. You almost look like the most stupidly blissful man in the world, but not quite. You almost look like you might commit suicide any second, but not quite."

"Oh, is that all?" I ask.

"Are you being sarcastic?" she says.

"No. Isn't there anything more revealing about my inner self? Less superficial? More meaningful?"

"Oh, you want the *meaningful* ones. In that case, I might as well show you the list I made of the meaningful optical illusions contained in you." She opens a drawer and takes out a white sheet of paper, folded in two. She hands it to me.

The paper contains the following information, written by hand:

Jeremy Acidophilus, Optical Illusion Man

1. He doesn't talk much, but when he talks, it's too much. (Ow. I'm terribly insulted.)
2. He looks weak and unhealthy, and yet if the end of the world ever came, he somehow looks as though he would survive us all, like a cockroach.
3. He looks easily manipulable, but also looks like he could be unexpectedly stubborn.
4. His face is often very pale, and his mouth is big and red, which sometimes makes him look like a vampire, sometimes like a clown, sometimes like an old-fashioned sensitive gentleman, but, surprisingly, never like a homosexual. On other days, his mouth looks much smaller, more normal-sized, and is less red, and his skin

is less white, and one wonders if one imagined his big
red mouth from the previous day or if it really existed.

That is the end of the list, but it was too long for my taste, and I feel as though I have just received four punches in the face.

"When you wrote cockroach, perhaps you meant maggot?" I ask her, not out of bitterness but out of genuine curiosity; my appearance always reminds me so vividly of a maggot that I wonder whether she might not find it a revelation if I mention it to her.

She looks at me, a bit surprised, and says, "No, I meant cockroach." She takes the paper from me and returns it to the drawer.

"Are you an O.I.W.?" I ask.

"I don't know," she says. "Do you think I am?"

I try to think of something she almost is, and finally I say, "You are almost rude, but not quite."

"I didn't mean to hurt your feelings," she says. "I'm dreadfully sorry if I did. But sometimes I get passionate about my art, almost angry, and I can't stop myself from saying or writing things that might be too harsh, because I feel that what I say is the truth."

"Will I still see you, now that you've finished painting me?"

"Of course. I want you to keep seeing my friend Laura. She doesn't have many friends, and I think you two could like each other a lot."

"I don't think she liked me much. She barely spoke to me," I say.

"She liked you a whole lot. She told me so herself."

"I'm not fond of . . . what she does."

"What about you? Do you do something so fascinating that it allows you to be so judgmental and picky?"

"I'm a fact checker. At least that's something people do. I don't know what you intend. Do you want me to get involved romantically with her?"

"That would be nice. If you like her, that is."

"I like you."

"I know, but you can't. I like Laura's brother, Damon."

Damn. I knew it.

"You must understand," she continues, "I'm encouraging you as a favor to her. Sort of tit for tat. I help her find a guy, and she puts in a good word for me to her brother. I actually don't know her that well. I met her recently, through her brother. I'm not incredibly fond of her. I find her quite ordinary, to be honest, which I know may surprise you, now that you've seen her show. Though she has qualities that would please most people. She's sane, well-balanced, stable, wholesome, calm, easygoing, even-tempered, relaxed, serene. Her brother, on the other hand, is splendid."

When I get home, my cat, Minou, is almost smiling, looking at me through half-closed eyes. Her fur is all fluffed up and disheveled.

Oh, Jeremy, darling! You look very good today, she says. I've been waiting endlessly for you to come home.

Why?

First tell me, am I pretty?

Yes, as usual.

You're not even looking at me.

I look at her, and she stretches luxuriously on the floor.

How about now? she asks. Do I look pretty now? She purrs violently, but I can tell she's making a tremendous effort not to purr while talking, because she knows it annoys me.

Yes, you're pretty, I reply. So why have you been waiting for me to come home?

Because I think I have my heety-weety.

What's a heety-weety?

Oh, Jeremy, you are sooo slow.

Okay, I'm slow. So what's a heety-weety?

A heety-weety is my heat. Why aren't the males coming?

Well, how do you expect them to come? All the windows and doors are closed, and we live on the third floor.

That doesn't matter. They're supposed to come anyway.

You mean by walking through walls?

I don't know. They find ways.

She meows a lot and looks as if she's in pain. I feel sorry for her, so I say, Don't worry, you'll never have to go through this again. We'll get you an operation, and you'll feel fine and normal for the rest of your life.

Are you insane? I want to make love. And I want to have children.

But you're going to start peeing everywhere.

I promise I won't.

She goes on and on, horrified and indignant, and I begin to feel like a monster. She makes me swear never to have her operated on, but I cross my fingers to keep the option open.

She calms down and says, Pet me, Jeremy, pet me. More. Don't stop. Oh Jeremy.

chapter five

Three days later, for the first time, I visit Henrietta for no reason other than friendship. In fact, she is the one who suggested it. I thought it must be because Laura would be there. But no. Instead there is a good-looking nude man, being painted by Henrietta. He is lying in the most comfortable position he could find, unless that rule applies only to the imperfect models, like me. Henrietta says hello but is so absorbed by her painting and marzipan cats that she does not pay much attention to me. Her daughter, Sara, takes my hand and pulls me to her bedroom to show me her Humpty Dumpty collection.

There are many different Humpty Dumpties sitting on her shelves. Many of them are real eggs with painted faces and string arms and legs pasted to them.

"I made them," says Sara.

"They're very well painted," I tell her.

She points to one of the eggs. I look at it and I am shocked. She says, "This one is my latest. I finished it this morning. It took me nine hours to make, during three days."

The face painted on the egg is my face.

"Do you like it?" she asks.

"Is it me?"

"Yes."

"It's very realistic. You're so talented."

"Thank you. Whenever I meet someone I like, I make an egg out of them."

"I'm very flattered."

"That's not all. There's a show that goes with it."

"Oh?"

"Yes. Are you ready?"

"Yeah."

"Okay." She stands tall and straight, facing me, next to the Humpty Dumpty of me, and starts reciting: "Humpty Dumpty sat on a wall. Humpty Dumpty had a great fall . . ."

At this point she slides her finger behind the little egg with my face on it, and pushes it off the shelf. It falls and breaks on the wood floor. Thick red shiny goo pours out of it.

Sara continues her recitation: "All the king's horses and all the king's men couldn't put him back together again."

I stand there stunned, feeling insulted.

"Wasn't it nice?" she asks.

"It's too bad you broke my face."

"But wasn't it nice, the show with the blood? Wasn't it surprising?"

"Very surprising. How did you make the blood?"

"Mercurochrome and olive oil."

"It's too bad you broke my face, though. Especially if it took you nine hours to make. It was so well done."

"Don't worry," she says, picking up a closed half-carton of eggs. She opens the carton, and I am confronted with six more Humpty Dumpties of me, each one expressing a different emotion, which I can more or less decipher as Fear, Surprise, Anger, Sadness, Boredom, and, the last one, Guilt, with bright-red cheeks of shame.

I look at the little broken face on the floor, the seventh egg, and I realize that it was Happiness.

"They're beautiful," I tell her.

"Don't think it took me sixty-three hours to make all these eggs of you. It took me nine. You can have one, but I must warn you that the one you pick will reveal more about your personality than would nine hours of conversation."

I try to decide if I should pick the one I like most or the one that will incriminate me least. The one I like most is Guilt. It is the funniest and most expressive, with its bright-red shamed cheeks, but it also happens to be the most embarrassing one to choose, so I decide to pick the least incriminating, most innocent one.

"I think I'll take Boredom," I say, pointing.

"It's not Boredom; it's Sleepiness. It's extremely revealing that you interpreted it as Boredom. But you're lying. It is not your favorite one, because it is obviously the least well painted. This is very revealing, Jeremy, and doesn't put you in a very good light. It shows that you are a bit of a coward and dishonest. Admit it. The bored one is not your favorite."

I find her unpleasantly clever for a child her age.

"You're right," I say, hiding my annoyance. "I chose the bored one because I didn't want you to think I was afraid, surprised, angry, sad, or guilty."

"You're revealing more of yourself every minute. Why in the world would you not want me to think you were surprised? That's not a negative or embarrassing emotion, but obviously it is for you, for some deep, strange, and mysterious reason."

She caught me. She's right. I did not want her to think I was surprised by her behavior toward me, by her excessive familiarity, which troubles and confuses me. I must lie. "No, you're right; surprise is not a negative or embarrassing emotion. I just happened to think of boredom first. I was negligent."

She looks at me suspiciously through half-closed eyes. "So tell me, which *is* your favorite egg?"

"The happy one that's on the floor."

"That's too easy. Anyway, I can't give you that one; it's broken. Which one in this carton do you like the most?"

"That one," I say, pointing to the guilty one. "I like his red cheeks."

"You don't need to justify your choice by saying you like the red cheeks. There's no reason for you to feel guilty about choosing guilt."

"I'm not justifying my choice. I really like the red cheeks."

I visit Lady Henrietta twice a week, every Saturday and Wednesday night, because she says I can stop by whenever I feel like it. She must enjoy my presence. I think our relationship is growing deeper, slowly but surely. I hope her affection for me will become romantic soon, if it isn't already.

Laura is starting to show up once in a while. She tries to talk to me a bit, saying nice normal things, like: "Jeremy, I loved that movie you chose, *We Are the Taurus*," and "Jeremy, I like your jacket," and "It's a beautiful day, isn't it?" To Henrietta and Sara, she says, "Your painting is coming along nicely, Henrietta," and "Are you learning interesting things in school, Sara?"

I grab the first chance I get to play with Sara, which I like a lot more than talking to Laura. I don't know why I'm so repelled by her. Well, one reason is that I hate the feeling of getting matched up. I've hated it all my life, ever since my mom used to make me play with the yucky little neighbor girl. My mom and her mom would sit together, look at us, and say, "Oh, it's so cuuuute!"

Often when I visit her, Henrietta is painting one of her models. So far I've seen only the beautiful models, no ordinary men like me. While Henrietta paints, her daughter, Sara, also does artwork. She sits at the coffee table and draws men's clothes, sometimes from imagination or sometimes getting the model's clothes from the dressing room and laying them out in front of her. She makes quick but very good sketches of the trousers, ties, shirts, and shoes, while nibbling on some of her mother's marzipan animals.

"I didn't know you were also an artist," I tell her.

"I'm not really. I only draw men's clothes."

"Why?"

"I think they go well with my mom's paintings."

I interpret this as some deep disturbance she has about her mother painting nude men. I express this opinion, in private, to Lady Henrietta, who says, "I doubt it's a 'deep disturbance.' It might be a slight puzzlement. Sara feels her drawings nicely complement my paintings. I think it's charming."

So I decide to ask Sara herself what she thinks: "How do you feel about your mother painting nude men?"

"I think it's great," she replies. "Nudity is the most profound subject in the world."

"Are you bothered by it?"

"No; on the contrary. I think I'm lucky to have such an intelligent and relaxed mother."

I'm not convinced. What Sara does and what she says are two different things. I would think that if she approved of her mother's paintings, she would try to imitate her by drawing naked things, like her dolls, naked.

Sara is always holding Barbie dolls, so finally one day I ask Lady Henrietta, "Isn't she a little too old to play with Barbie dolls?"

"Yes, of course," says Lady Henrietta. "That's why she does it. She likes to be unconventional, which is something truly admirable in a child, because at that age they are so cruel to each other. She likes to do things that will arouse her classmates' scorn, and she confronts them with it. She's so strong."

"That's why she dresses in these very childish clothes?" (Which she does.)

"Yes, that's why. On top of it, she sort of likes Barbie dolls. They stimulate her imagination."

That's when I decide to buy Sara a Barbie doll, to please her mother.

I go to F.A.O. Schwarz, thinking they will have the biggest selection. I want to buy the best Barbie doll Lady Henrietta has ever seen. I want to impress her with my choice. I bet she has never bothered to go to F.A.O. Schwarz for a Barbie doll. I bet F.A.O. Schwarz carries Barbie dolls that are more beautiful and realistic than any she has ever seen. I can already imagine the effect that my choice will have on Lady Henrietta. I bet Sara will tell her mom that it's the best Barbie doll and say something like: "Your new friend, the O.I.M. one, has exquisite taste."

I am now in the Barbie section. They do have a rather large selection. I start looking carefully at all the boxes, trying to find the most impressive one.

I see *Barbie Flight Time gift set. Pretty pilot changes into glamorous date! Wings for you. And a paper doll too.*

They have the same model in three versions: the black-skinned doll, the blond doll, and the brunette, who has a prettier expression than the other two because her mouth is closed.

They have *Barbie Wet'n Wild Surf Set. Dolls not included.*

Also *Wet'n Wild Water Park. Dolls not included. The ultimate pool and super slide! "Drinking" Fountain! Spraying Jet Stream!*

I try to figure out why they put the word "drinking" in quotation marks. None of the other words are in quotation marks. It must be a typo.

There are about a dozen more boxes, with Barbie cars, houses, workout centers, picnic sets, etc. I am a little disappointed. None of the dolls are realistic or beautiful or interesting. I feel I should give up my idea of buying Sara a Barbie doll. Maybe I should get her a Humpty Dumpty instead.

I am about to leave, when I see that off to one side are some dolls that look like Barbie but are called Jane.

The first Jane box I come upon is *Jane does makeup, but can't get it right, so picks up telephone to call her friend over.* In the box there is a little telephone and a Jane doll with her mascara and lipstick smeared ungracefully around her eyes and mouth.

I go to the next box. *Jane goes on a diet*. The Jane doll is chubby.

The next one is *Jane walked in dog poop on her way home, and she must get it off her new shoes before her date comes to pick her up in five minutes*. There is a brown glob on the pink shoe of the Jane doll.

The next one is *Jane goes to the movies with boyfriend, and he kisses her. Dolls not included*. In the box there are two movie theater chairs and nothing else.

The next one is *Jane chooses a hobby. She starts painting*. Nude men. That would have been good.

A saleswoman comes up to me and says, "Do you need help?"

"I'm trying to find the best doll for a little girl."

"You should look at the Barbie dolls right over there. They're much better than the Jane dolls."

"I already saw the Barbie dolls. I must have missed the better ones. Where are they?"

"They're all better." She then lowers her voice. "I know I'm not supposed to say this, but personally, I think the Jane dolls should be banned. They're unwholesome."

I buy *Jane does makeup* and *Jane goes to the movies with boyfriend*, still wondering why they put the word "drinking" in quotation marks.

I give Sara the Jane doll, and she jumps around my neck and kisses me and hugs me, which still makes me feel uncomfortable, so I decide not to give her presents anymore. But whenever I go there, she keeps throwing herself at me anyway. She really likes me.

Lady Henrietta does not ask to paint me again, but she seems to like my visits, even to think they are normal and should continue. I have become one of her friends.

Her daughter adores me. She hugs me when I come in, and kisses my cheek. She forces me to watch movies with her, especially one called *Donkey Skin*, or, in French, *Peau d'Âne*. Both Lady Henrietta and her daughter speak French well. Sara goes to a French school. The movie is in French, with English subtitles. It's a fairy tale. A humorous fairy tale. Catherine Deneuve plays the princess.

The little girl knows the words to all the songs, and sings along, with a very beautiful voice. In fact, she knows the words to the entire movie and talks at the same time as the actors.

The story is about a king who falls in love with his daughter. He wants to marry her. She loves her father but doesn't want to marry him. To discourage him, she tells him she will agree if he gives her a dress the color of the weather. To her surprise, he succeeds. She tells him she wants a dress the color of the moon, thinking it'll be too difficult, but he succeeds. She tells him she wants a dress the color of the sun. He succeeds. She tells him she wants the skin of his magic donkey. He is indignant at this request because he loves his donkey, which defecates gold. But he kills the donkey and gives her the skin, thinking that now she will marry him. She wears the skin as a disguise and runs away. Eventually she meets a prince.

Once, Lady Henrietta watches the movie with us. She tells me that the fairy tale was written by Charles Perrault, the same guy who wrote the stories of Sleeping Beauty, Little Red Riding Hood, Bluebeard, and Cinderella. Henrietta says she often wondered why "Donkey Skin" never became as well known in America as the others. She suspects that it must be because the subject of a father being in love with his daughter is too shocking and objectionable to Americans. And of course, she says, it *is* shocking and objectionable in real life, but does that mean you can't have a fairy tale about it? Bluebeard killing his wives is even more shocking, and yet Americans don't object to that. Interesting phenomenon, she muses.

The little girl is very intelligent, but strange, quite articulate for her age. One day I'm sitting on the couch and she comes and sits on my lap, wraps her arms around my neck, and rests her head on my shoulder.

Holy shit, I think.

From then on she often sits on my lap. She sometimes kisses my cheek passionately. She even gives me hickeys on my neck and cheeks, which I don't feel but notice in the mirror when I get home. I realize then what the red marks are on my neck and cheeks.

Every time I go to their apartment, Sara has thought of new things to tell me, more imagery like the time she told me I was a poor naked turtle. Or the time—it really beat all the others—she said I should be kept in a cage. "You are a creature to be owned" were her precise words. "To be shown to guests."

Other times she says things like: "I love you because you're not embarrassed to buy me Jane dolls. And because you think of me."

She's wrong. When I buy her Jane dolls I am thinking of her mother.

A m a n d a F i l i p a c c h i

I could never be intimate and comfortable with Sara, and I feel bad that she will be disappointed.

Henrietta, who is often present during her daughter's strong displays of affection for me, doesn't seem to think that her behavior is in the least bit strange, and I guess maybe it isn't. I don't know. I'm confused. Children are allowed to be affectionate: It's their innocence. But this girl is so pretty, and there's something so sexual in her affection. I'm not sure if it's really there or if I'm just a pervert. She often comes in scantily dressed. But then I think, is it really scantily dressed, or am I just choosing to see it that way? After all, shorts and a T-shirt are a perfectly proper way of dressing, but on her they seem like a provocation. Maybe it's because she wears them every single time I see her. She's not letting me catch my breath. I feel like saying, "Give me a break! Refresh my eyes for once. Wear a potato sack."

But no, she keeps at it, she keeps at it. Her arms are smooth, and there's a strange glow to her skin that more mature women don't have. It's almost magical, again like a cartoon.

I'm madly in love with Lady Henrietta, but I'm starting to feel sexually attracted to the daughter, which horrifies me. I try to become cold to her, to make hints. I stand up and say, "Come on now, act like a lady, you're not a baby anymore."

She looks at me uncertainly for a moment, but then jumps up, putting her arms around my neck and says, "Yes I am."

Lady Henrietta often leaves us alone together, which annoys me. She continues to see Damon, and I continue to be jealous, but I don't hear of any real intimacy growing between them, which makes me feel better.

One day Sara invites three of her friends "for tea." The girls are basically rather unattractive, but on top of it, their hair is disheveled, they wear very ugly, unflattering clothes, and two of them are overweight. Sara, on the other hand, looks more beautiful than ever. I understand her little trick right away.

When her friends leave, Sara asks me, "Which part of my appearance do you dislike the least?"

"Don't be so modest. You mean, which part do I like the most?"

"Well, yes, assuming that there's any part you like."

"Your hair."

When I get home from work the next day, I see a long flower box at the foot of my door. There's a card with it, which I open. I don't recognize the handwriting, and there is no signature. It says, "Here is a lock, a token of my affection."

I open the box, and a wave of nausea sweeps over me. I feel as though I'm holding a decapitated head, except that the head is not there.

Pee-U, yucky ducky. Where is the *head?* is my instinctive thought.

There are two long blond braids lying inside the box. They look like a corpse. Disgusting. Sad.

I pounce on the phone and call Lady Henrietta. She answers. I say, "Sara cut her hair?"

"Yes."

"She gave it to me in a flower box."

"I know."

"How could you let her do it?"

"My daughter can do anything she wants as long as it doesn't hurt anyone."

"But she had beautiful hair."

"She wanted to cut it. It looks very pretty now."

"Do you want the braids? I don't want them; I think it's disgusting. And it'll probably mean more to you than to me."

"You can do what you want. Though you should be touched. She did it to be nice. It's a really big deal, her gesture."

"I know. That's what's so annoying. It's indecent. Yeah, I'm touched, but I'm mostly troubled and worried about her mental and emotional health. I'm surprised you're not worried also."

One day Lady Henrietta says something that horrifies me beyond belief.

She says, "Would you do me an enormous favor?"

"Yes," I answer, overjoyed at the opportunity to please her.

I wait for her to tell me what the favor is, but instead she gets her handbag and takes out two plane tickets. She stands there, not saying anything, just looking at me. I open the tickets and see that they are for Orlando, Florida.

"What is this?" I ask, suddenly deeply excited, because I am thinking that maybe she wants to go on a vacation with me.

"I would like you to go there with my daughter next weekend."

What the hell's going on? "Why?" I ask. "What's there?"

"Disney World. I think things are finally moving forward between Damon and me. I'd like to have a very intimate weekend with him, without my daughter. She's always wanted to go to Disney World. This way I'll be rid of her but won't feel too guilty about it. Will you please do it?"

I am crushed by the news about Damon. On top of it, I am not happy about what she wants me to do, not in the least. I feel that Lady Henrietta is now being really obnoxious, but I mean really. For the first time since I met her, I find her annoying.

Before I can respond, she says, "You are one of the few people I trust. And you are one of the few people Sara likes. So it's perfect. It would be such a help if you could do this. I would owe you for life. And anyway, Disney World is supposed to be pretty fun for adults also."

"I don't know," I say. "I think it's a little strange."

"What's strange?"

"I mean, I'm not her father after all. Is this an acceptable thing to do?"

"She doesn't have a father," says Lady Henrietta coldly. "If you don't want to do it, it's fine. I'll have her stay with one of my other male models, whom she hates, but she'll have no choice."

I have a feeling she's inventing this little threat to make me feel bad.

"I don't know," I say. "It's not that I don't want to do it. It's that—" I can't finish the sentence. What am I going to say: "It's that don't you think she's acting a little too affectionate"? Or: "I don't know what I might do"? No, I can't say these things, or she'll think I'm a dangerous maniac and will never want to see me again.

Finally, I say, "It's that people might think it a little strange."

"Nonsense. You'll just say you're her father."

I don't say no. I just sort of slide into it, not knowing how to refuse. I don't want her to be upset with me and to dislike me. After all, I still have hope that she'll break up with Damon. Just because she's going to spend one weekend with him doesn't necessarily mean that she'll spend the rest of her life with him. And in a way, it's sort of good that she trusts me with her daughter.

Maybe it means that unconsciously she wants me to be the father and she's getting me ready for that role. This possibility may seem farfetched, but I always like to fantasize about the best possible thing that a seemingly negative situation might bring.

The next day I get a good idea that makes up a tiny bit for having to take Sara to Disney World alone. It's to bring my mother to Disney World with Sara. This would kill three birds with one stone: (1) I would be doing the favor for Lady Henrietta. (2) I would be pleasing my mother, who wants to spend time with me. (3) I wouldn't be alone with Sara.

When I mention the idea to Lady Henrietta, she does not seem thrilled, and I can't figure out why. I thought she would feel even better about the whole thing. Instead she says, "Oh. Why do you want to bring your mother? You think you'd be bored just with Sara?"

I am annoyed at her, and I feel like replying, "No, you idiot, that's the problem: I'm afraid I wouldn't be bored at all."

But I say, "My mother has been wanting to see me for a long time, so I thought this would be a good opportunity. I'm sure she'd love Disney World. On top of it, I'm surprised you're not glad that an older woman will be there to help me look after Sara."

She does not say anything more, but she doesn't seem very pleased about the idea. Nevertheless, the next day she gives me another plane ticket. I offer to pay for it, even though I can't really afford it, but Lady Henrietta says she won't hear of it. I try not to feel guilty, reminding myself that she's rich.

"At least you won't have to pay for an extra room," I say. "Sara can share a room with my mother."

"No," replies Lady Henrietta. "You will all three have your own rooms."

London Bridge is falling down	Off to Disney World we go
Falling down	World we go
Falling down	World we go
London Bridge is falling down	Off to Disney World we go
My fair lady.	Shit fuck shit-fuck.

My girlfriend, Charlotte, thinks the whole thing is a little strange, but she doesn't pay as much attention to it as I was afraid she might, because she happens to be very busy right now. She says she's even sort of glad she'll have the whole weekend to work, with no distractions.

chapter six

My mother is at first very glad, but her happiness at spending four days with me fades when she starts taking it for granted. She gets cranky about everything.

Yes, I did say four days. Lady Henrietta first told me it was just for the weekend, probably because she wanted to give me the bad news in small doses. Once she felt confident I had accepted the idea, she said it was Sara's Easter vacation, and the more days she, Henrietta, could have alone, the better.

She gives us a lot of money to spend at Disney World. She says it's very expensive there.

At Disney World, everyone looks at Sara. Men look at her because she's so beautiful. Women look at her out of curiosity, seemingly intrigued. It starts at the hotel, with the sleazy porter. He looks as if he smells bad, though he doesn't. He has a five o'clock shadow, or even a twenty-four-hour shadow; it wouldn't surprise me. Perhaps I am judgmental because I don't like him. The way he looks at Sara as he's pushing the cart with our bags. He looks at her with too much familiarity. He touches the small of her back when we get out of the elevator. And he asks her impertinent questions, like, "How old are you?"

"Eighteen," she answers.

"Really? You look seventeen."

Sara smiles at me.

"What grade are you in?"

"Seventh grade."

"Really? Isn't that a little backward?"

"Yes. I'm not very intelligent."

"Hmm. Anyway, ladies only need to be pretty, and *that* you certainly are. And docile is good too."

"You've got a great ass," says my mother to the porter. She puts her hand on his bottom.

The porter stops walking and looks at her with eyebrows raised. I do so also. Sara is trying not to laugh.

"Are you married, honey?" my mother asks him.

"Yes."

"I'm not surprised. A cute little prick like you. I'm sure your wife must be proud to have a hunk with such nice buns."

And she taps the porter's bottom before continuing down the hallway. He looks at me.

I don't know what to say, so I just nod to him.

The hairy, sleazy porter, looking confused, continues his journey down the hallway. He puts my mom's bag in her room, my bag in my room, and then he heads toward Sara's room. I go with them, not wanting to leave her alone with that man. He does nothing else irritating, to my relief.

Sara is not interested in seeing the Magic Kingdom, which, she asserts, is for babies. She wants to go to EPCOT Center which, the bus driver informs us, stands for Every Person Comes Out Tired. She wants to go to Future World. That's when my mother tells us what *she* wants to do. She says she had no desire whatsoever to come to Disney World, that the only reason she came was to spend some time with me, and that therefore we should go to The Living Seas first, as it is the only thing that might put her in a good mood. So that's what we do. We see big fish swimming in aquariums.

My seventy-one-year-old mother may seem conventional and proper because she does not like my messy apartment, but she is not ordinary at all. She's like a little bull. Short and stocky, less fat than muscular. A small rock. Her body looks hard, like if you poked your finger at any part of it, even a presumably mushy part, your finger wouldn't sink one millimeter. A compact creature. Which is perhaps why, when she runs, her flesh doesn't jiggle, as one would expect in a person her age. Or perhaps this is due to her running method, very low to the ground, knees bent, "for speed," she says. She doesn't bounce. But she *can* jump, and she does, sometimes, and does it well, even with her short, stubby legs. Children occasionally cross in front of her unexpectedly, pulling toy animals on long leashes. I cover my eyes. But my mother leaps over them smoothly.

She loves to run, especially when it's not necessary. Her favorite scenario occurs when she sees people about to get into line ahead of us. She'll run to beat them to it. When she visits me in the city, she runs to make the lights before the Don't Walk signs stop blinking. But the city doesn't offer as many opportunities to run as Disney World does, and running to make the lights is not as much fun as running to get in line before someone else does. There are so many lines to run to!

And yet, when we walk, she leans on my arm with all her weight. When we climb stairs, I practically have to carry her. It's all an act. Sometimes she gets bored with hanging on to me. She lets me go and walks by my side with a spring in her step. And at the first glimpse of someone heading toward our line, she bolts away to get there first.

When she has won her place in line, she tries to regain her composure. She organizes herself, straightens her shirt and skirt, smooths her hair, feels herself all over, and clears her throat.

My mother looks like an older me. Which is to say that she looks like a man. She has a huge complex about this, has a mortal fear of one day being mistaken for a man. Her face looks like a man's when she smiles, and also when she doesn't smile. She has long, deep lines running from the wings of her nose down to the corners of her mouth. However, certain aspects of her face look less like a man's than like a toad's—let's say a male toad's. She has moles and no lips, just a slit. But since there could be no greater insult, in her mind, than being taken for a man, she does things to herself, wears signposts, to guarantee that no one will be confused. Most women her age try to look as young as possible. My mother's concern is merely to look like a woman. In itself, this is such a hard thing for her to accomplish that it would be ridiculous to expect her to try also to look like a *younger* woman, or a *pretty* woman, or even *not a toad*. And she doesn't worry about those things. (Good for her.) She doesn't dye her hair. She wears it gray, but she puts pink bows in it: signposts of womanhood. And she wears frilly things, and perfume, and lots of jewelry: not the expensive kind, which she can't afford, but pastel plastic. She says it's more classy than fake gold. She never fails to wear bright-red lipstick, but without much success, due to her lack of lip. She does this not to look pretty, just to look not masculine. And blush on her cheeks. She doesn't bother with eye stuff anymore, because she doesn't have the patience. Anyway, her eyes are her best feature: "best" as in "impressive," or even "intimidating," not as in "attractive." They are black, wide open and alert, flashing here and there like lightning. She never looks sleepy but always wears a frown.

One day (I don't know what possessed me) I remarked, "If you didn't always frown, you wouldn't look so much like a man." Although I didn't believe a word of this, I picked on her complex to eliminate the frown more efficiently. Well, she seemed so hurt, and was in such a bad mood for days afterward, that I never said anything of the sort again.

My mother's behavior with the porter surprised me. I'd never seen her act that way before, and I wondered what brought it on. I did not want to ask her about it when Sara was with us, because my mother might have felt too inhibited to answer me sincerely. But now is the perfect time. We are alone, standing in line for Journey into Imagination, which the guidebook describes as "an imaginative ride through the creative process." Sara has left us to go to the bathroom and buy a snack.

I know I must formulate my question in the shape of a compliment. It would be a mistake to simply ask, "Why did you treat the porter that way?" My mother would automatically take it as a criticism, get angry, and scream at me.

"That was wonderful, the way you treated the porter," I remark. Anyway, I *did* think it was wonderful.

"Thank you," she says, and does not say more, even though I give her a good full minute to do so.

"Sometimes you surprise me by doing the most wonderful things," I tell her.

"Well, I would hope that my wonderful things don't come as such a *great* surprise. They're not *that* rare, after all. Why do you have to be so surprised?"

I sense that this will be one of our convoluted conversations. In the past, I've tried every method imaginable to get out of them, but nothing ever works. My best bet is patience. I look at the people standing in line near us, hoping they all have many distractions and won't be tempted to listen in on us. They would think we belong in a mental institution. In front of us is a mother talking loudly to her three children, who are playing loudly together. Good. I glance behind us. There are two men, about my age, thirtyish. They look rather sophisticated for Disney World. Tall. Educated. One of them has longish brown hair. They are both wearing shorts. They are tan. The other one is blond. They are the types of men women would prefer to me. I could not imagine living creatures more out of place at Disney World than these two men, especially their combination. They are talking to each other. Anyway, they look discreet, as if they wouldn't stoop to eavesdropping.

"I'm sorry," I tell my mother. "I didn't express myself clearly. I simply meant that such wonderful behavior is rare in anyone. I know very few people who would have had the courage or the wit to even attempt to treat the porter that way, not to mention the mastery with which you carried out the operation."

Amanda Filipacchi

"Oh, spare me, Jeremy."

"I mean it."

"So do I."

When she talks, my mother is sure of herself. She articulates well. Her tone is clear, confident, authoritative, and powerful. It makes anything she says sound intelligent. I did not inherit her talent, but sometimes when I speak to her, I feel I'm able to imitate it.

"I'm sorry," I say. "What interests me is this: I've never seen you treat a man the way you treated the porter, in that clever way. I'd like to know if there was a specific reason."

"Yes. It's because I never really knew men before."

"What an intriguing thought. You've piqued my curiosity."

"It was already piqued."

"Right again."

"I was not right before. How can I be right again?"

I look around in embarrassment. The two men are still talking.

"Because you are *always* right," I tell my mother.

"But not in a specific way in this conversation."

"Right again."

"This time it fits, because I was right before," she says.

"What did you mean when you said you never really knew men before?"

"Okay, you want to get back to the subject. Giving some sort of warning is more polite than just barging rudely back in."

"I'm sorry."

"I don't care if you are. That's not the logical thing to say at this point. I'm merely teaching you something that you should already know."

"Would you like to get back to our conversation?"

"It's that sort of warning I mean, but you do it so clumsily. A better way is to say, 'As we were saying . . .' Or, even better,

N u d e   M e n

'I don't mean to interrupt you, but our conversation was so agreeable that I would love to continue it from where we left off, if you would like to.' "

I glance back. They're still talking.

"As we were saying," I say, "what did you mean when you said you never really knew men before?"

"You chose the less good way. I can't believe it. Just to upset me. I told you the second way was better than the first way, and you went ahead and used the first way."

"I'm sorry, but the second way was too hard to remember. It was long."

"I marvel at your lack of shame in admitting the weakness of your mind. What is even worse than having a weak mind is not having the shame to hide the fact."

"I don't mean to interrupt you, but our conversation was so agreeable that I would love to continue it from where we left off, if you would like to."

"You're now using the second way, which means you lied when you said it was too long to remember. What is even ruder and more obnoxious than having a weak mind and not having the shame to hide it is to purposefully reveal the fact that you lied at an earlier point in a conversation."

We're already in it so deep, I may as well just charge ahead, even if they're listening.

"Yes," I say. "What did you mean when you said you never really knew men before?"

"I meant that recently I have discovered them in a new way."

"Oh, really."

"What way," says my mother.

"What?"

"What way," she repeats.

"What do you mean?"

"What way."

"What way?"

"Through books," she says.

"Through books." I take a Kleenex out of my pocket and wipe my forehead.

"No need to repeat what I say. You can come up with something a little more original."

"What aspects of men have you discovered recently through books?"

"You don't need to repeat 'through books.' We've already said it many times."

"What aspects of men?"

"A certain aspect. A certain way that they think about women."

I nod encouragingly.

"I need sound," she says.

"Hmm."

"I mean words."

"Go on."

"Men, in the books I've read, say and think things like: 'That cute little cunt Cindy.' And the narrator says, concerning the main character: 'Intelligence in women has never much interested him.' And then this one: the male character thinks, 'She does know something. All cunts know something.' "

"I read that book!" I exclaim. "It's John Updike's *Rabbit Is Rich*, right?" I don't mind if they hear me now. In fact, I'm sure they'd be impressed that I was able to recognize a novel simply by hearing some of its sexist lines. I glance back to check if they're listening. They're not talking, but they're not looking at us either. They're watching people walk by.

"So it shocked you also," she says.

"That's not the word, exactly—"

"Don't deny my feelings."

"I'm not. I'm expressing mine."

"Well," she says, "it was unpleasant to learn such things from those books. And the only way men will change—and I'm not talking about you; you're not a man—is for women to talk about men in the same way. And we'll just see how pleasant men find that."

The children in front of us are playing more loudly than ever, and their mother is screaming at them. Good. Hopefully, their noise completely muffled what my mom just said.

"What do you mean, I'm not a man?" I ask softly, close to her face.

"Don't change the subject."

I grab her arm, a bit tightly. "What do you mean, I'm not a man?" My voice wavers. I knew she had a low opinion of me, but this beats everything.

"Why do men find it so upsetting to be told they are not *real* men?" she says, disengaging her arm.

"It has nothing to do with gender," I tell her. "Women find it upsetting to be told they are not women. What do you mean, I'm not a man?"

"Don't take it so badly. I meant it as a compliment. I meant you are a person. People are individuals, first and foremost. Then they have ages. Then they have nationalities. Then they have race. Then they have religion. Then they have social class. Then they have childhood and education. And then they are females or males, but that's far down the list. You are a person. You don't have all the jerkiness that the majority of men have. Or do you? Do you ever act or think in any way that is degrading to women?"

"I don't think so."

"I *know* you don't. That sole quality makes up a hundred times for all your other weaknesses combined."

"Thank you." That's got to be the nicest thing my mom has said to me in years.

I glance back. To my great embarrassment, the two men are staring at me silently. I smile faintly, to seem at ease, and turn away.

Disney World: Bright pastel colors everywhere. Everything so happy. The people so fat, and so much flesh uncovered, and thick lips eating hot dogs, and shorts bunched up in the crotches because the big thighs pull them up at every step, and the other fat families taking turns being pushed in the wheelchairs that you can rent.

Sara tells us she has a new philosophy of life. She explains it like a scientist: "The solutions to problems are in the words themselves. For example, the solution, when you're depressed, is that you've got to take a *deep rest*. Get it?"

"How tall are you?" my mother asks Sara.

"Five feet seven and a quarter."

I'm sure she's telling the truth, because I'm five ten, and she's just about three inches shorter.

"That's very tall for a girl with such a low number," says my mom.

"What number?" asks Sara.

"Your age. Eleven is a low number, wouldn't you say?"

"No. I'd say it's a young age."

"No. It's a low number. That's more objective. Just because you've only lived a few years doesn't mean you're young. Especially in *your* case," she says, sweeping her eyes very noticeably over Sara's body. "It just means your number is low."

Sara nods, as though she understands, accepts, and likes this.

We go to pavilions called Horizons, Universe of Energy, and World of Motion, in which there are little train rides, meant to be educational. We are all sitting there, in the vehicles, watching with great boredom the fake-looking Audio-Animatronics (these are life-size dolls that move a bit, accompanied by spoken words). Not one of us three wants to be here, not even Sara. I am certain, I instinctively know with every shred of my being, that she insists on going on these rides to find opportunities of getting closer to me, of manipulating me and charming me in every imaginable way. My mother goes on these rides because she doesn't want to miss a moment of being with me. I go on these rides because we are a sandwich, and I am the baloney.

Some of the lines are long, thirty minutes or more. My mother is complaining, so I tell her she can go walk around with Sara while I stand in line. Sara says no, she wants to wait in line with me, but she encourages my mother to walk around. My mother leaves us (to my great surprise, because for the first time on this trip, she is going to miss a few minutes of my presence). Sara is in a fine mood. She is nice to me.

"How much do you weigh?" my mother asks Sara.

"About one hundred and fifteen pounds."

Sara acts languorous, like a cat, draping herself over the seats of the rides. Every chance she gets, she hugs me with fright. She plasters her body against mine.

My mother says, "Look at that cute little prick over there. Nice and fresh. Right out of the oven."

But what's the point? No one hears her. I guess she's just venting her anger. I guess it's just the principle of it.

To Sara, it's like a game. She tries to be seductive when my mother is not looking. It makes me very uncomfortable, to say the least. She gives me furtive kisses, not on the mouth but, still, nearby. I want to say, "Mommy, did you see what she did to me? Make her stop." The few times that my mother does see something, she says, "Aw, it's so cute."

Sara says, "When you're solitary, and it's a problem, the antidote is in the word. *Soul it airy.* Which means you've got to make your soul more airy and light. People will like you more if you're less serious, and you won't be solitary anymore."

I am very physically attracted to Sara. She is extremely sensuous, in addition to being beautiful. Very supple. What she wears looks absurdly, grotesquely sexy on her. Just shorts, not particularly tight, not particularly short. Flat shoes. She also wears miniskirts, but they are not tight; they are full and loose and totally appropriate for her age. She wears no makeup and looks all the more stunning for it. She is very physical with me, always touching me. I wonder if she's the type of person who is always touching everybody or just always touching me. In any case, she's not always touching my mother.

She sometimes gets mad that I don't respond to her caresses and kisses and cuddles. She tries to make me jealous by pointing to older men she finds attractive. Also very old men.

My mother makes kissing sounds to passing men.

"That's not in those books!" I tell her.

"No, but it's all coming back to me now."

We buy Mickey Mouse masks. Mickey Mouse for me, Minnie Mouse for Sara. My mom refuses to get grandma Minnie Mouse, even though they have one. She gets no mask.

I try to flirt with women, so that Sara will see I'm interested in women my own age. I also try to get her to be interested in little boys.

Sara points to an old man in a wheelchair and says, "Isn't he good-looking? He's so charming."

I look at her, shocked, and realize it's not only to make me jealous that she does this; it's to show me that she likes older men and that if I don't give in, another man probably will.

A few minutes later I point to a five-year-old boy and say, "Isn't he good-looking? He's so charming. You should go talk to him."

She bangs her shoulder against mine and says, "Oh, yeah, right."

"Hello," says my mother, in a small, suggestive voice, to men who walk by.

Sara has the face of a child. I cannot be in love with that beautiful child's face. It's just too young.

"Pretty," says my mother to men.

My mother does not have a very high opinion of me. She finds me socially inept and retarded. "What is even worse than being incompetent with your career and your love life," she tells me, "is being inept at everyday life." She feels sorry for me and is probably very embarrassed by me, but she doesn't want to hurt me. She feels it's good for me to be with her, that it can only help me. When she's harsh, it's not because she dislikes me. In fact, she often says, "I love you and just want what's good for you. You need to be shaken up a bit." I don't take it too personally.

My mother complains to Sara about me. Sara complains to my mother about me, saying things like: "Don't you think he should let himself go a little more? Don't you think he's too stiff and constipated?"

"I agree," says my mom. "That's what I've been telling him for years."

"He's always so worried about doing what's proper."

"Couldn't agree more."

We go back to the hotel at around five, because Sara has a headache and wants to rest.

Right after dinner, my mother goes to her room to sleep. Sara comes to my room and begins to talk about things; I'm not sure what things, because I'm so tense. She seems very relaxed.

She keeps talking about me, analyzing me, telling me what she likes about me. She shows off her flesh. I'm not sure if she's doing it on purpose or if it's just me, old pervert that I am, noticing it. If she *is* doing it on purpose, she has a talent for it, because it looks very natural. She reeks of childishness. Smooth cartoonish skin. Even the slightly uncoordinated movements of children. She looks like putty, like if I press her arm, it'll change shape and stay that way.

As we talk, she insists on sitting next to me, with my arm wrapped around her. She cuddles in the hollow of my armpit. "You're my teddy bear," she says, which is music to my ears. That's the kind of attitude I like. The innocent, friendly one. At one point she walks over to the door and spins around. She starts singing "Tonight" from *West Side Story*. She walks slowly toward me, perfectly serious, with an intense expression on her face, singing: "Tonight, tonight, there's only you tonight. Tonight there will be no morning star. Tonight, tonight . . ."

She finally reaches me and begs me to sing with her. I object quite energetically, telling her I can't sing at all. She insists even more energetically, and we start singing the duo, her cheek glued to mine, my voice sounding like I don't know what. In fact, I'm not really singing, I'm talking.

She finally goes to her room to sleep.

The next day Sara wants to do Horizons again. So we do it again, even though Mom doesn't really want to.

We then go to MGM Studio, taking the shuttle bus at around 4:00 p.m. We take a ride called "Backstage Studio Tour." We only do the first half, which is on trams and lasts twenty-five minutes. There's a scary part when our tram goes over a bridge, which starts shaking, and fire appears everywhere, and a huge amount of water comes crashing toward us. The fire is hot, and the people on the left side of the tram get wet. We are on the right side. The second half of the tour, which we don't do, lasts forty-five minutes and is on foot.

Sara's face is young, but she has the body of a tall, sensuous woman.

My mother says loudly, so people can hear her, "Intelligence in men has never much interested me."

Sara tries to act very sexy, to move sexily, to make me desire her.

What does she want from me? How far is she trying to go? Not that I would accommodate her.

At one point, during a rare moment when Sara is not with us, my mother tells me, "I don't understand why this little girl likes you so much. But I'm very pleased about it. It's charming, her affection. I'm sure it builds your confidence. I must say I'm a bit jealous of her. I hate her a bit."

We go on the rides. We go on the little trains, and we see the little shows.

When my mother is beyond hearing range, Sara says to me out of the blue, "I've got to warn you that I've got big boobs for my age. Or for any age. I'm afraid you'll faint if you see them."

"Then I hope I will never see them."

We go on the little trains, we see the shows, we stand in the endless lines (half an hour, an hour), we go in the stores but buy very little, we eat at the little restaurants, some of which are good, surprisingly.

Sara often has headaches. I don't know if it's because she thinks they're an attractive feminine quality or if they're real.

"Look at that sexy prick over there. Not bad-looking. But not right for me. He's old enough to be my husband."

"If the word is 'infatuated,' meaning that you're infatuated with someone and it's a problem because the person doesn't like you back, well, the word tells you that your problem is *in fat you ate,* meaning that you've got to eat less fat, so you'll *be* less fat, and the person you want will want you back. The last piece, *id,* just means that the solution is sort of psychological."

Sara is like those freaks in circuses, like women with beards. She's a child with the body of a woman, or a woman with the face of a child.

She is a goddess. She's unreal. She's so beautiful. Her womanly curves are wrapped in child's skin. It must hurt the young child's skin to be stretched over all those curves. It must itch. It looks as though it might burst. I have never seen a woman's body with skin so tight. It looks very strange. It looks strangely much like a Barbie doll. I am overwhelmed by her and in awe of her. I am even sometimes intimidated by her.

I am not in love with her. I cannot be, because of her unmarked face, her low number, and her body, which doesn't have enough defects for my taste. She also hasn't enough past for my taste. Past is an attractive quality, you know, which people often don't realize because they are seldom confronted with too little of it.

If her head were perched on the body of a child, her face would not seem particularly innocent. But perched on the body of a woman, it looks like the face of a newborn.

"If the word is 'ugly,' meaning that you are, or you think you are, ugly, the solution is *uh, glee,* meaning that you must try to be gleeful and you'll seem more attractive to people. The *uh* just means that the solution is not obvious."

I feel comfortable with her, just as she feels comfortable with me, because we are both freaks. I've noticed, these past few weeks, that I depend heavily on her affection, for emotional support, when I'm depressed. When everything in my life seems to be going badly, I have one consoling thought: "At least Sara loves me."

I sense that in a way she is vulnerable, that she is uncomfortable and embarrassed about her body. I want to console and protect her.

Tonight, like last night, Mom goes to bed and Sara comes to my room and talks for two and a half hours. She makes me sing songs in French from the *Donkey Skin* movie, and in between the songs, sometimes even in the middle of the songs, she suddenly says, "I want you to like me, and I want you to love me." We sing *Donkey Skin* some more, and then I go out on the balcony to get some air. When I come back in, she climbs up on my knees, for the hundredth time since I've known her. She kisses my cheek, lays her head on my shoulder, and whispers near my ear, "You are a little boy in the body of a man. I am a woman in the body of a little girl. We are perfect for each other."

She got that wrong. She's a little girl in the body of a woman. I swear to God. Her body is the body of a woman. In fact, so is her inside, I mean her soul. Her soul is a woman, not a little girl. She is a woman in the body of a woman.

She plops down on the bed and says, matter-of-factly, "My mother took me to the doctor a few weeks ago to get a vaccination and a checkup. I took off my clothes and put them on a chair. The doctor picked up my panties, which were lying on the chair with my other clothes, and brought them to my mom and said, 'Her panties are soaking wet. She's ready.' "

I look at her, open-mouthed, thinking: Huh, I didn't know doctors did that. The world really isn't as I had imagined. I got it all wrong.

Then Sara says, "I'm only kidding. That was just a dream I had. A really awful and embarrassing dream."

She climbs back on my knees and whispers in my ear, "Eighteen to thirty-six, fifty to sixty-eight, seventy-two to ninety. Do you know what these numbers are?" And before I can answer, she says, "They are the difference in our ages. I calculated them all. There's not such a big difference at all. Eleven to twenty-nine is the only one that seems big, but it's only an illusion."

I stare at her, paralyzed, not knowing what to do, not even able to wonder what to do. I feel like an object without the power of thought. Finally, a clear thought comes into my head, and I say, "You should get interested in boys your own age."

"What I'm talking about is a little more than 'interested,' " she says.

"Well, whatever, then, but do it with someone your own age."

"I love boys my own age, but in a different way."

"In what way?"

"Oh . . . I would like to kiss them."

I don't dare ask her how she loves *me*, so I ask, "Why don't you, then?"

"I don't have the guts."

I raise my eyebrows. "You *don't?*"

She catches my meaning, smiles, and tries to explain. "I admire them too much. They make me shy."

"I'm sure you don't mean all of them. You mean one, right?"

"I guess."

A moment later, she says, "When I'm at home, in my room, I sometimes wish a man, a stranger, would come and make love to me. He is not you, but that doesn't matter."

"Is he one of your mother's nude models?"

"He could be, or he could not be. In my mind I think he mostly comes from the outside."

I am silent while I think this over.

Then she says, "I'm not in love with you. I don't admire you. Do you mind?"

"No, I'm delighted."

"But I love you like a best friend I don't respect, a best friend I feel sorry for."

Ow. Terribly insulted. Hurt feelings. She's not very nice, but I don't feel it would be proper for me to express my pain, under the circumstances. The circumstances being her advances toward me, most of the time. I'm surprised that such a young girl can play with my mind, and hurt me, as successfully as a woman three times her age.

She finally goes to her room. She calls me on the phone.

"Can you please come to my room?" she says.

"Why?"

"I want you to show me how to turn on the TV."

"It's very simple."

"No; I can't figure it out."

I sigh. "Okay." I hang up and leave my room.

I am staring at my bare feet, which are pounding the carpeted hallway, and I think to myself: I will be immensely surprised if there isn't a little plot simmering behind her request.

I open her door. She is standing in the middle of her room, kissing the hairy porter. She even has her arms around him. She's kissing him on the mouth, looking at me.

My first instinct, when I see them, is to say, "Oh, excuse me," back out of the room, and close the door. But I don't. I just stand there. The porter pulls away from Sara, frowning, and rushes out.

I notice the TV is on.

"Your TV is on," I tell her.

"He showed me," she says.

I leave without saying anything.

In the morning we do the Indiana Jones Epic Stunt Spectacular. We pass a store that can put your picture on the cover of a magazine. We don't really want to do it, but then I see that they have *Screen* magazine as one of the choices, and I decide we simply must do it. So we all three have our picture taken, and they put it on the cover. The picture is horribly ugly of me and not so good of my mom, but it's great of Sara. She's giving me a kiss on one cheek, and my mother is giving me a kiss on my other cheek. Next to our faces it says "Hot Stuff." Mom wants me to tear up the picture, but Sara says she wants to keep it as a souvenir for her mother. To this I object energetically. I don't want darling Lady Henrietta to see that monstrous picture of me. But Sara wins. We let her keep it.

If she did nothing, I would have no desire for her. But it's her behavior. She's so seductive. And I feel she loves me, with a strange and deep affection. She may say that she's not in love with me, and I guess I believe her. It doesn't make me feel good; not that I want her to be in love with me, but the fact that she says it hurts me. It reinforces my inferiority complex, the idea that no woman could be in love with me, no woman could find me attractive. I act too insecure, meek, cowardly, nerdy, effeminate, petty, mediocre intelligence, no sense of humor, immature, uptight. But I feel she loves me because she feels sooo comfortable with me and is sooo unintimidated by me, because she has sooo little admiration for me. Nevertheless, she loves me. I am her best friend. And I am grateful for her love. It's something I have not had, and have missed.

My mother goes back to the hotel after lunch. She's had enough of Disney World, and the lines, and the men, and Sara's word games.

Sara tells me she wants to go to a seed auction.

"What?" I ask her.

"Yes, I really want to do that."

"But what is it, and where do they have one?"

"It *is* what it *sounds like*. And the closest thing to it they have here, I think, is a shop where they sell seeds and nuts and things. They have one in Wonders of Life."

So we go to the seed shop. She buys some seeds. Then she says she wants to see the ducks.

"What ducks?" I ask her.

"I don't know. Just ducks. I think I saw some on a pond somewhere."

We wander around and come upon some ducks on a pond. Sara picks up a rock and throws it at the ducks. They fly away.

"That's not nice!" I tell her. "Why did you do that?"

"I must see duck shun."

She must see duck shun. I don't even bother asking her why she must see it. She's just being eccentric, trying to seem mysterious. Just let her be. She must see duck shun. And what else, may I ask? Really!

And then, of course, I get it.

And then I understand the other one as well, the seed auction.

On our way back to the hotel, she sucks on something endlessly and loudly, as though she wants me to ask her what she is sucking on.

"What are you sucking on?" I ask her.

"Seeds." She sticks out her tongue. Two little sunflower seeds are lying on it.

"Why are you sucking them?"

"Figure it out yourself."

She's sucking seeds. I'm not getting anything.

Seeds are sucked. Make it simpler.

She sucks seeds.

Succeeds.

We have dinner with my mom at the Coral Reef restaurant in The Living Seas. There are four big glass panels on one side of the room, through which one can see sharks, a swordfish, stingrays, a jewfish (which is huge: it's sort of a grouper), and many smaller fishes.

Mom is in a slightly better mood, but all we talk about are

the fishes in the aquarium, and pet fishes in general, and my girlfriend Charlotte's dead goldfish, the one I gave her, Al.

I hope Sara will not come to my room tonight. I don't want to see her. As I am thinking this, there is a knock on the door. Maybe it's my mother. I have never been so happy at the thought that maybe a knock on my door is from my mother paying me a surprise visit.

"Who is it?" I ask softly, standing a few feet away from the door, because I don't want to be near, or touching, something that Sara might be near, or touching.

"It's me," answers Sara in a singsong voice.

"What do you want?"

"Open the door."

"I'm very tired. I was already falling asleep."

"Aw, come on. I have a surprise."

I bet I know what it is. I bet she bought me a pair of shorts and she'll request that I try them on in front of her.

"I really don't feel well right now," I tell her.

"I don't either. I can't fall asleep, so I just want to chat for a few minutes, and then I'll be sleepy." She begs, just like my mother when she pays me surprise visits in the city.

"Are you sure you can't just read or something?" I ask.

"Yes, I'm sure."

I open the door with dread. She walks in, wearing a white terry-cloth bathrobe.

"I was only joking," she says. "I don't have a surprise. I just wanted you to open the door."

She takes off her bathrobe and drops it on the floor. She is naked.

I clutch the closet, to prevent myself from dropping to the floor like her bathrobe. "What are you doing?" I ask.

"I'm hot. Don't mind me."

She lies down on my bed, turns on the radio, and starts flipping through the hotel Bible restlessly, to the beat of the music, like a metronome. It's classical.

I pick up her bathrobe and throw it over her. "Please put this back on or get out of my room. You should not show yourself naked in front of me."

She kicks off the robe. "Why? I'm only a little girl. Children are allowed to be naked. You look so funny when you try to be harsh."

"You're not going to put it back on?"

"No, I'm not. I'm hot."

"And you're not going to leave?"

"No. I want to chat. I can't fall asleep."

I suddenly get a very clever idea, which I am very proud of. I am gloating at how it will disappoint her, and there will be nothing she'll be able to do about it. I open a drawer and take out one of my long black socks. I walk to the chair by the window, grinning, not looking at Sara, though I can see from the corner of my eye that she is following my movements, probably with curiosity. I sit on the chair and tie the sock around my head, over my eyes. I wonder if she will voice her disappointment or hide it.

"You're very prudish, you know, Jeremy?" she says.

"That's nice. Otherwise what's new?"

"Nothing is new."

"That's too bad. So what did you want to chat about?"

I hear her slam the Bible down on the night table. Now that I am blindfolded, I remember the body that I saw, and I look at it in my mind. I cannot take my eyes off it. It is the most flawless and beautiful body I have ever seen.

Sara laughs and sits on my lap. She's quite heavy for a supposed little girl.

"I got you now," she says.

"Oh, don't do this," I whine.

"You can't see me, so what does it matter? I could be wearing a space suit as far as you're concerned."

She strokes my hair, plays with the end of my sock.

"What do you think I should do to help me fall asleep?" she asks.

"Imagine you are slowly falling down a dark hole, like Alice in Wonderland."

She kisses me on the mouth, for the first time. My lips are tightly shut. I am not breathing.

"Relax," she says. "Imagine you are falling down a dark hole, like Alice in Wonderland."

"You should do this with someone your own age," I say.

She slides her hands under my sweater and caresses my bare skin. I am paralyzed. I am excited by her, and that is why I am paralyzed. I can't help having these thoughts: Well, she really *wants* to do it. It's not as though she didn't try. She sure tried hard, for weeks, she did everything in her power for this to happen. She would be terribly hurt if I rejected her now. It might even scar her for life.

And I become red with shame at the thought of what society would think if it heard my thoughts. But the thoughts come back; I can't keep them away: Why shouldn't she have sex at eleven? She certainly seems ready.

And as though agreeing with my thoughts, Sara says, "I got my first orgasm six months ago, just a few weeks after I got my first period. Isn't that interesting. I'm ready."

My thoughts continue: What openness. What brass. Who knows, she might be advanced like those girls in Africa. They do it when they're like five, I heard. Apart from that, I can tell that she's dying to do it. This isn't just innocent platonic childish affection. It's excitement and lust. That's undeniable. I don't know what to do.

I take my Bic pen out of my pocket and rest my front tooth on the tip of its cap, even though I swore I would never do it again.

She puts her hand on my crotch, over my pants, and this causes sudden, automatic, conditioned disapproval on my part. "You should do this with someone your own age," I say, taking her hand away and putting my tooth back on the tip of my pen.

My pen slips and stabs my palate. Blood gushes out. I don't even bother to swallow it quickly. My mouth fills up.

"Oh, you hurt yourself," she says. "It's my fault. I made you nervous, and now you're bleeding. Do you forgive me?"

I nod my head and feel a drop dribbling out of the corner of my mouth.

She kisses me. She unbuttons my pants, unzips them. She gets up and lowers my trousers and underwear as far as she can. I am erect.

"Oh, so that's what a thingy looks like," she says.

I wish I could give her a look of disapproval, but since my eyes are covered I need to do all the expressing with my mouth, so I sort of scrunch up my lips in reproach.

"I'm only kidding," she says, "Remember, I live with nude men. I know what these things look like."

She tries to pull my pants from under me with all her strength, but doesn't succeed.

"Do you think you could bounce a bit?" she asks.

I stay paralyzed. I do not allow myself to "bounce," even

though I would like to. She tugs one side of my trousers, then the other. I know that she's not making any progress, because I can feel my pants bunched under me, blocked by the weight of my bottom. But I do not help her. It would be a crime; I would be participating.

She suddenly stops pulling and laughs. "You look so funny."

I can imagine that I do look funny. For a second, I experience a surge of inward laughter. I expect it to seep out, at least in an irrepressible smile, but a mixture of panic and desire quenches the smile before it is born, like a stifled sneeze. Not the slightest muscle or wrinkle twitches on my face. I have never been as sexually excited in my entire, goddamned life. I am taking this whole thing much more seriously than she is.

I hear paper tearing. It sounds like a candy wrapper. I feel her hands. She is putting a condom on me. That I did not expect. Under my sock, my eyes are open wide with surprise.

"You've done this before?" I ask.

"No," she says, her voice filled with pride. Pride at her skill, not pride at never having done this before. I explain this because I know it with absolute certainty, and it might be misunderstood.

Yes you have, you lying piglet: This is a delirious thought on my part, with no foundation whatsoever and no thought behind it.

"I don't want to catch an incurable disease from you," she explains. "Or an incurably fatal disease, or a fatally incurable one."

How romantic.

"I thought of all the combinations," she says.

Yes, I see.

"For that matter," she continues, "I wouldn't like to catch a baby from you either, because then I'd have to go on one of those TV shows with many other girls who have small numbers and who caught babies. I'm going to take your blindfold off now."

"No!" I cry. "I would rather not see your face."

"But I want you to see us."

"No, because I must not see your face."

"You're so difficult, you spoiled little chicken," she says, annoyed.

She gets up. I hear her walking around the room, rummaging through things. She comes back to me, straddles me, and takes off my blindfold. I scream. Mickey Mouse is sitting on me. No, it's just a mask. Sara is so ingenious. Now I don't have to stare at her face, I can stare at Mickey Mouse. She puts me into herself. The mouse is grinning at me obscenely; he looks as if he's having fun, but I imagine that under the mask, Sara must be squinting with pain, clenching her teeth. I do not take my eyes off the glimmering black eyes inside the mouse's eyes, and they are fixed on me as well. I wish I could see her expression, to know if she truly is grimacing, as I imagine, or if it's different. I can tell nothing. The mouse keeps smiling, and the music keeps playing, and she even knows that you're supposed to move. I don't move. I feel selfish not to, but it's against my principles.

She slaps my arm. "Move! I know you want to."

If she's going to start beating me, I will not stupidly stick to my principles. That would be too much. So I move.

Afterward I accompany her to her room, and I ask, "Did it hurt?"

"Yes," she says.

I leave her and go out of the hotel. I walk in the night and I cry. I'm a pervert. Would a normal man have been able to get excited by an eleven-year-old girl, even if she threw herself at him? Probably not. I think about what will happen now. The little girl will tell her mother, the mother will tell the police, and the police will come and get me and put me in jail for the rest of my life, and I won't fight them because what I did was horrible. It's not as though I didn't know it was horrible. Society pounds it into your head from your earliest days. I knew very well that it was a horror for little girls or little boys to have sexual intercourse with an adult, or with anyone. A horror. It's called child molestation, even rape, when they're that age and you're that age. Because children do not come on to adults, they simply don't, it's a fact that everyone knows, unless it's in total childish innocence that they come, to get the affection of a father or mother. But they do not think about sex at all, they do not have any sexual urges, they just have curiosity. I knew all this, but I chose to ignore it. I will not resist the police. I will simply wait for them to come and get me. Or maybe I should just kill myself now.

chapter *seven*

The next day we return to New York. No one says anything unusual, and my mother suspects nothing. Sara goes home, my mother goes back to her house in the country, and I go to my apartment. Charlotte greets me when I arrive. I had forgotten that she had moved into my apartment. I expected to be alone. She asks me how the trip went. "Good," I say, and answer her questions absentmindedly.

Minou is in the middle of her second heat. She peed on my kitchen counter. Thick, concentrated pee, in small puddles. I am much too preoccupied by the previous night to ask Charlotte why she allowed the pee to dry without cleaning it.

I clean the counter and wait. It's five o'clock, and I know that Lady Henrietta may call me at any moment, as soon as Sara finishes telling her what I did. Or maybe Henrietta won't even bother to call. Maybe she'll just send the police. I am a pervert, and I am waiting with relief for the police to come get me.

You might think that this is a perfect opportunity for me to make a wish on my little white elephant. I could wish that Sara never tells Henrietta what happened. But I don't. It does not really occur to me to make a wish regarding this problem. When one is hopeful that a certain bad thing will not occur, one does not use one's white elephant, because to do so would seem too trivial, too pointless, childish, hopeless, which should demonstrate to you that I am not as empty-headed as I may seem, my head is not so very much in the clouds. I *am* a down-to-earth person when life gets serious.

Henrietta doesn't call that evening, and the police don't come. The next day I wait. Sara must have hesitated before telling her mother. But she's going to tell her very soon, I'm sure.

The phone doesn't ring that day.

The next day I wait, and the phone rings. I answer. It's Lady Henrietta. I am barely breathing, my eyes are closed, I feel that the end of my life has come.

"Hi," she says, cheerfully.

Her tone surprises me. "Hi," I answer.

"How are you?" she asks.

"Okay."

"I wanted to thank you for what you did."

"Oh."

"I know you really didn't want to go to Disney World, and it must have been such a bore for you, but now things are going great between Damon and me. We're quite involved. We had the most romantic weekend in the world. I owe you for life."

"That's okay."

She talks a bit more. I'm not really listening. We hang up.

Sara didn't tell her mother. What is she waiting for? This is a new development I must deal with. But it makes sense. Children who have been sexually abused very rarely tell anyone. They are too ashamed; they think it's their fault. Or maybe Sara simply didn't feel like telling her mother because she thought she would get in trouble.

I sit on my couch all evening, staring blankly in front of me. It gets dark outside. I don't turn on the light. Sara could tell her mother any minute, any day, any week, any month, any year. The police could come and get me anytime between now and ten years from now, or even when I'm eighty, they could come. I don't know what to do.

I live, that's what I do: meaning, I brush my teeth, I go to sleep, I wake up in the morning, I eat, I go to work, I file, I live. Charlotte notices that there's something wrong with me. She makes a comment, and I make a comment, and we drop it.

I live for three days. Then I live for a fourth day. Then I hesitate a little, and I make it to the fifth day. I then sit on my couch and live through a sixth day. And then I sit on my couch again, and I stop living. I cannot brush my teeth or go to bed anymore. I cannot go to work and file. On the seventh day, my buzzer rings. It must be the police.

"Who is it?" I ask in the intercom.

"It's Sara."

I let her up. When I open my door, Mickey Mouse is standing there in front of me. It's a nightmare, a punishment. Sara walks in and says, "Why haven't you called me? I thought you would call me. I've been waiting for your call."

"What do you want?" I ask her.

"The usual."

"What is the usual?"

"Isn't it obvious? Isn't it written all over my face?"

I stare at her mask and say, "No, that is *not* the usual."

"Well, it should be. It will be. And it is in my mind. Your girlfriend isn't home?"

"No."

"Where is she?"

"Having dinner with friends."

"When will she be back?"

"In a few hours."

"Can I have something to drink?"

"What do you want?"

"You choose. Surprise me."

I go to the kitchen and try to think of the most unsexual drink I know. Coffee? No, it excites one. Tea? No, that has caffeine too. Herb tea? Yes, that's good. Mint? No, that's also a stimulant. Sleepy-Time? Yes, it'll make her drowsy. But on second thought, no, because "Sleepy" is too much like "Let's sleep together." Chamomile? Yes! There is nothing more unsexual than a digestive aid.

When I come back out with the tea, Sara is not naked. Good. What a relief. We're off to a fine start. My spirits rise slightly.

Sara is petting Minou, who's rolling around on her back. "Why is your cat acting so strange?" she asks.

I certainly don't want to tell her that Minou is in heat, or it might inspire her. I could tell her Minou is distressed because my mother saw her fur balls on the floor. Or I could tell her she's rolling around with happiness because she's getting along splendidly with my girlfriend, who just moved in.

Finally, I answer, "She's just hot, that's all."

"But why does she want so badly to be petted? She's completely frantic."

I reply the first thing that pops into my mind: "She likes to be petted when she's hot, because it aerates her fur."

"What do you mean, 'aerates'?"

"You know, it ventilates it."

"I wouldn't mind getting my fur aerated," mutters Sara.

I pretend I didn't hear, and we leave it at that. We drink the tea and talk about the weather. She's the one who brings up the weather, and I'm glad; I could not have thought of a more wonderful subject to discuss with her. Deliciously impersonal. Perhaps if we get sufficiently into it, we can talk about the weather until Charlotte gets back in a few hours, and I will have survived this visit. After a while, though, the conversation is becoming one-sided. I'm the one talking about clouds, various clouds, and how I wish I knew the names of all the different types of clouds. And I tell her about rain, and the fact that one should not drink rain, because even though one might think that it's the purest water in the world, actually it's not, especially in the cities, because it picks up the pollution from the air as it falls from the clouds. And I tell her about snow, that I used to eat snow, and that one should probably not eat snow either, especially in the cities, for the same reason that one should not drink rain. And I tell her, "Could you please pour me a tall glass of warm summer rain." And I laugh. Sara is starting to look at me strangely. I don't know how I know this, since she is wearing the mask, but I do know it. Perhaps through the particular quality of her silence. A silence with her breath restrained, her breath just hanging there in the middle of her lungs, not going out very much and not going in very much.

I don't dare ask her why she's wearing that mask. If I'm lucky, maybe she'll forget she's wearing it. Or at least, maybe she'll forget *why* she's wearing it, which is what matters.

Finally, she says, "Did you have a good week?"

"Yes. Yes, I did," I lie, and nod. "And you?" I see the danger of that question as soon as I have uttered it, and I wish I had kept my mouth shut, because she either did or did not have a good week, both of which possibilities are probably my fault for reasons I don't want to hear or know.

"I had an interesting week," she says, "other than waiting nervously for your phone call. I had to write a story for school. The teacher gave me an A-plus on it, but then she called in my mother for a private conference because she thought the story showed that I might have problems at home. She's a stupid teacher."

I suddenly get very scared and wonder if her story is about a little girl who goes to Disney World and has an affair with a grown man.

"What was in your story that made your teacher think you might have problems at home?" I ask.

"Beats me."

"*Who* beats you?"

"No. Beats me, as in: I have no clue."

"Oh. Well, what was your story about?"

"Thank you for asking. The title was, quote: The Unauthorized Biography of the Late Humpty Dumpty. The True Story Behind His Great Fall. His Secret Addiction, His Hidden Obsession, His Torturous Temptation, His Dilemma: To Hatch or Not to Hatch? That is the Question. End of quote. Do you like the title?"

"Yes, but why did your teacher think you had problems at home? What was your story about?"

"Thank you for asking again. Once upon a time Humpty Dumpty had a temptation, a great desire. He wanted to be sat on by a hen. After all, it was normal, for he was an egg, and being sat on by a downy bird butt is an egg's natural destiny and desire. There was a big beautiful hen near where he lived. She was always sitting, and never on any eggs, and therefore she had plenty of vacant space under her for him. Humpty wanted ever so badly to go slide himself under her soft sitting bird butt, but he knew it was dangerous, it was a risk, for if he indulged in the pleasure of being sat on, he would soon hatch and would no longer be an egg, and he liked being an egg, and he wasn't sure he'd like being a chick. Do you like it so far?"

"Yes; go on," I tell her.

"Okay." Sara puts down her tea, walks over to me, takes my teacup from my hands, puts it on the table, and sits on my lap.

"What are you doing?" I ask.

"Telling you the rest of my story. So Humpty went to ask the advice of his brother, Lumpy Dumpty, who told him to have willpower, to resist the temptation of getting sat on, or he would hatch. 'To hatch,' said his brother, Lumpy, 'is undesirable. It's the unknown, it's probably immoral, and it's tremendously harmful psychologically *and* physically, if not downright fatal. It breaks you, it scars you for life, and that's if you're lucky enough to get glued back together again by the king's horses and men, but if you're not, then just forget it; you're in pieces. Getting sat on is sinful. Above all it's indecent. It shows the lack of any basic eggly decency.' Do you like it so far?"

"Yes," I reply, though I'm wondering if she's not indirectly trying to insult me through her story, since I am now being sat on by her.

"Humpty Dumpty knew that his brother Lumpy was probably right. However, one day he circled the hen many times, trying to imagine her downy bird butt feathers covering his hard bald shell, and he got chills of pleasure thinking of it. The hen frisked her downy bird butt in his direction and made soft bird sounds. Finally, he could resist the temptation no longer."

Sara slides her hand into my shirt and caresses my skin softly and says, "Humpty slowly slid himself under the hen, feeling each feather, one by one, move over every millimeter of his hard bald shell as though he were submerging himself in a warm, delightful bath. The bird smell was intoxicating, and he knew it was dangerous, knew that once eggs are drugged by the bird smell, they have no more will or desire to escape before they hatch. But Humpty was not drugged yet. It takes a while. Every few minutes he would turn himself over, to have every side of his body exposed to her warm feathers, much the way one might turn over a piece of food in the frying pan so that it will be cooked on both sides. That's what was happening to him, he realized: he was cooking. The longer he was sat on, the more the monster within him would grow, and soon it would come out."

Sara slides her hand out of my shirt and slowly starts unbuttoning my shirt buttons as she goes on: "Humpty gathered all his willpower, slid himself out from under the divine hen, and walked over to his meditation wall. He sat on the wall for days, and thought, and tried to make a decision. 'To hatch or not to hatch? That is the question,' he told himself. 'To be sat on or not to be sat on? That is the other question.' He did not think he could go through life without being sat on. Life simply would not be worth living. It felt so natural, so right, how could it be evil or immoral or harmful? After all, we all have a need. Some of us need to be sat on, and some of us need to get our fur aerated. Anyway, Humpty felt his soul shriveling under the strain of trying to resist something his body needed. He was becoming grim and bitter. Permanent wrinkles of unhappiness appeared on his hard bald shell of a face." Sara caresses my face. "But he still sat on his wall, thinking. Finally, he started rolling on his side, back and forth, with indecision and restlessness, and he had his great fall off his meditation wall. And all the king's horses and all the king's men couldn't put him back together again. Do you like it?"

"Yes, it was a very good story."

"It's not over. All the king's horses and all the king's men couldn't put Humpty Dumpty back together again. So they carried his pieces to the castle and . . ."

At that point Sara unbuttons my pants, slides her hand inside my underwear, and begins to stroke me, and I instantly stop hearing the rest of her story, as though I have become deaf or she started talking in another language. But her story is fascinating anyway, so I tell her, "Stop that. I can't concentrate."

"Stop what?"

"That."

"What I'm doing or what I'm saying?"

I can't answer her, because I'm not sure. I'm confused. That question requires quite a bit of thought and concentration, but I can't think clearly enough, no matter how hard I try, so I say, "You know which."

"No, I have no idea."

I make a superhuman effort to focus my mind, and I finally think of the proper, correct answer. "What you're doing."

"I can't, or *I* won't be able to concentrate on my story."

"Well, tell me a bit more. Tell me what happens."

She continues stroking me and tells me more of her story, not one word of which I hear, even though it's fascinating. So I tell her, "Speed up the pacing. Get to the point more quickly. You're too slow. It's boring. I can't concentrate."

She strokes faster.

I still can't hear what she's saying. "Blah blah blah blah," I tell her. "Hurry! Get to the point."

She strokes faster and continues her story.

"Louder! I can't hear you!" I say.

She talks louder and strokes harder. Suddenly, something feels strange.

"I can't concentrate! I can't hear you!" I cry out, panicked. "I haven't heard a single word you've said in the past five minutes, do you realize that?"

"I'm not offended," she says.

"You talk too loud and too fast, and you don't articulate well enough, and you skip vital information. It's unclear, it's too intense." I look at her, and I am startled. "My God, you're *nude*! When did you get so undressed?"

"When Humpty Dumpty was getting reconstructive surgery to remove his scars."

"I don't remember that part. I couldn't concentrate on your damn story, which is a shame cause it was so good. I wish I had heard it."

"Let's do one thing at a time, then," she says, and slides her hands inside my underwear again.

I take them out. "No, let us *not* do one thing at a time. Let us not do anything at all except get you dressed. Get dressed."

"Never."

"Never?"

"Ne-ver." She lowers my pants and my underwear, and I feel terribly awkward, being exposed like this. Sara's nudity never seems as naked as my nudity, for some reason.

"That's it. It's over," I tell her. "You're finished. We're finished. I'm calling your mother right now. This minute. I'll tell her everything that happened, and I'm bringing you back home."

I pick up the phone, but Sara slams my hand down. "Stop it, Jeremy! You *know* you want me. And you *know* the only way to get rid of a temptation is to yield to it. Resist it, and your soul grows sick with longing for the things it has forbidden to itself, and sick with desire for what its monstrous laws have made monstrous and unlawful."

"Where do you *hear* these wisdoms? From your mother?"

"No, Lady Henrietta did not say that. It was Lord Henry in *The Picture of Dorian Gray*. And I've put that quote at the beginning of my Humpty Dumpty biography. It's the message of the story."

"No wonder your teacher thinks you're having problems at home."

"Well fuck you. Doesn't that quote have any effect on you? Don't you see the truth in it?"

"Yes, it does have an effect on me. It snaps me back to reality with the word 'unlawful.' The word 'monstrous' causes a nice special effect in me as well. Would you like to see what it is?"

"What?"

I pick up the phone and say, "To call your mother."

Sara grabs my cheeks, squishes them angrily in her palms, and desperately shouts in my face, "But you're *misinterpreting Oscar Wilde*!"

"Let go," I say, articulating with difficulty through my squished cheeks.

She lets go, huffs, raises her arms, and slowly starts turning around, swinging her hips and undulating her body. As she turns, she snaps her fingers and rolls her wrists and stamps her feet like a Spanish dancer. Her beautiful breasts jiggle like Jell-O.

Calling Henrietta is not such a good idea, after all, especially while Sara is trying to distract me. So I take out some blank paper and a pen.

"What are you doing, Jeremy?" asks Sara.

"I am writing a letter of confession, which I will mail to your mother as I escort you back home."

I write down "Dear" on the paper, and then wonder if I should write "Henrietta," "Lady Henrietta," or "Lady," or "Ms. Lady Henrietta," or what. Sara grabs the pen from my hand and draws the face of Mickey Mouse on my letter.

She hands back the pen and says, "Now you can write the letter around it, and I'm sure Mom will appreciate the drawing. Letter reading is more fun when there's an illustration that explains the text."

I tear up the letter and start again on a new sheet. I write, "Dear Henrietta," and a comma. Sara tries to grab the pen from me again, but this time I am quicker than she is, and I hold the pen out of her reach. She lunges for my letter, but I beat her to it and press the letter and my pen against my chest and remain stiff and motionless in my chair.

She stands behind me and encircles me with her arms. I feel her cold plastic mask pressing against the side of my face. "I want to kiss you, Jeremy, but I can't because of this awful mask I'm wearing."

"Don't take it off!" I cry, because I am afraid to see the childish face of the person who is arousing me.

She slides her hands in my shirt. I push her away and snap, "Stop that."

"What?"

"That!" I shout.

"What I'm doing or what I'm saying?"

"*Both!*" I scream in her face.

But she does not stop, so I push her away again, but she comes back on me, so I finally leap up from my chair, rush to my bedroom, and come back with a long black sock, perhaps the very one that served me so well at Disney World. And now, for the second time, the faithful sock is coming to the rescue. Except that the last time, come to think of it, the sock didn't serve me so well after all.

I stand in front of Sara, near the couch, and say, "Sit."

She sits on the couch.

"No. On the floor."

She obeys me.

"Lie down."

"Oh, goody," she says, and lies on the floor, her bright, white, nude body shining up at me, glowing teasingly.

"Raise your arms above your head," I tell her.

She raises them, and I pass them on either side of the foot of the couch, and then I tie her wrists together with the sock.

"Wonderful," she says. "Now we're doing a bit of tying up. That means you're excited, right?"

I ignore her and go back to my letter.

"Jeremy, you were supposed to stay here," Sara says.

"No I wasn't."

"Okay, then I'll come and see you." And she easily slips her hands out of the sock knot and is all over me again.

The sock has failed me for the second time. I will not use any fabric softener at the next wash. Not because had the sock not been so well softened, Sara could not have slipped her hands out. No, I am not so dumb as to think that the extra lack of softness would have made any significant difference in the ease of Sara's escape. The reason I will not use fabric softener at the sock's next bath is, of course, to punish the sock for repeatedly failing me.

I go to the bathroom, climb on the toilet, and bring down my handcuffs from the ceiling.

When Sara sees the handcuffs, she sucks in her breath sharply and says, "Wow, Jeremy. Handcuffs. You're an exciting person."

With the handcuffs, I lock Sara's wrists around the foot of the couch, in the same position as before. She does not resist. She seems to be enjoying it, probably feeling a sense of power and challenge, and thinking: You can do anything you want to me, Jeremy, but you'll see, I'll still get you.

I go back to the table and stare at the "Dear Henrietta" on the page.

"Jeremy?"

I ignore her and try to concentrate. I wonder if I should start with: "I have committed a terrible crime" or "This is a letter of confession"?

"Jeremy, look at me."

I look at her. "What?"

"Can't you sit a little closer?"

"No." I look back down at the page. Or should I start with: "I'm very sorry to have to write this confession to you"? Finally, I cross out "Dear Henrietta" and write underneath: "My Lady." It's the most respectful greeting I can think of. Then I could begin with: "After you read this letter, I won't blame you if you'll want to kill me."

Sara says, "I've never had so much fun. This is exciting. But don't be too much of a tease. Don't keep me locked up too long."

I ignore her, but Minou doesn't. She is looking at Sara with great curiosity. She's never seen anyone lying on the floor like this before. But soon the novelty fades, and she goes back to rolling on her back with heat.

Sara is silent for a while, and then hums a bit, and then says, "His strong arms were resting on the table. His large right manly but sensitive hand was holding a pen. He was writing a letter to her mother, a letter describing all the sordid details, the sin that had occurred at the park of amusements. The pen, the lucky pen, held by those long graceful male fingers, was sliding against the page the way she wished his cheek would slide against her stomach. She, poor young woman, was lying naked as a worm on the cold hard floor, hands handcuffed around the foot of his couch. If only it was his foot, and not his couch's foot, she would feel consoled. The mask was on her face, the mask which he cruelly forced her to wear because he could not bear to see her ugly face. But her body, oh, her body was beauty itself, a swan, a naked princess."

Sara is silent again. Then she says, "Jeremy, unlock me."

"No," I answer.

" 'Jeremy, unlock me,' she repeated," Sara continues. "She said it over and over again, but he kept saying no, no, no. 'Jeremy, unlock me, unlock me, unlock me.' "

I ignore her. And then I hear a heavy sliding noise. I look up, and she is slowly dragging the couch across the slippery wood floor. She grips her bare feet to the floor and pulls her body forward and advances toward me, on her back, legs first, dragging the couch behind her. Her progress is very slow. She groans under the strain. Minou is absolutely horrified by this spectacle. She's not used to the couch moving around and making noise. She runs to the kitchen and hides.

I go back to my letter, and Sara says, "So the poor soul, the poor desperate little bird, started dragging the couch behind her, which was terribly straining her skinny, puny arms. It was making a loud grindy-like noise, and it was scratching his floor, which upset him more than the damage it was doing to her body. She might not even be able to have babies in the future, because her poor lovely delicate lustful body was being stretched like a rubber band so much."

"Stop dragging the couch," I tell her.

"Her body was burning with desire, and so was his. They both desperately wanted to get their fur aerated. He tried to concentrate on his letter, tried not to look at her, but it was hard."

What she says is true. She goes on. "Her skin remembered his touch from the park of amusements, and her skin was begging him; if only he'd look up from his letter, he'd see every one of her little hairs kneeling in prayer, praying that he would become rational and come to her."

I glance at her and look back down at my letter, my mind hot, as in a fever. I am aroused. I take a deep breath and read "My Lady" out loud, hoping that the sound of my voice will help me to focus my mind. Then I read as I write: " 'I am very sorry to have to write you this letter.' "

" 'Unlock me, unlock me, my lord, I implore you,' she cried, but he did not listen, or pretended not to."

" 'Something happened at Disney World which should never, *ever* have happened, something terrible,' " I read.

"He was terribly excited, was dying to get up and come to her, but was fighting the temptation with all his power, and he was a strong man, a strong, muscular man with rippling muscles and a hard manhood between his legs, a manhood that he wanted to give her but daren't, because he knew that it wast sin. I knowest that it ist sinst, he thought to himself."

" 'Your daughter and I had a good time at Disney World, but then one night we got carried away and lost our minds, or rather, I should say, *I* lost *my* mind, since she's a minor, and we did it, we made love.' "

I stop reading, because this particular scene I am living right now strikes me very strongly with déjà vu. I have seen this scene before somewhere, or a very similar one, hard as that may be to believe, for this scene is so strange, but I'm sure of it. And then I remember. It was in the film *The Exorcist*. Sara reminds me of the little girl possessed by the devil, who moved furniture. The girl was tied to her bed, just as Sara is chained to the couch. I am the priest, reading from the Bible, trying to destroy the devil with holy words, while the devil-girl is speaking to me, trying to tempt me, her face a mask of evil. The girl and the priest both talked at the same time to each other, each trying to win, trying to overpower the other.

Suddenly, Sara stops pulling the couch. She is close enough to me now that the tip of her foot can touch my foot when her leg is completely stretched out. She is lying there, below me, on her back, silent and panting, and she finally says, "He has finished his letter. He has revealed the whole truth, and he looks down at her and knows he's supposed to bring her home now, but he just doesn't know if he's going to be able to do it, because he knows that as soon as he unlocks her she will pounce on him, and then he won't be able to resist her, so why even try? Why even try? But he really should take off her handcuffs now. Her wrists must be sore from having dragged that heavy couch all that way, and he's not as cruel as he seems, he has a noble decent heart under that virile manly exterior. He really should look at those little wrists of hers. They might be bleeding, and then he would get in trouble with her mother. He should tend to those wrists if they are bleeding, before they get infected from the dirt on the floor. So he gets up."

Minou is sitting in the kitchen doorway, looking at Sara from a safe distance. She seems to have forgotten her heat for now. Things evidently got a little too weird for her taste.

Sara is silent for a moment. "He gets up!" she repeats, louder. She is silent again and then says, softly, "Jeremy, please get up."

I get up.

"And he walks over to her," she says.

I slowly, softly, walk over to her head and stand there, towering above her, looking down.

"And he crouches next to her face."

I slowly bend down.

"And he feels pity in his heart. He wants to give her a reassuring pat somewhere, but he's not sure where, because there's no place on her body that's not erotic in the position and the nudity she's in, so he takes the little key out of his pocket and unlocks her handcuffs."

I unlock her handcuffs.

She says, "He looks at her wrists, and they are rather red and irritated, but not bleeding."

I look at her wrists. Her description is accurate.

"She sits up," says Sara, and sits up, "and looks into his eyes for a long moment, through the holes of the Mickey Mouse mask."

Sara looks into my eyes. "She gets up and pulls him to his feet."

Sara gets up, takes my hand, and pulls me up. I yield.

"She leads him to the bedroom," says Sara, and leads me to

the bedroom. Halfway there, she stops and says, "*He* leads *her*
to the bedroom."

I lead her to the bedroom.

Sara says, "She wants him to aerate her fur the way a real
man aerates a real woman's fur."

I ask, "Not like the last time?"

"He asked. 'No,' she answered. 'The last time we aerated each
other's furs the way a woman aerates a man's fur.' "

"Really?" I say. "Is that the way you see it? That's how you
think women make love to men?"

"He asked. 'Well, if not that,' she answered, 'it was at least
the way little girls make love to men.' "

I must make love to her the way a real man makes love to a
real woman. But she is not a real woman. And I suppose one
could argue that I am not a real man.

I wear a condom and lie on top of her and make love to her.
Minou looks at me having sex with this mouse. I have an incredible urge and need to kiss Sara's face, but I don't dare take
off her mask for fear of seeing extreme youth underneath. I stick
my tongue in the eyes of her mask and in the mouth of her mask,
and my tongue gets quite cut up in one of the eyes from the
sharp edge of the plastic. It bleeds, and some drops of blood fall
on the mask and run down its cheek, making Mickey Mouse look
as though he's crying blood, which disturbs me greatly, so I close
my eyes and concentrate on being a real man.

Afterward Sara goes in the bathroom, runs the shower, and
stays in there for half an hour. I start getting nervous that
Charlotte might be coming home soon. When I knock on the
door and ask Sara why she's taking so long, she answers, "Do

you mind? I'm washing my femininity." I ask her to hurry up, but she doesn't, so I finally tell her to end her shower, but she tells me she hasn't finished washing her femininity yet. So eventually I get a knife to unlock the door, thinking there might be something wrong. Sara is sitting on the closed toilet, reading my boyhood diary, which she took down from the ceiling.

"It's a very interesting story about the little white elephant," she says.

"Yes," I say, taking my diary from her and closing it.

"Do you still have the elephant?"

"Yes."

"Do you ever make wishes on it?"

"No, of course not."

"Can I see it?"

"No. I don't know where it is, and I have to take you home now."

I take Sara home by cab. Just before getting out, she says, "My mom will be out with friends tomorrow for the whole evening. I want you to visit me at around five o'clock and aerate my fur again."

"No, I won't come," I tell her.

"I'll be waiting," she says, and gets out.

The cabdriver looks at me in his rearview mirror with a suspicious frown, I think. Then I go back home.

I have not sent the letter to Henrietta yet, because I must decide whether calling her might not be a better idea.

chapter *eight*

The following day I skip work again. I must stay home and decide whether I really will confess or not. It's not a light decision. After thinking about it all morning, I conclude that maybe I don't need to confess after all, because Sara was obviously not harmed, and I will never do it again. I have no more desire left in me. I can go on with my life.

At two o'clock, however, I start to feel some desire again, and this frightens me. These first twinges of longing slowly but inexorably grow. I feel like Humpty Dumpty, getting closer to hatching. There is a monster within me, a monster of lust, and soon he will come out, and he'll gladly accept Sara's invitation to visit her at five o'clock to aerate her fur. I am afraid of myself. I must confine and restrain myself before I hatch. I must enchain myself now, while I'm still ambivalent, still vacillating.

I take down my handcuffs from the bathroom ceiling and bring them to the kitchen. I handcuff my left wrist to the oven door and sit on a chair. I throw the key far into the living room. Minou pounces on it, thinking this is a game, and plays with it, eventually knocking it out of my sight. I will wait like this until Charlotte gets home at five-thirty and unlocks me.

Minou, having finally become bored with playing with the key, sits in the kitchen doorway, contemplating me. She says, I hope I'm not prying if I ask what you are doing.

I swear, sometimes you remind me so much of Henrietta's doorman, with your smug sentence structures, I reply.

Okay, she says. How's this: What the hell are you doing?

Leave me alone. I'm hatching.

I see. Let me know when you're done.

I have almost reached the point where if I were not handcuffed I would visit Sara with no hesitation. I have only a tiny drop of doubt left, a tiny grain of guilt. I say: I'm going to crack at any moment.

That's useful to know, answers Minou.

Oh my God, it's really happening. I just felt the first crack.

Is there anything I can do?

I bury my face in my hands. I want Sara, no doubt about it, no guilt about it; I wish I were not handcuffed. I can't believe I even considered going to jail for sleeping with her. It wasn't really so very wrong. It wasn't *that* dreadful, *that* horrendous. Let's not exaggerate. Why do I let myself be so tortured by it?

I know I will visit Sara tonight. It may be a bit wrong, a bit undesirable and unbecoming and unpraiseworthy, but it's not *that* despicable a crime. I sigh deeply and lift up my head and say, Okay, it's finished. I've hatched.

You have?

Yes.

What now?

I wish you could get me that key.

I can understand, she says.

Will you try?

Cream. Heavy, that is. Every day for a month. In exchange for the key.

Okay, I say.

Minou smiles, lies down, and falls asleep.

You useless piece of catness, I tell her.

Yeah, yeah, attaboy Jeremy, she replies in her sleep.

My only choice now is to wait for Charlotte to come home and unlock me. What will she think when she sees me like this? She'll want an explanation. Perhaps I could tell her that I was depressed and was testing a theory that says you should lock yourself to a famous tool of suicide to no longer be depressed. One's forced proximity to suicide tools revives one's taste for life, I'll say. Ovens are a classic suicide tool, even though they can't be used that way anymore, but it doesn't matter, it's the symbolism that counts, the connotations that ovens strike up in our minds. Most of this is subconscious, you know.

And Charlotte will answer, "Yes, I know," because she's a psychologist and will therefore agree with anything that contains the word "subconscious."

Five o'clock comes and goes. The phone rings. My machine answers, and I hear Sara, who says, "Knowing you, I bet you didn't go to work today. It's five-fifteen, and you're late. I want you to come and aerate my fur *this second*, do you hear? I'm waiting." She hangs up.

I must not let her words agitate me too much. I try to focus my mind on something else.

The suicide tool excuse might be a little too farfetched. I could simply tell Charlotte that I was playing with my new handcuffs and accidentally threw the key too far away. She'll ask me why I bought handcuffs, and I'll tell her I thought they would be fun. But she might put more meaning into it than I intended, and she might say, "You're right, we could have a lot of fun with handcuffs. Let's play with them after dinner." This thought fills me with such frustration and disgust that tears well up in my eyes. I angrily pull on the oven door like a desperate child, and it slides right off its hinges, as easy as you please. For a second I wonder if it's not an optical illusion. I didn't know oven doors could just slide off their hinges. You just pull them, and they slide. Presto! If I had known, I would have handcuffed myself to the refrigerator. But right now I thank God for my ignorance.

I rush to the living room to get the key to unlock myself from the oven door, but it's not there. Minou must have played with it until it got knocked somewhere unreachable. I look for it but can't find it, and I'm getting so impatient to see Sara that I finally just leave my apartment carrying the oven door like a briefcase. I feel quite embarrassed to be visiting Sara like this, for it will make me seem desperate and pathetic, but oh, well, whatever points of attractiveness I will lose by showing up with the oven door I can try to regain by concocting a witty explanation for it. If Sara, due to her young age, believes it, all the better.

When I arrive, Sara is wearing a white terry-cloth bathrobe, and though her face is hidden by the Mickey Mouse mask, I can plainly see that she seems truly taken aback.

"You're staring at my oven door," I remark.

"What's it for?"

"It's just a trinket I bought for myself, a trivial ornament of little value called an Imitation Handcuff Bracelet, to which one can attach various charms of one's choice. Today I happened to choose this nice faux oven door. Next week I might add to it a refrigerator door. It's a pleasingly masculine bracelet because, as you can see, the charms are not overly dainty or delicate."

"Poor Jeremy. You tried to resist me, didn't you? I told you it was useless."

And she throws herself in my arms, and I hug her and kiss her neck. She yanks off her Mickey Mouse mask and flings it across the room in a gesture of complete liberation, and I yank up my oven door to shield my face from the sight, but unfortunately I can see her through the little window. Sara approaches me and kisses me on the oven door. I force myself not to feel horrified by her youth. But what is finally even more striking than her youth is the fact that her features are no longer frozen in a tight Mickey Mouse smile. Her face floods my eyes with expressions of her thoughts, almost as though I can read her mind. She seems quite changeable and serious compared to the paralyzed hilarity I had gotten used to.

She takes my hands and lowers my oven door the way a man might lower an Egyptian woman's veil. She kisses me on the lips, softly at first, and then ravenously, which is understandable considering we've been so deprived of kissing each other's faces.

We lie down, me on my back, and try to make love, but I am unable to become aroused because I can't bear the sight of her face, which is so immediate and overpowering, so pure and undiluted. Feeling somewhat embarrassed, I pull the oven door over my face. Although I can still see her through the glass, I am able to deal with this maskless reality because we are protected from one another by the pane which prevents us from touching each other. The glass squishes my cheek, and crushes my nose to the side, but it comforts me, it relaxes me, it enables me to make love to her. I stare at her with one big eye as my breath fogs up the window. She knocks on the glass to get my attention, which she already has, and shouts to me in the oven, "Is it strange for you to be squashing your face with your charm, or do I just still have a lot more to learn about sex?"

I don't reply.

Afterward, when I'm getting ready to leave, Sara says, "Mom will be out tomorrow evening again. You can come at five and aerate my fur."

"No, I won't come."

"I'll be waiting."

I go back home, disgusted with myself for having slept with Sara a third time. And what will I tell Charlotte when I get home? How will I explain to her this oven door attached to my wrist? Perhaps I could tell her I accidentally picked it up instead of my briefcase when going to work this morning, that I was just absentminded. Terrible lie. I don't know what I'll tell her.

When I get home there's a note from Charlotte on the living room table, saying she had to go out for dinner and that she'll be back later. I'm so relieved. I scramble all over, looking for the key, and finally find it under the radiator. I unlock the handcuffs and slide the oven door back on its hinges.

I skip work again the next day. I stay home, sit on my couch, and think about what I should do. Eventually I handcuff myself to the refrigerator. After a while, I hatch. Hatching can be repetitive, I've discovered.

A m a n d a   F i l i p a c c h i

At five-fifteen Sara calls and says into my machine: "Why are you late today, Mr. Acidophilus? I know the way your mind works, and I'll bet you anything that you are handcuffed to the fridge right now. I checked the door of our fridge to see if there's any way you can escape, and I think your only chance is to unscrew the handle. If you do not succeed, then just wait for your girlfriend to get home and think of a good excuse to give her as to why you're attached to the fridge. Then erase this message, for the tape will not self-destruct like in *Mission: Impossible*, and come and aerate my fur. But don't bother coming if you're carrying the fridge door. It's just not worth it."

I can't unscrew the fridge handle because I placed all the screwdrivers and knives out of my reach.

Charlotte gets home. She comes into the kitchen and looks at me with great surprise, then walks up real close to make sure her eyes aren't fooling her.

"What are you doing?" she asks.

"I'm on a special diet that uses reverse psychology. It says that you're supposed to handcuff yourself to the refrigerator. It tries to disgust you with allowance and freedom and permission, making the forbidden fruit no longer forbidden. The motto is: 'You want it, you've got it, now get sick of it.'"

"You're kidding."

"No. And it says that it's not enough to merely yield to the temptation; you must lock yourself to it. With this diet, instead of locking the fridge, you lock yourself to the fridge. Most of this is subconscious, you know."

"Yes, I know," she says. "But it's weird psychology."

I ask her to please unlock me. She gets the key and does. I go to the answering machine and erase Sara's message. I suddenly realize that I will not visit Sara tonight, because Charlotte's mere presence is arousing my shame and stirring my conscience beyond my tolerance, not to mention the fact that this same mere but proper presence of hers always has the curious ability to moderate my sensual appetite in a fascinatingly implacable way, to put it mercifully.

The next morning I'm sitting on my couch, knowing that I will want to see Sara again, knowing that I'll have to handcuff myself to the fridge again, and I decide that I cannot face another day of being chained like a creature with rabies.

I pick up the phone and dial Henrietta's number, knowing it's the only solution and not allowing myself to think about it for one instant.

Henrietta answers.

"There's something I must talk to you about," I say.

"Oh, yes?"

"Yes."

"What is it?"

"Something happened in Disney World."

"Really?"

"Yes."

"What?"

"Something bad that will make you very upset. Something bad happened to Sara."

"She seems very happy. What happened?"

"I did something to her."

"Yeah?"

"Yeah."

"What?"

"I must have been insane at the time. I must have lost my

mind. We got along really well. She was very nice to me and very affectionate, and I lost control. We had sex."

"I know. Thank you. She wanted to for a long time. She had a crush on you from the first day she met you."

I pull the receiver away from my ear, and I stare at it. I put it back to my ear and I say, "What do you mean?"

"Don't worry about it, Jeremy. You did nothing wrong."

"I had sex with your eleven-year-old daughter at Disney World!"

"Don't shout. It doesn't matter. I'm all for it."

"Why didn't you tell me this right away? You knew I'd be feeling guilty and living through hell, waiting for the police to knock at my door, and then trying, but failing, to resist your daughter's repeated attempts at seducing me. Why didn't you tell me right away when I got back?"

"I didn't want to invade your privacy or make you uncomfortable if you didn't want to talk about it. But obviously you do want to talk about it, so we will, but when you've calmed down. You can come see me this evening, and I'll explain things."

"I don't want Sara to be there."

"Of course."

She hangs up. I remain sitting on the couch. Charlotte walks toward me slowly from the bedroom and says, "You had sex with an eleven-year-old girl?"

I stare at her. I had forgotten that this was Saturday and that she was not at work.

"I overheard the whole thing," she says. "It is horrifying. I'm going to tell your mother."

"Why my mother? Why not the police?"

"Because it's family business."

She heads for the phone. I step in front of her.

"I can call from anywhere," she says.

"I don't want you to call my mother."

"Yes, I will, darling. It's for your own good."

I feel all the rage toward her that has gathered in me over the months. The drop that overflows the glass. I give her a tremendous slap, with the intention of knocking her out.

She is on the floor, motionless. I feel guilty immediately. I feel I am sinking to greater depths, first by having sex with an eleven-year-old girl, then by purposefully knocking out my girlfriend. What am I going to do with her now, kill her? It wouldn't surprise me. And yet the slap has made me feel much better. Some of the rage is out of me.

I kneel beside her. She lifts her head.

"I'm sorry," I say. "You can call my mother if you want to. *I'll* call her."

I pick up the phone, but she prevents me. "It doesn't matter," she says.

Things seem to return to normal. Charlotte goes out shopping. An hour later my mother calls me.

"Charlotte told me everything."

I can't believe it.

"I can't believe it," she says. "You had sex with Sara when we were in Disney World?"

"Charlotte called you?"

"Yes, thank God. You must be punished." She hangs up.

I will break up with Charlotte. I can't stand her anymore. I will make her leave my apartment.

I go and see Lady Henrietta.

I ask her, "How could you approve of your daughter having sex at eleven years old? No mother accepts that."

She answers, "I've always been very open with my daughter, and she's very open with me. I've encouraged her to talk to me about whatever she wanted, about boys she had crushes on, about what types of relationships she hoped to have with them.

"I am for children's sexual liberation," she goes on. "Why should it be wrong for children to have sex if they feel like it? What right do we have to prevent them? But of course, they must feel like it. That's what determines the line between children's sexual liberation and child molestation. I am as strongly opposed to the latter as I am in favor of the former. I wanted to have sex when I was twelve. But I didn't, because society said it was wrong, and I thought: Society must have a good reason for believing children should not have sex, a good reason that I don't understand because I'm too young. But in a few years I'll understand it, and I'll be glad I waited.

"I remember lying in bed," she continues, "when I was thirteen, wondering how I'd be able to wait until the acceptable age, which I thought was around eighteen. The thought of waiting five years was hell. When I was sixteen, I almost did it but decided not to, because it was not quite the acceptable age. I still didn't know why I shouldn't do it, and I thought I must still be too young to understand. I am now thirty years old, and I haven't yet discovered the reason why I had to wait until I was eighteen to have sex, and I'm angry about it. I decided not to make my child go through that nonsense. Everyone is different. Some people don't find the idea of sex pleasant until they're nineteen or twenty. Some never find it pleasant. Others want to start when they're even younger than I was. And I'm not talking about innocent curiosity here. I'm talking about full-fledged sexual excitement, identical to what adults feel."

She looks at me in silence for a moment, and then says, "Before you came on the scene, Sara never expressed any desire to make love to anyone. She often talked about certain boys she wanted to kiss or even cuddle with. But when she met you, she started speaking to me about you immediately. She said she thought you were wonderful, that she was in love with you and wanted to make love to you. I wasn't sure exactly how I felt about you back then. You're not exactly run of the mill. I thought you were rather strange, no offense, especially when you first came to my studio to pose. I saw blood in your mouth. It scared me a little. I thought perhaps you were a bit disturbed. I always wanted to ask you about that. How did your mouth get full of blood?"

"I was resting my tooth against the tip of my pen," I explain, "and it slipped and stabbed my palate. The blood came out quickly, but I thought I was swallowing it fast enough for you not to notice."

"Well, that's a simple explanation, much less spooky than I feared. When I got to know you better, I realized that I had been right. You are not the run of the mill. But I also realized that you were better than the run of the mill, that you were gentle and kind, and that there was no one I would have preferred my daughter to fall in love with than you. Nevertheless, I thought that her interest might fade. To tell you the truth, I even hoped it would, because although it seemed perfectly clear to me that Sara should do whatever she felt like, there remained a part of me, from the old days, that thought that maybe I was still too young to understand why children shouldn't have sex. Anyway, Sara's interest in you certainly did not fade; it became a passion. By then I had gotten used to the idea that she had made up her mind to charm you. I started worrying about how disappointed she would be if you did not reciprocate her affection. I was virtually certain that you could never be interested in her because she was so young and because you were interested in me. I told her this many times. I didn't want her to get her hopes up. I told her she should set her mind on someone her own age, but she wouldn't give in. That's when she came up with the idea of Disney World. It was her idea, and she spoke in such a rational, intelligent, and mature way that she convinced me to let her go with you."

The more I listen to Lady Henrietta, the more I feel my guilt and tension leaving me.

"How old were you when you first wanted to have sex?" she asks me.

"About ten."

"How old were you when you did?"

"Twenty-one."

"Was the wait bothersome?"

"Yes."

"Frustrating?"

"Yes."

"To say the least?"

"Yes."

"May I go so far as to say that it was a form of torture?"

"Yes."

"Children should be educated, not kept in ignorance. The only danger for them is pregnancy and disease."

"I don't want to see or hear from Sara anymore," I reply. "Tell her to stop calling me. *You* may not think that what happened was wrong, but I don't want to live my life this way. I was hoping you'd put an end to it. In a way, you did. I can never again do what I did with Sara, knowing that you know about it."

* * *

I feel much better, but I realize I do not like Lady Henrietta as much as before. As a result of having been traumatized, I crave normalcy now.

I go back to my apartment. Charlotte's there.

"You called my mother," I accuse her.

"You told me I could."

"But you said you wouldn't."

"I changed my mind."

"So did I," I say. "I think we should not see each other for a while. I would like you to leave my apartment. I want to live alone again."

"Oh."

"I want you to be gone by tomorrow evening. I'll sleep on the couch tonight."

The next day I am in the supermarket, buying food. I'm at the lemon stand, looking at all the plump yellow lemons. Whenever I see lemons I get a strong feeling of identification, and now, as I gaze at a whole pile of them, I get a feeling of belonging, of acceptance. It's only with lemons that I feel this way, because we share bitterness. A woman stands next to me and says, "You're tall; could you please grab me a box of those garbage bags up there?"

"Do you want the tall kitchen garbage bags or the bigger kind?" I ask.

"The tall kitchen kind."

I hand her the box.

"Thank you so much," she says. "I'll use these garbage bags tonight to teach my daughter how to throw things away. She's eleven, and she never throws anything in the garbage. Yet she's not dumb. She's quite mature for her age, but of course not mature enough to go to bed with a man."

The woman turns around and walks away. I stand there staring at her back. I have never seen her before.

When I get home, I ask Charlotte, "Have you been sending a friend of yours around to bug me?"

"No; why? Has someone bugged you?"

"A stranger came up to me and spoke to me about little girls and sex."

"It's your guilty conscience punishing you."

That evening, Lady Henrietta calls and invites me to visit her the next evening. I hesitate.

"Why are you inviting me?" I ask.

"Because I want us to remain friends. I don't want what happened to spoil our friendship. Laura will be there. I'm sure she'd love to see you."

I am exasperated. Will this Laura thing never end?

"Laura and I don't click," I say. "She is the dullest person I've ever met."

"You're wrong. She's just shy. Once you get to know her better, she becomes downright interesting. I promised her you'd come over again soon. See her at least once more, and then we'll drop it."

"Will Sara be there?"

"Yes."

"Then I would rather not come."

"I think you should see her. I think there are things she wants to tell you."

"I'm sure."

"It won't kill you. See her at least once."

It's 10:00 p.m., and Charlotte is still in my apartment, reading peacefully in bed. I confront her.

"I asked you to be gone by this evening."

"I don't agree," she says.

"We're broken up now. We're not boyfriend-girlfriend anymore."

"I don't agree that we broke up."

I'm too tired to fight her. I'll wait till she's in a better mood. I sleep on the couch.

My mother calls me just as I'm falling asleep.

"Did you enjoy my lemon woman?" she asks.

"What are you talking about?"

"My supermarket lemon woman with the garbage bags?"

"You're the one who sent that woman to talk to me?"

"Correction. I hired her."

I feel relieved that I'm not going insane. But I don't feel the anger she probably expects me to feel. I am indifferent and tired.

"What do you want?" I ask.

"What I want is to know if you enjoyed my lemon woman."

"No, but obviously you did."

"You're wrong, Jeremy. This is not a game I'm playing. I'm spending my life savings to hire people to punish you. This is the only way I can help you and save you. You need to be taught a good lesson."

"Don't waste your money on me."

"Nevertheless, that is what I will do, which should prove to you how much I love you."

"I appreciate the gesture, but really it's not necessary."

"I think it is."

"Then do as you wish."

The next day, as I'm walking home from work, a man bumps into me in the street. He turns around and says, "I'm sorry."

"It's okay," I say.

He starts talking: "I always feel so bad when I bump into people, especially men, because I'm afraid they think it's a threat, like in the movies. Especially western movies, I think. I often see those movies with my stepdaughter. She's twelve. So pretty and affectionate, but I could never be sexually attracted to a little girl. No normal man can."

And he rushes off. I stop walking and stare at his figure as it disappears behind a corner.

When I open the door to my apartment, my phone is ringing. I pick up the receiver.

"Did you enjoy *that* one?" asks my mother.

"Clever. Do *you* write the scenarios?"

"Yes."

And she starts criticizing me, telling me how horrible what I did in Disney World was, how could a child of hers do this, etc., etc. I say I know, it's true, it was horrible, unforgivable, I *am* a monster, etc., etc. And I mean it. We hang up. I smell pee. I look around, but I don't see anything. Then I see. I am sitting on it. Minou began her third heat by peeing on my couch. I spend the next hour trying to wash it out, first with hand soap, which doesn't work, then with too much Woolite, which I can't rinse out afterward. It's slimy and keeps foaming up.

That evening, I go to Lady Henrietta's place. Laura is not there yet, but Sara is. Her mother leaves us alone.

Sara speaks first: "I'm afraid that maybe I made a mistake."

"I made a mistake too," I say.

"No, you didn't. I did. I put our friendship in danger. Our friendship means more to me than anything, and I would never have tried to . . . charm you if I thought it would ruin things."

"I'm very sorry about what happened," I tell her. "I'm a weak man, and what I did was very bad."

"I'm not sorry. Being with you those times was wonderful."

I stare in silence. She continues: "I understand that you feel embarrassed with me now. I should have thought of that beforehand, but I didn't. I know you can't love me the way you would an older woman, so all I ask for is your friendship. We can forget about what happened, and I promise I won't try to charm you anymore. I'll just be very frank and very direct. There won't be any more teasing or flirting. There won't be anything that will make you uncomfortable. So will you still see me sometimes, when you come visit my mother?"

"Of course."

"Thank you," she says.

We then carry on a bit of small talk, and she leaves.

Henrietta comes back, and Laura arrives. The moment I see Laura, I realize she is exactly who I need. The very traits in her that I had found unpleasant before, I now crave. Her sanity, her normalcy. I love every word she utters. I love it when she says, "How've you been, Jeremy? I haven't seen you in a long time."

"I've missed you," I tell her, barely believing that I'm saying this. I glance at Henrietta to see if she heard me. She is staring at me with surprise. I won't let it embarrass me.

Laura looks at me with surprise too, but mostly with pleasure.

"How have *you* been?" I ask her, as we go to sit on the couch.

"Fine, thank you."

I ask her about her show and rack my brain to think of other things to say, but can't come up with anything, and she can't either, because we don't have much in common. It's wonderful to find someone to whom you have nothing to say. It's so normal and sane. Much better than exchanging dozens of twisted little comments with Henrietta.

The next day I'm with Tommy (my crotch brooch friend) in a bookstore. We're buying Cliffs Notes for him. An old woman with an umbrella walks toward us. We watch her coming, not really paying attention. She stops in front of us. She takes the handle of her closed umbrella in both hands and holds it in the air like a baseball bat. She swings her umbrella and gives me a tremendous blow on the hip.

"Ow!" I say, holding my hip.

Tommy steps back, expecting that he'll be next, but the old woman pays no attention to him; all her interest is focused on me. She stares at me viciously and says, "You are an abomination to your family! You are a monster."

A few people are looking as she walks away.

"Do you know her?" asks Tommy.

"Not really."

"What do you mean, not really?"

"No—I mean no."

"Why didn't you tell me that you were an abomination to your family?"

"I don't really have a family."

"Except for your mother."

"Yeah."

"Poor Jeremy. Things like this only happen to you. She seemed to know something about you. Did you do anything very naughty that could cause such a venomous reaction?"

"I've never even seen her before. She's insane."

"You didn't answer my question, so I must assume that you did do something very naughty."

An hour later, I am back at my apartment, kneeling on the floor, scrubbing the newly pee-drenched couch, when the phone rings.

"What about *that* one?" says my mother's voice, which has become nauseating to my ears.

"It hurt," I answer. "Was the violence included in your scenario, or did your employee improvise?"

"Nothing is improvised."

"What are you going to do next? Have one of your agents run me over with a car?"

"How dare you speak to me that way. How dare you even insinuate such a thing!"

She hangs up but calls me many more times, bugging me. I waste practically my whole evening talking on the phone with her. I finally warn her that I will change my number if she doesn't stop phoning me.

Notice that I do not make a wish on my little white elephant for the agents to stop coming. Why? Because I know it's pointless. But then why am I so filled with hope when I make a wish for certain people to love me? And more important, why am I not repelled by the idea of making a certain person love me unnaturally, against her will, by using magic? Wouldn't I prefer it if her love for me was genuine?

Charlotte is not moving out of my apartment. I keep asking her to, ordering her to, but she doesn't do it. She refuses to acknowledge that we're broken up.

I try to explain to her the concept of breaking up. "You don't need two people to do it. In a couple, if only one of the people wants to be broken up, then the couple is broken up."

"I don't agree."

"Anyway, I'm involved with someone else."

"Is it a little boy this time?"

I've been thinking a lot about Laura. The thought of her normality soothes my mind. I often go to Lady Henrietta's apartment to see Laura.

One day I invite her to have dinner with me at a nearby restaurant. As we walk there, a woman passing us bumps into me lightly. She turns around and says, "I'm sorry."

"Leave me alone!" I growl.

She walks away, looking bewildered. Laura looks no less bewildered. "What's wrong?" she asks.

"Oh nothing, I'm sorry; I made a mistake."

"What mistake?"

I try to think of an explanation. "Oh, I don't know. I was in a daze, and she caught me by surprise."

Laura raises her eyebrows at my unconvincing explanation and stops questioning me.

At dinner, we talk of nothing interesting whatsoever, and I love it. I learn that she is one year younger than I am. I did think beforehand of a few things to ask her, so we could make a bit of conversation. I ask her how many students she has. She says ten. She also tells me that recently, to her disappointment, three children dropped out when their parents found out what it was, exactly, that they were paying for.

I tell her my childhood story of the little white elephant, thinking it might interest her since it has to do with magic. She thinks it's sweet. But I don't tell her that I still keep the elephant on my night table. We're not close enough for that.

After dinner, as we walk in the street, an old man stops us and says, "Excuse me, but could you please tell me where Bloomingdale's is?"

I stand there gritting my teeth, while Laura gives him directions. I look at him with tentative hatred, dying to tell him to fuck off but knowing I can't risk a second mistake in front of Laura. After giving him the directions, Laura tells him, "But Bloomingdale's is closed right now."

"Oh, I know," he says. "I just want to make sure I know where it is, because I'm taking my granddaughter there tomorrow. She's eleven, and I can't let her go there alone, or some pervert might try to pick her up and have sex with her. Do you think I should let that happen?" he asks Laura.

"No," she says, and starts pulling at my arm, to get us away.

I yield with great joy to her pull.

The man calls after us, "Wait a minute, mister, what about

you? Do you think I should have sex with an eleven-year-old girl?"

I am perspiring as we walk away. The rest of the evening unfolds very pleasantly. We get heavily involved romantically that very night, because it feels too right to wait.

Back home, the ordeal begins again.

"What about that one?" my mother's voice crackles.

I hang up. Ring. I pick up, hang up. Ring. Pick up, hang up. Ring.

Charlotte is obnoxiously serene, reading a book, paying no attention to the phone.

Notice that I do not make a wish on my white elephant for Laura to love me. This is because I feel she probably already does, and since this is the case, I would not want to think her love for me is caused by magic, that she's under a spell. If, on the other hand, I did not sense that she already loved me, and I desperately wanted her to, I would not for one moment hesitate to use the white elephant, even though it never worked in the past when I tried it on certain people.

Ring. Pick up, hang up. Ring.

I escape outside, into the night, but I realize I can't be alone, no matter where I go. Any of the people walking in the street, or shopping in a supermarket, or sitting in a movie theater, could be hired by my mother.

I must take control of my life. I go to a store, buy an avocado, walk to the park, and sit on a bench. I bite into the avocado, skin and all, and then I twirl the piece in my mouth, detach the skin from the flesh with my tongue, and spit out the skin. I once saw an Oriental woman eating a kiwi that way in the subway.

I eat three more mouthfuls using this method, then I place the bitten avocado next to me on the bench, I take out a scrap of paper and my Bic pen, and I make a list of things to do:

1. Have Minou spayed.
2. Kick Charlotte out of my apartment.
3. Get an unlisted phone number.
4. Keep my apartment clean.
5. See more of Laura.

I try to think of other resolutions I might want to add. I want a real list, a juicy, meaty list. Suddenly, a sixth resolution comes to my mind.

6. Ask for a promotion at the magazine.

When I get home, I take out my little ivory elephant and think to it: If you are magic, I make a wish that when I ask for a promotion at work, they will give it to me eagerly. In fact, they will somehow be grateful that I finally asked.

The next morning, when Charlotte has left for work, I get my locks changed. I take all of Charlotte's belongings and put them in the hallway outside my door. I then call the veterinarian and make an appointment for the following day. And then I call the telephone company to have my number changed. They will change it in three days. Better than never.

I go to work. I will ask them today. How should I act? Strong and confident? Or nice and charming and humble? Asking for a promotion is in itself a strong and confident thing to do, so maybe I should be nice and charming in the execution of that act.

I knock on my superior's open door.

"Yes?" he says.

"Do you have a minute? I'd like to talk to you," I ask, smiling.

"Okay."

I sit across from him and wipe my moist palms on my knees. Annie comes in to arrange some books on the shelves. It disturbs me that she's here, but my superior pays no attention to her and waits for me to talk, so I begin. "I feel that I have paid my dues," I tell him. "I've filed for a long time. I've done a little fact checking, but not much. I was wondering if I could get a promotion." I glance at Annie. She glances back at me with skepticism; perhaps even contempt; at the very least condescension.

"Really?" asks my boss, looking surprised.

"Yes. Why do you seem surprised?"

"I don't know. To what position would you like to get promoted?"

"I guess full-time fact checker. At least."

He nods thoughtfully. "I'll have to discuss this with Cathryn," he says. Cathryn is the editor in chief. "I'll let you know what she decides."

"Okay," I say, wiping my palms on my trousers once more and getting up. "Well, thank you. I appreciate it." I nod to him and leave the room.

I file nervously, telling myself not to be nervous. The worst they can say is "no," right? And why would they say that? I'm a nice person and I file well. I may be meek and boring, but certainly no one can say I am not nice. Prepare yourself for a long wait, I tell myself. Don't expect them to get back to you today. And probably not tomorrow either. It may take a week before they give you their answer. They may even forget. I'll have to remind them, if they haven't gotten back to me in a week.

Time flies more quickly than usual. About two hours later, Annie comes to me and says, "He can see you in his office now."

"Oh, okay," I answer, dazed.

She follows me into the office and again arranges the books on the shelves.

I sit across from my boss.

"I just spoke with Cathryn," he says, "and after some deliberation, we both agreed that your services are no longer needed."

"What do you mean?"

"We would appreciate getting your resignation tomorrow morning, if that is convenient for you."

"I'm willing to keep on filing."

"That is not convenient for us. We would prefer to get your resignation. We would be grateful."

"Why? What made you decide this?"

"My talk with Cathryn. We discussed your proposal and came to the conclusion that actually we do not need you for filing any more than we need you for fact checking." He stares at me blankly.

I glance at Annie, hoping to get a look of sympathy from her, but her back is turned to me.

I go home. I was assertive, and look what happened. How much worse can things get? Bastard elephant.

Maybe it's for the best. I'll look for a new job, which will probably be better than the old one. Most jobs would be. But first I'll take a break. A week or two, before I start sending out my résumé. Just enough time to take hold of myself and get my life in order.

Notice I'm speaking of my elephant as one would of God. "Maybe it's for the best" is the excuse one gives when God goofs.

When Charlotte gets home from work, she sees her belongings in the hallway, tries to open my door, can't, starts ringing, shouting, banging, calling, insulting, crying, kicking, threatening suicide, threatening to call the police, to turn me in, and finally falls silent. I look through the peephole. Her things are still there, but she isn't. I open my door an inch, and she jumps up and flings herself against it. I was prepared for that trick, so I am not caught by surprise and am able to close the door easily.

The whole thing starts over: the bangs, the screams, the insults, the tears. I take a bath with earplugs in my ears. I let the hot water relax my muscles. A couple of minutes later I remove one earplug. She's still banging.

"I got fired!" I shout to her from my bath.

The banging stops for a moment, but then it starts again.

"I don't have a job, and I'm not going back to work," I scream, hoping that this information will make her less eager to hold on to me. "Did you hear me?" I shout.

"Open the door," she shouts back.

"Did you hear I got fired? Did you hear?" I scream at the top of my lungs.

"Yes, I heard, but you'll get another job . . ."

I squish the earplug back in my ear and close my eyes, content. She heard. That's all that matters.

I hear the phone ringing through my earplugs. I don't answer it. In just three more days I'll have peace from the phone, and maybe from my ex-girlfriend, and maybe from my cat, and even, if I'm lucky, from the strangers in the street, though I'm not getting my hopes up for that one.

The next morning I go to work carrying my resignation. I walk with my tail between my legs, my shoulders drooping. I'm a loser, a failure.

No I'm not. *They* are. Their lives are so empty and dull that they entertain themselves by performing petty cruelties. I must walk in there like a king. *I* must be the disdainful one, for once, the contemptuous one, the condescending one.

I march into the magazine, holding my head high, my nose stuck up in the air, and place my resignation on my boss's desk. He's out of his office. I certainly will not wait for him to return to say goodbye. As I walk toward the exit I pass Annie, sitting at her desk, and say, "Ciao, Annie. Happy filing."

I take Minou to the vet and have her spayed. Two days later, she's lying on my desk, looking at me blankly. I pet her head, but she's as unfriendly as an ice pick. I try to pick her up, but she growls and stiffens, so I let her go. She settles back down, and I notice something orange peeping out from under her.

What is that? I ask.

Fuck off, she says, covering the orange object more completely with her body.

What is that thing? I repeat.

She turns her head away.

Don't you dare scratch me, I say, sliding my hand under her.

She turns around ferociously and bites my hand. It bleeds. I shout. I feel an irresistible urge to grab her and fling her across the room, but I control myself because she has just had surgery.

You are a monster, I say.

You only said not to scratch, not not to bite, she answers smugly.

I pull the orange object out from under her. It's the kitchen scissors.

What is this? I ask.

The kitchen scissors.

Did you drag these all the way here?

Yes.

You shouldn't drag heavy things after your operation. What are they for?

To cut your balls off.

Since yesterday my mother hasn't been able to call me because of my change in phone number. Charlotte is finally leaving me alone, Minou is getting nicer, but people are still coming up to me in the street and talking to me about little girls. I call my mother and ask her to stop sending her employees over. She refuses.

I see more of Laura and less of Lady Henrietta, because recently things have changed. Sara is not as nice as before, and she has health problems. She gets severe headaches and often throws up. This makes her moody and spoiled and affects her mother. Lady Henrietta invites me very rarely these days, and when I do visit, she never seems pleased to see me. I feel concerned for Sara, but I guess she has a stubborn flu and needs to be left alone with her mother.

I am pleased to announce that Laura is officially my girlfriend and I'm her boyfriend. It's been the case since the first night, in fact, but I'm mentioning it now in case it wasn't clear. We are very good for each other. She makes me more normal, and I make her less normal. I've told her about sleeping with my elephant. She took it well.

She also took it well when I "quit" my job. Although she works only for the respectability, not for the money, working is not something she requires of others. She's extremely well balanced. People who are very well balanced don't need ambition to be happy. They don't need goals. They appreciate life. They live one day at a time and love each day. She evokes this same serenity in me.

Laura is tallish, but not extremely tall for a woman, which is good because I'm not very tall for a man. She is perfectly proportioned, and she's as beautiful as a magazine model, her body too. She has light-brown hair and warm brown eyes. She's a brown person: brown as in brown haireyes. Very sensible, but sensitive; down-to-earth, but warm; moderate, but able to be extravagant. In addition to being a brown person, she happens to be so gorgeous physically, mentally, and emotionally that any man would marry her instantly if he were lucky enough to be the object of her love, like I am.

Her face always glows with health, and her cheeks are pink. She has healthy-looking teeth that are not too white: they are very real-looking and blend well with the color of her skin. One eye wanders out sometimes, but ever so slightly and imaginatively—I mean "rarely"—that I always think it's my imagination. It gives her an air of reality, of being a human, alive, who will die, which humans do.

Her personality, as well, is brown. Brown as in earth, down to earth.

We spend most of our time together at her place, not at mine, because although I keep my apartment clean these days, hers is bigger, more comfortable, more luxurious, paid for by her parents. It's a big, pale apartment with lots of light and few cumbersome objects, except for a shiny black piano. She does not play it well but loves to play, anyway, and likes the look of the instrument. She says she has always felt happy in a room with a piano. We sometimes toy with the idea of living together but decide to wait until the perfect moment, a time when it will happen naturally, almost without our thinking.

I go to practically every one of Laura's shows, to be nice and because I love her. I privately feel sorry for her and wish I could help her. It makes me suffer to see someone make such a fool of herself. Especially someone I know. Especially someone I like.

I finally decide I cannot let her go on with her pathetic show without at least trying to shake her up a bit. So one Sunday afternoon, at her apartment, I introduce the subject by making a casual comment.

"You know, I was thinking, it might not be a bad idea to show the empty boot first, before you take the flower out of it."

"My foot's in it. Isn't that enough proof the boot is empty?" she asks.

"Of course not," I say gently. "You know, I was wondering: You never told me if you know how to do any traditional magic tricks."

"You don't like my show," she states flatly.

"Yes I do! I just thought it might perk it up a little to do some traditional magic, like when things seem to really disappear and stuff."

"I don't do that sort of thing. I do modern magic."

"It seems more like baby magic to me," I say. "Any kid can do it. No offense."

"That's what ignorant people say of abstract art. This is abstract magic, modern magic, postmodern magic, naïve magic, experimental magic, avant-garde magic, an acquired taste. The dancing makes my work slightly more accessible and commercial. I could add singing, but that might overwhelm them."

"To do modern stuff, you have to know the traditional stuff," I tell her. "You can't resort to modern stuff just because it's easier. Good modern stuff is done out of choice, not out of inability to do anything else. Picasso was able to do extremely realistic portraits of people. He simply chose not to concentrate on that style."

"I just don't *do* realistic magic. It's not my thing."

"I know, but do you know *how* to do it?"

"Of course."

"Could I see some of your tricks?" I feel like a policeman. Could I see your driver's license?

She stares at me for a few long seconds and then goes into her bedroom to get her equipment.

She comes back and stands in front of me, holding a top hat and a wand. She proceeds to do the well-known, traditional magic trick, which one has seen a dozen times in the subways and on TV, of pulling a toy rabbit out of a top hat, after having shown me the empty hat first. She does it stiffly and clumsily. She truly has no talent for it. Not very coordinated.

"Pretty good, pretty good," I tell her. "I wouldn't compare you to Picasso, but pretty good. Can't you do anything better than that, though?"

She makes an ugly face at me and does the well-known trick with the silver loops, of attaching them and detaching them, when they seem unattachable and undetachable. The tip of her tongue is stuck out in concentration. Truly nothing impressive. It's almost worse than the baby magic she does onstage. You need a minimum of grace and assurance.

"Isn't there *any* trick you can do well?" I ask, in a joking tone. I don't want to seem too harsh, but I don't want to be too soft either, or it won't help her.

"You are ruffling my feathers, Mr. Acidophilus." She really is offended. It's nice she can joke about it and put on a light air. Perhaps I poked at a sensitive spot of hers. Perhaps she has a terrible complex about being incompetent at magic.

But she calmly proceeds to do the trick of making a card disappear under a handkerchief. She moves like a robot. She does it so badly that I can almost guess where she hid the card: in the lining of the handkerchief, or in her sleeve, or wherever cards are hid.

"Don't you do *anything* well?" I ask.

She angrily slaps a coin into her palm, and it disappears before my very eyes, while her hand remains open.

"There, that's more my territory," she mumbles.

I look up at her face. She quickly looks away and repeats the traditional trick with the silver loops. I stop her.

"Laura, that thing you just did. What was it?"

She blushes, pouts, looks distressed, and quickly blurts out, "You just pushed me too far. You humiliated me. I wasn't think-ing. Let's erase the slate. I want to lose consciousness."

"I'm sure you do," I say, stunned. "I'm sure you do," I repeat involuntarily. "That seemed mighty much like real magic to me."

"Of course not. That's the only trick I'm good at. I just happen to do it well because it requires no sleight of hand."

"*It requires no sleight of hand?* Then it sounds even more like real magic to me."

"Well, it's not."

"Then show me how you did it."

"It's too complicated to explain."

"Try."

"No. Magicians are absolutely never supposed to reveal their tricks, no matter what. But you can go to any magic store and buy the kit with the instruction book."

I do exactly that. Early the next day, I go to a magic store and ask for a trick that enables you to make a coin disappear while your hand is open. They do not sell such a thing, of course, because such a trick can be performed only by fairies or witches or TVs. When I get home, I tell her I didn't find her trick for sale.

"Yeah, well, I didn't think you'd go check," she says. "I just wanted to get you off my back. It was actually my grandfather who taught it to me."

"I don't believe you for one second, just for the record."

"The only reason you're obsessed with it is because it involves a coin, like when you were little," she says. "If it had been a button in my hand, or a thimble, or a ring, or a pebble, you wouldn't have given it another thought."

"Not true."

"Yes true."

"Not not not."

"Yeah yeah yeah."

"No, I tell you."

"Yes, absolutely."

"Not on your life."

"Yes on my life."

"Forget it," I say, waving my hand. But I then turn toward her eagerly and exclaim, "Do it again!"

"Never. Drop your fixation."

"Never."

We stare at each other, almost panting. I suddenly plop down on the couch, exhausted. "I understand your dilemma," I drawl. "You're obviously not good at traditional magic, and it would be too risky for you to do your *real* magic, because even if you tried to make it look like fake magic, there's always the chance you could get discovered. So all you can do is your postmodern baby magic. I understand your problem, and I now respect your decision." I close my eyes. My case is closed: There is nothing you can say that will make my words untrue.

"Oh, *please!* Give me a break," she says. "My *real* magic? Yeah, right, Jeremy."

Nothing you can say.

We just are.

We stand in the street, Laura and I, at a corner, without moving, without touching each other. We just are, together. The pleasure of being together is so intense that it is painful to bear. We must slow it down. We must slow down our existence and our heartbeats.

When we are together, we get very excited about touching people without their noticing it. It is almost a contest between us: Who can touch people most. The best is when we both touch someone at the same time. The most convenient place to do this is in line.

We never speak to each other about this behavior of ours. It isn't some sort of game that we consciously set out to play. It started so gradually and imperceptibly that I couldn't tell you on what day I touched my first person, or even what week. Touching clothing is good, it counts, but touching the *person* is much better, though it is of course more difficult to avoid being caught. Touching people without being noticed is exciting, daring, dangerous, yet warm, loving, and close. Even bumping or brushing against someone in the street is wonderful. And it does not matter if they feel it, because they'll just think it's an accident and won't know it was planned, that we did it on purpose.

When Laura and I touch each other, the pleasure is so intense that it is painful. That is why we are able to enjoy this pleasure much more fully when it is diluted by an intermediary. The pleasure we get from touching someone at the same time is so exquisite and perfect in its subtle sensuality that the person in question need not be unaware of our touch. When we receive a visitor, we often stand on either side of him, holding his arms, patting him, bumping against his sides playfully, whispering in his ear (because even our breath against the side of his face adds to our pleasure), ruffling his hair (justifying our behavior by saying we like his haircut), and feeling his clothes (justifying our behavior by saying we like them). We do this rather expertly, so our guest attributes our behavior to deep affection.

This is not to say that we don't make love. We do, but not as often as people who are less in love. For us, making love is a dangerous pleasure that we must, should, and do try to resist, because it leaves us feeling sick and stunned afterward.

I observe Laura carefully whenever I'm with her, to try and catch her doing some of her real magic. I often wonder if I might have been wrong about that coin trick. Perhaps she can't do real magic. Perhaps the quarter did not truly disappear from her palm as I thought it did. Maybe I hallucinated, though I'm convinced I didn't.

How strong is her magic, I wonder. What other tricks can she do? Can she make a chair disappear, or only small things? Can she make things appear, or only disappear? Can she make people love her?

Can she make people love her? Am I under her spell?

I sometimes ask her to show me more of her real magic, and she tries to ridicule me, to make me stop pestering her. She'll say things like: "I can't believe you, Jeremy. You're such a baby! You still believe in magic. How many times do I have to tell you I'm not a fairy?"

You would think that since she's so eager for me to drop my fixation, she'd simply reveal to me how she performed her coin trick. But she doesn't, which I'm convinced means that there's nothing to reveal, no solution, no secret; it's just pure, undiluted magic.

I keep going to her shows, and I sometimes fall asleep halfway through. One evening I wake up suddenly from my doze because I hear clapping. What? What? What are they clapping at? The show's not over yet. So what are they clapping at? I sit forward in my seat and squint at the bright lights stinging my sleepy eyes. I don't notice anything strange or different. Did she do her real magic? Could that be it? No, I doubt it, because if she had made things really disappear onstage, in front of their very eyes, using no sleight of hand, they wouldn't be clapping; they'd be fainting, or getting the police, or running out, or screaming madly, or kissing her feet and worshiping her like a god. Perhaps I'm getting carried away. But at the very least, they'd be staring at her with complete astonishment, like me when she made the coin disappear. They would be too stunned to clap.

I did not notice what she did to deserve the clapping. I missed it. Oh well, I'll have to ask her about it later. But suddenly there is clapping again, and my eyes are not closed, and I can tell you that she did *nothing* to deserve it. It's her same old marble-out-of-mouth trick. For the rest of the show, there are two tables of people who clap at every lousy rotten trick she does, and I stare at them with disbelief and then look at Laura to see if she is troubled, or pleased. She does look a little stunned. She has trouble concentrating, I can tell, takes longer than usual to accomplish every trick and every interlude of dance. Sometimes she glances at the clapping tables and then quickly looks away. But she does not look displeased. Her eyes are brighter than usual, and her lips are blushing and smiling in a lovely soft manner.

The clappers look like students. Some are older, and wiser-looking, as if they might be graduate students. They have beards.

After her show, I tell her I don't understand. She says, "Maybe it's you, Jeremy. Maybe you bring me good luck."

At her next show, three nights later, there are five clapping tables.

The waiters have to bring in more tables, and they eliminate the open dancing area. Her show goes from ten minutes to twenty to half an hour, but not more. She doesn't want to overdo it. She wants to leave them unsatisfied, dying for more. And then we realize that she is an overnight sensation.

But don't think it's her same old dumb tricks that are attracting so much attention. No. It's her new tricks, which are even more moronic. Laura has great instinct and intuition about people. After her first successful evening, she was able to sense which tricks people were clapping at particularly loudly, and she went in that direction. Her most admired tricks are the ones that are barely perceptible as tricks, the most subtle ones, like when she takes off her brown jacket and reveals that the inside is red.

Her tricks get progressively more idiotic, and the clapping and the number of clappers increase. Laura unwraps a candy and smells it, and people clap. Such tricks cannot even be called magic anymore, yet people call them that with delight, and calling them that contains a message about modern life and society, which goes something like this: In our times, routine, habit, drudgery, and repetition are so ingrained, so inescapable, that it seems as though nothing short of magic can break the pattern of eating the candy. Breaking that pattern, by doing the unexpected, even ever so slightly, like smelling the candy, is so unusual and extraordinary that it is certainly worth being called magic and certainly worth clapping for.

When Laura takes a Kleenex out of her pocket and wipes her forehead with it, everyone roars with clapter because the primary function of a Kleenex is to receive a nose's wind. By wiping her forehead (a less common, secondary function), Laura is fighting drudgery and expectation.

The most refined people are those who can detect the subtlest tricks, and they clap. If someone claps wrongly, at one of Laura's "trick tricks," like when she looks at the time on her watch, well, she'll shake her head ever so slightly, and the person is horribly humiliated, given crushingly subtle looks of disdain and contemptuous clucks of the tongue by the other members of the audience. If, on the other hand, someone claps alone in the right place, Laura's lips twitch into a slight smile, and everyone joins in on the clapping and bestows on the first lucky clapper looks of endless respect and admiration.

A typical evening consists of the following repertoire of basic tricks:

Laura winds her watch. One courageous clapper dares a few claps. She smiles slightly. They all roar, with clapter, and reward the fortunate first clapper with smiles and "Ah!"'s of awe. The primary function of a watch is to indicate the time, which is worth no respect because it only contributes to the monotony of modern life. To be wound is a watch's secondary, less common, function and is worth great respect.

Laura takes a comb and brush out of her box of objects and starts combing the hair out of the brush. One clapper claps, she twitches her lips, the entire room claps.

She takes off her pearl necklace and puts it on the table on the stage. Someone claps, she turns her head one inch to the side, which everyone knows is a negative response, and people cluck, snort, and snicker to the now ruined first clapper. People have become bold. Sometimes they even allow their disdain to be expressed verbally. You'll hear "God," "Really!" and "He's out of it."

One of the reasons her show is so beloved is that there's a lot at stake for the audience. People can build or destroy their reputation with a single clap. It's the quick way to success. Or failure.

After her show, people talk to one another enthusiastically, saying things like: "She's a genius; her choice of tricks is superb, exquisite. The vocabulary is rich, and the language, my goodness, the language is sublime. When she revealed the red inside of her jacket, I thought I would die!" The ultimately chic thing to say is: "How did she do that?" and to ask her directly, "Is there any chance you might ever reveal how you did that jacket trick?" And she wisely answers, "I'm sorry, I never reveal my magic tricks. I'd be out on the street without a job. You understand."

"Of course; how thoughtless of me." And the person walks away, saying, "Ah! The deceptive simplicity of it! I *love* the way she magics."

How real is her magic, I wonder. How big are her powers? Can she make people love her? Are they under her spell?

Tables are reserved weeks in advance. People order a meal, but many of them barely touch their food, they are so moved and affected by the show.

People send their kids to her for lessons. She has so many students that she has to divide her class into three levels of difficulty. The lowest is for traditional magic, where ordinary tricks are taught, such as pulling rabbits out of seemingly empty hats. These basic tricks provide a good foundation and background. In the second and slightly more difficult class, students learn how to take flowers and wands out of their boots, and marbles out of their mouths. The last and most difficult class focuses on tricks like taking off jackets whose insides are of a different color than their outsides.

It feeds into the system, the fact that the beginning classes are more difficult than the advanced classes, the fact that students progress from learning sleight of hand to smelling candies to winding watches to wiping their foreheads with Kleenexes. They love it that way, the parents and the public, but the children have trouble understanding this system and are told they are too young to understand; it's experimental, abstract, avant-garde, intellectual, an acquired taste.

After I broke up with Charlotte, I got a few short letters from her, which I didn't mention because she is too unimportant in my life right now. They all said pretty much the same thing: "I do not need you. Thanks for breaking it off." Or: "I do not need you. I'm dating other people." And then I didn't hear from her anymore. And still haven't. And I don't care. She was almost a stranger, even though I had been with her for a year.

Don't think my mother's agents have stopped coming up to me. Certainly not. But I've learned how to deal with them. Actually, I'm quite proud of myself, because I don't merely *deal* with them, I fluster them. It's quite fun: the same sort of fun children have when they set insects on fire.

One of these annoying little bugs reveals himself to me one evening at Défense d'y Voir, during Laura's show. He's an elegant man, with white hair, sitting at a nearby table. He leans back in his chair and asks me if I have a match. Even though neither Laura nor I smoke, I do happen to have a lighter on me, for reasons too complicated to get into right now. Actually, if you must know, I saw a scary movie recently in which a man got buried alive in a coffin, and I decided a lighter could come in handy in a life-or-death situation. The buried man had a lighter and was therefore able to see where he was and to understand what he was going to die of. And then he died.

The elegant man lights his cigarette with my lighter and says, "I forgot mine at home, because I left the house in a rush, very upset. My eleven-year-old granddaughter drives me mad. She—"

"Really, she's eleven?" I interrupt him.

"Yes. She—"

"That's such a wonderful age. They still love their parents at that age. And they make lots of friends," I ramble. "They start throwing parties, becoming conscious of fashion—"

"Yes, actually that's part of the problem," he interrupts. "They start becoming attracted to the opposite sex, and unfortunately, the opposite sex becomes attracted to them. Even older members of the opposite sex, if you catch my meaning."

"Oh, exactly. And then they start fighting with their parents, and the parents become unreasonable, and the problems don't quit, you know, even as the years pass. And then sometimes the parents send agents to pester their children."

The insect is on fire. The elegant man is flustered. He takes a long drag on his cigarette, nodding and frowning, probably racking his brain for something to say or do.

"Yes, exactly," he says, and turns his back to me.

I put my hand on his shoulder and add, "But what the parents don't realize is that the children love it when the agents come to them. It's so much fun. Someone should let the parents know that."

The agent clears his throat and says, "I'll keep that in mind." He gets up and leaves the restaurant.

Another time, I'm in a video store, picking out a movie for Laura and me to watch that evening, cuddled up cozily in her bed. A middle-aged woman is standing next to me, also looking through the movie boxes. She pulls one off the shelf, turns to me, and asks, "Have you seen this movie?"

The movie she's holding in my face is *Lolita*. How unsubtle can one get? I almost burst out laughing.

"I think I did, a few years ago," I reply.

"What did you think of it?"

I try to come up with the best possible answer to this delicious question. I could tell her, "I think you should tell my mother to stop pestering me."

Or I could turn to her and say, "I thought it was the most romantic movie I've ever seen." (Which, in case you're interested, isn't true; it actually left me quite indifferent.)

Or I could tell her she's ugly, that she has no sense of fashion, that one should not wear one's collar *up*, the way she wears hers. I could tell her *anything* in the whole world. Because one can take liberties with fake strangers. One can be delirious, unrespectable, ridiculous. My answer must be outrageous.

I puff out my chest and say, "It's a monstrosity! It should be banned. I was so shocked I don't think I ever recovered."

"I see," she says. "I have a daughter—"

"Eleven?"

"Yes. She—"

"Absolutely. Eleven-year-old daughters definitely have a tendency to sleep with dirty old twenty-nine-year-old men who constantly try to seduce them. I myself start drooling when I see one of those eleven-year-old nymphs. Exactly like the big bad wolf. I want to tweak their fannies."

"That's not good. You should—"

"Well, I'm not *only* interested in your daughter; I also find *you* very attractive. I love the way you wear your collar up. Raised collars excite me." I slide my hand behind her neck and start stroking the back of her collar. "Would you like to come to my apartment? We could watch *Lolita* together. You could describe your daughter to me. Is she well developed? They should not be *too* developed, or it defeats the whole point, you see, and then one might as well settle for a big girl like yourself," I say, looking at her chest.

She blinks at me and says, "I was warned that you'd be a tough one. Tom was very upset. He's a gentle and sensitive man, and he still talks about how obnoxious you were to him, when all he did was ask you for a light. And then you touched him on the shoulder. And now you're touching my neck. You have a tendency to touch. You take liberties. We don't like that. You should be kinder to strangers."

The following day I call my mother, because I haven't spoken to her in quite some time, ever since I changed my phone number. I want to try once more to convince her to stop sending me her insects.

The first thing she says after I say hello is: "You are pestering my agents. I want you to stop pestering my agents. They cost a lot of money to hire, and you are ruining their work."

"But they are so charming, I can't help myself."

"It's not gonna work."

"What's not?"

"Telling me you're enjoying it, telling my agents to tell me this. It's not gonna make me stop."

"Good, because I really *am* enjoying it. Please don't stop. If you stop, I'll hire my own agents to come and talk to me in the street."

She hangs up.

My relationship with Laura continues to develop and deepen. I think she is as in love with me as I am with her. Not only is she so normal, within her strangeness, but she's good-natured, natural, and cheerful. Very compassionate. She often gives money to beggars.

About a month has passed since I "quit" my job, and I haven't yet started looking for another one. I'm enjoying life so much right now that it seems a shame to change it in any way. My savings are not being depleted very quickly, since Laura insists on paying for things whenever we're together, "Because I'm rich," she says, "and you're not, and I love you, so it's only normal." If my savings do run out, she says she'll support me until I feel like going back to work.

One day I tell her what happened at Disney World. She says she knows about it; Lady Henrietta told her. She says it does not change her feelings toward me, and that although she does not think it was a wonderful thing, I am not completely to blame, considering the circumstances, and Sara is obviously mature for her age. What Laura disapproves of is the way Lady Henrietta and Sara manipulated me into it, without explaining anything to me beforehand.

I am her boyfriend. Yes, I am her boyfriend. You are right to look at me. She probably wouldn't have become famous if it wasn't for me. She told me so herself that first night, when she said, "Maybe it's you, maybe you bring me luck."

I'm very happy and content. I am a happy doggy, as one of my mother's friends would say. I don't think I've ever felt so well balanced in my life. Notice that I'm not talking to my cat anymore. Nor does she talk to me. This does not mean she's not happy. No, she's as affectionate as ever, but she simply stares at me dumbly most of the time, which makes me feel intelligent, normal, and sane. My greatest wish right now is for things to remain exactly as they are, and I do make that wish on my little white elephant. I've never made such a passive wish before, such an easy wish for you to accomplish. I'm not asking you to *do* anything. Rather, I'm sort of asking you not to do anything. Of course, there is the little cloud of Henrietta and Sara being unfriendly to me, but who cares? It'll probably get cleared up by itself.

At Laura's shows, I sit in my chair and prop my feet up on another chair, to be supercomfortable. I'm the only one in the entire room who dares to do this. I even bring a nice little flat mushy pillow from home for my back, and it feels almost as if I'm in bed. My body tingles with warmth and comfort, and I sometimes fall asleep, which is why I always sit in a dark corner, to be less conspicuous. I drink Shirley Temples, hot chocolate, ginger ale, eat Jell-O. I don't drink alcohol because I don't like it, and I feel too comfortable to care what people think. If they ask me why I drink those childish sweet things, I can always say I'm an alcoholic and must abstain, which I think is more respectable than saying you just don't like alcohol. I don't like very prickly bubbles either, so I don't drink Coke. I am basking: I think that's the perfect word. Yes, I am basking.

I look at the people to see if they are looking at me. I wonder if they know who I am, that I am the lover of the woman they love. I'm not jealous of her success. The pretension of the whole thing baffles me. I don't feel she deserves her success, which makes it all the more wonderful. What could be better than getting something you don't deserve?

Her show has become a sort of cult, like *The Rocky Horror Show*, only infinitely more intellectual and dignified. Her magic is ever changing, ever improving, ever metamorphosing. She introduces tricks whose effect lies not in secondary function, as opposed to primary function, but rather in simple and slight unusualness. For example, she takes off her boots, and her feet are bare. She has spurned the expectation that one wears socks under boots. She pushes the top hat off her head and lets it dangle down her back like a cowboy hat. If not quite startling, this effect is at least uncommon.

Laura also adds frills to her show. She comes down to the audience and takes things from people. The interest here lies in the fact that she chooses the one thing that each person will miss least, like a pack of cigarettes, a pen, a plastic lighter, a handkerchief, a shoelace, a button. And she is always right in her choice. The problem is that even the thing they will miss least is sometimes something that they will miss too much. Therefore, people start bringing wrapped presents for Laura, which they place on their tables for her to take, which she does. After the show, Laura and I unwrap the presents and find a nut, a pebble, a thimble, a coin. People often give her nice presents too, like silver lighters, gold earrings, silk scarves, makeup, tickets to musicals, because they love her. Sometimes the presents are bribes. One evening, accompanying a pretty pendant, there was a letter: "I am a middle-aged man with gray hair. At your next show I will be wearing a yellow tie so that you can easily recognize me. I would be grateful if you would do tricks that no one would normally clap at. I will clap at them enthusiastically, and you will smile in approval to make people think that I'm a talented and perceptive clapper. I need this boost in my social life right now. There's plenty more where this necklace came from." There's an address and phone number at the bottom of the card. Laura does not accept bribes. She returns the pendant.

One evening, among the presents, we find a diamond ring with a note that says, "Marry me," signed by a certain Paul Tops. The following night she asks the audience, "Is Paul Tops here?" A man's hand shoots up. She goes to him, returns the ring in its box, and says, "No. I'm sorry, I love *him*." And she points to me, sitting in my dark corner, with my legs propped up on the other chair, a Shirley Temple in my hand and a dish of green Jell-O jiggle on my table, and everyone looks at me, and I am caught off guard, and I try to straighten up a little and look less as if I'm in bed, but it's hard because of those feet of mine propped up on that chair. I smile at the people, and they clap at me. When their attention goes back to Laura, I sink back in my dark corner and sigh with relief.

Another frill she adds to her show is to answer people's thoughts. She asks everyone to think of a question that is important to them. She then comes down in the audience and plays fortune cookie. She stands in front of someone and says, "It all depends on if you're healthy," or "You would have to be more intelligent," or "Don't be in such a hurry," or "Sometimes in life you can't do that," or "Okay, but first go to the hairdresser." Although people do not seem displeased with her answers, one day I ask her to answer one of *my* silent questions, to see how good she really is. She accepts. I think: Will Henrietta ever love me?

Not that I want her to. Just asking out of curiosity, out of lack of imagination, out of my inability to think of a more interesting question. "Not as long as I live," Laura answers.

Hmm. Interesting response. But it doesn't prove her authenticity one iota.

In her frilliest gimmick, Laura comes down to the audience and touches faces. She'll stand in front of people, her face very close to theirs, squinting, scrutinizing their features while breathing softly on their nose, and finally, with the tip of her index finger, she'll touch a particular spot on their face. It is the most aesthetically pleasing spot to touch on that particular person, on that particular day, at that particular moment.

Perhaps she was inspired by our game of secretly touching.

She'll touch a spot on a chin, on a jaw, in the hollow of a cheek, above an eyebrow, on the tail of an eye, on the horizon of a mouth, on the sorrow of a nose, on the joke of an eyelash, on the imagination of a mustache, on the laziness of a beard. I get carried away. The men find it very exciting, I'm certain, when she breathes on their eyes and squints into their pores. One evening she does it to me in front of all those people, who are holding their breaths at the romance of it, and my heart melts with love, and so does my stomach, and I become aroused and feel as though I'm wilting. I wait with anticipation while she makes up her mind as to where she'll touch me. I hope it won't be somewhere funny, like the tip of my nose. I don't want this to be comical.

She touches my right temple. My throat constricts. I'm slightly disappointed. I was hoping she might do something different, something special, to me, like kiss me, but she obviously wants to be professional, wants to show no favoritism, no lack of discipline, no flagging, meandering, or pussyfooting. She takes her touching seriously.

* * *

One day, in the subway, a man is doing magic tricks. We watch him pull a rabbit out of a hat, and Laura laughs.

"Why are you laughing?" I ask.

"I'm thinking of what my audience would think of that. They would find that so vulgar, so base."

Laura has eliminated the dancing from her show, as you might have noticed by now. ("The more cultured the person, the more stark they like it," she explains to me.)

Articles come out on her magic.

There are imitators, but they are not accepted by the most cultured people. She is considered the best, because the first.

Two ballet companies have been fighting to get her.

"But it's not ballet," I tell her. "You don't even dance anymore."

"That's the whole point. Just as it's not magic."

Nevertheless, people still call her "The Dancing Magician."

Laura has raised magic to equal the most important art forms.

How big are her powers? Can she make people love her? Are we under her spell?

I often catch myself not wondering if I can have a happy life with a woman who may have cast a love spell on me. I really should wonder about such a thing, logic tells me. So I wonder about it.

chapter *nine*

I haven't visited Lady Henrietta in almost two weeks; she hasn't invited me. When I tried inviting myself, she said she was too busy. She sounded depressed. Now she finally says I can come, so I am entering her apartment, about to go say hello to her in the kitchen, but I am arrested by the sight of Sara, standing at her mother's easel, painting men's clothes, which is not what arrests me, because she often does that. She is wearing a sparkling yellow floor-length dress with a huge crinoline. I have never seen anything so radiant. A large blue and white parrot is perched on the easel.

I go up to her and say, "What is all this?"

"I'm glad you're here," she says. "You can meet my new parrot. Mom bought it for me yesterday."

"Why?"

"Because I wanted it."

"That's nice. It must have been expensive."

"Ten thou."

I'm pretty knowledgeable about pets, so I know that she's probably not lying.

"All you're interested in is money," she says. "Don't you want to know his name?"

"Yes."

"Richard."

"Why Richard?"

"It was the name of my old dog, who was named after my previous dog, who was named after my previous cat, who was named after my blue blanket, who was named after my father."

Ah, her father, that mysterious thing called her father. What a strange foreign word coming from her mouth. Well, that should certainly satisfy people who think this little girl's father is an important absence in her life, you Freudian jerks.

"Say hello, Richard," she tells her parrot.

The parrot is silent.

"He hasn't learned to talk yet," she explains. "Ask me how much my dress the color of the sun cost."

"How much?"

"Two thou. All *you've* ever given me was a Jane doll. Do you realize that?"

"I hadn't thought of it, but now that you mention it, you're right."

"Aren't you embarrassed?"

"It hasn't been your birthday or Christmas yet."

"Typical!"

"What's wrong?"

"I want something from you. I certainly deserve it, and not only that, I also demand it."

"What do you want?"

"Wait a second, I have to decide." A second later, she says, "I want a Humpty Dumpty made of gold, another one made of platinum, and a third one made of gold *and* platinum, with diamond eyes, an opal mouth, and sapphire dimples, wearing an emerald earring, a ruby necklace, and a hat of dried flowers, with yellow straw hair sticking out under, and I want him to be sitting in a crystal dish of potpourri."

"Is it okay if I just get you the potpourri?"

"No."

"I don't think such Humpty Dumpties exist."

"Oh really Jeremy? Well I thought you could get them at any old supermarket," she says sarcastically. "I don't want something that already *exists*, except for Richard." And she kisses her parrot. "These Humpty Dumpties must be custom-made. Like this dress the color of the sun." She slowly turns around to model her dress.

I squint, blinded by the sparkling fabric. "It's lovely," I tell her. "You look like a queen."

"You're stupid! I'm not a queen; I'm a princess. Queens are old and thick. So, will you give me those Humpty Dumpties? I love custom-made. I never knew it existed before."

"They would be too expensive."

"I feel sorry for you, Jeremy. You are little. You are a little piece of nothingness."

I do believe my hair is standing on end. She picks up her

skirts, grabs her parrot like a teddy bear, and calmly marches into her room, slamming the door behind her, majestically.

I'm gonna tell on her. I go to the kitchen. Henrietta is sitting at the table, on which is lying a large pink fish with blue eyes and green fins. A marzipan fish. The biggest marzipan thing I've ever seen. A striking resemblance to the Humpty Dumpty with sapphire dimples. Resemblance in mentality and roundness.

The fish's right fin is half eaten. Henrietta is picking off some more with her fingers. I am so full of my tattletale plans that I don't pay attention to her sullen air.

I begin, "So, was *that* custom-made too?" I point with disdain at the fish.

"Yes, actually." She keeps eating the fin.

For an instant, I feel like tearing off the whole tail, but then I don't, because I'm usually not the type who does uncontrolled violent things when I'm angry. So all I do is eat a piece of fin, without asking her permission.

"Why did you buy Sara that ten-thousand-dollar parrot and custom-made dress?" I ask.

"To make her happy."

"You're ruining her personality. She's acting like a spoiled brat, to say the least."

"But is she happy?"

"Oh, yeah, she's happy, but she's mean."

Henrietta continues picking at the fin and mutters, "As long as she's happy . . ."

"Yes, but next thing you know, she'll ask you for a dress the color of the weather, like in her movie *Donkey Skin*, and then what will you do? If you don't give it to her, she'll hate you."

"She already did ask me for one. And I did give it to her. She prefers the one the color of the sun."

I tear off a little piece of the tail and chew it angrily in front of her. Immediately, I feel sad for having ruined an uneaten section of her custom-made fish.

"I'm sorry," I say. "But you can't keep buying her everything she asks for."

I suddenly notice tears running down her face.

"What's wrong?" I ask, sitting down next to her and putting my hand on her shoulder.

"Sara is dying," she says, staring at the marzipan fish.

"What?"

"The doctor says she has a brain tumor."

"No."

She nods at the fish. I want her to look at me.

"She had pains in her head," she says, "and nausea. He did tests."

"Are you sure about this? Did you get a second opinion?"

She nods at the fish. As long as Henrietta keeps staring at that fish, I have trouble believing her words are not insane.

"There are cures," I tell her.

She shakes her head and tells the fish, "It's too far advanced. It can't be cured at all. She has only a few weeks or months left."

"Oh my God."

We sit in silence, both of us staring blankly at the fish.

"Does she know?" I finally ask.

"No."

There's a movement in the kitchen doorway. We look. It's Sara, standing.

A small voice in my head says: *She does now, ladies and gentlemen.*

We stare at her, stunned, waiting for her to speak, not knowing if she heard us talk. We soon realize from her expression that she did hear.

"Is that true?" she asks.

Is what true? I want to ask in return, but I remain silent instead.

Henrietta is unable to reply, which is a clear enough answer for Sara, who turns around and disappears into the living room. Henrietta rushes after her. I follow. The mother and daughter are holding each other, crying.

That night I tell Laura the news about Sara, and I cry. Her first reaction is incomprehension. Then she cries, too, and tries to comfort me.

The next day Henrietta asks me to come over while Sara is at school, so we can talk in private. We sit on the couch.

She says, "When the doctor told me the bad news, I recorded it."

"Why?"

"I can deal with bad news better if I own it and can play it whenever I wish. It makes me feel I can alter it, even though I know it's not true." She takes out a little tape recorder. "If you ever have bad news to tell me, please warn me beforehand, so I can record it."

She turns on her tape recorder, and from it comes the doctor's voice: "During the next two weeks the pain in her head will become much worse and will be constant, not just seizures like now. I cannot stress, sufficiently, how excruciating the pain will become."

"Oh, no," gasps Henrietta's voice from the tape recorder.

"Yes. *But*"—the doctor pauses—"there will be another symptom going on at the same time as the pain, which will make the pain more bearable."

He waits for her to ask "What?" The jerk.

"What?" she asks.

"This secondary symptom is nicknamed the Happy Symptom. It's rather rare, but it occurs in certain cases of brain tumor, such as Sara's."

"What is the Happy Symptom?"

"It *is* what it sounds like, which is, happiness. During the next two weeks or so, her tumor will be growing through a part of her brain that will cause excruciating pain, but it will also be growing through a part that will cause tremendous happiness. The more the pain grows—and it will grow each day, I assure you—so will the happiness become more intense."

"How is that possible?"

"Pain and happiness, just like pleasure and unhappiness, can coexist without discord. Notice that I did not say pain and *pleasure*, which form a different combination altogether, the pain usually killing the pleasure, beyond a certain point. The reason people have a hard time realizing that pain and happiness can live in perfect harmony is simply because that particular coupling of feelings does not happen very often. The most frequent cases in ordinary life of pain and happiness are women in labor, women who want their baby very, very much. You'll see, it's a fascinating phenomenon. People with the Happy Symptom often say uncommon things when they are in pain."

Henrietta is silent on the tape recorder.

"But don't worry too much," the doctor continues. "These symptoms won't last long. As soon as those two sections of her brain are vanquished, which, as I said, should take about two weeks, the pain will disappear quickly and entirely. And so will the happiness."

Henrietta is still silent.

"Do you have any more questions?" asks the doctor.

"Yes," she says. "How will it be before the end? Will she get much worse?"

"No. Pain will not come back, which is the beauty of her particular tumor. She won't get gradually weaker, or lose weight, or get numb. She will simply die. The unfortunate aspect is that you will have no warning. It will be very sudden."

"How do you mean sudden? She'll just fall down and be dead?"

"I don't know if she'll fall down, but she'll be dead. I suppose if she happens to be standing, she might fall down. Or she might sit in a chair first, and simply close her eyes. Or, if you're walking down the street, she might sit on the ground, or lie down on the sidewalk, and close her eyes."

The very next day, Sara's pain is already starting to increase. The times of no pain diminish in length and frequency. The happiness begins. Henrietta calls and tells me that Sara is suffering terribly. I go and see them. As soon as I step out of the elevator, I hear Sara screaming. When I enter the apartment, she's sitting on the couch, clutching her head and banging it against the pillow. There is a huge smile on her face.

"Jeremy!" she exclaims, as soon as she sees me. "I've never felt like this before. I feel as though my face is being ripped apart. It feels so real! It's better than any special effect I've ever seen."

Henrietta is sitting next to her, looking green. Sara howls with pain once more, and says, "That's the nail again now." Her face is contorted with pain and joy. "It feels as though someone very strong is slowly pushing a nail into my skull, and I really wish they'd just hammer it in quickly and get it over with."

"A nail?" I say.

"Yes. It's a long nail that moves toward the center of my mind, and when it reaches the center, I know I will die."

Henrietta finally speaks: "The doctor said the pain will stop long before it reaches the center."

"And that's not all, Jeremy," says Sara. "There's a third special effect that I've had since last night. It's that the back of my head is open and my brain is dribbling down my back. It is unfuckingbelievable! I even feel the wetness of my brain on the back of my neck."

I close my mouth, which has been open for the past few minutes.

The next day, not only is Sara fascinated by her pain, but the very idea that she's dying has become immensely attractive to her. Henrietta informs me that Sara has told everyone in school that she's dying, and people say she brags about it.

"I can't tell her not to be happy that she's dying," says Henrietta.

"No, of course not," I tell her.

"You know what she was heard saying in school?"

"What?"

"She was heard saying, 'Cool, man, I'm gonna *die*.' "

* * *

I finally call my mother, to tell her the tragic news about Sara. I do not look forward to this, because knowing her, I wouldn't be surprised if she said it was my sleeping with Sara that caused her tumor.

When I tell her that Sara is dying, she doesn't believe me. She says, "You're just trying to torture me. You're up to your same old tricks."

Me, up to *my* same old tricks!

"It doesn't matter if you don't believe me," I tell her sadly. "In fact, perhaps it's better if you don't. I just thought I should let you know."

A few minutes later, Henrietta calls to tell me that my mother just phoned to ask her if Sara was truly sick. When Henrietta assured her that she was, and dying as well, my mother expressed intense sympathy and offered words of support. My mother then asked Henrietta for my new phone number, saying she wanted to apologize to me, but Henrietta wasn't sure it was okay to give it to her, so she didn't.

Well, well, my mother wants to apologize. I'm not sure I believe her. *She* might be up to *her* old tricks. Anyway, after all she's put me through, she deserves to wait a bit, to be tortured a bit. I'll make her wait a few days, and then I'll call her.

The very next morning, however, my mother is ringing my buzzer. I let her up with no argument. She walks in, shoulders drooping, looking at me shamefully.

She goes to the window and stares outside, her back turned to me. She says, "I stayed awake all night, unable to sleep."

What does she expect me to answer: I'm sorry I told you the news? "I'm sorry," I tell her.

She shakes her head quickly. "No, I'm not saying that to make you apologize. I'm just devastated. I'm shocked. That's all I meant." She keeps staring out the window, and finally adds, "I want to apologize."

She doesn't add anything more, so I say "Oh?" and she goes and sits in a corner of my couch. She then looks at me frankly, squarely, and says, "I was a tyrant and a tormentor, and I repent."

It's a little late for that. It's easy to repent when a tragedy occurs. I remain quiet and look at my feet.

"I miss your messiness," she says. "I was hoping your apartment would be dirty today, so that I would get a chance to act like a wonderful person. I had it all planned out. I was going to come in, ignore the mess, sit on your couch, or, if your couch was too cluttered, sit in a corner somewhere, and I was planning to not utter the slightest word about, you know, the old fruits and fur balls. I was going to be admirable, but good intentions always come too late."

Sadness starts creeping into my heart.

"I'm especially embarrassed about the agents," she adds.

I can no longer bear it. "Don't be too hard on yourself," I tell her, unable to believe I'm saying this. "You felt that what I did was wrong, and you expressed your opinion sincerely."

She snorts sadly and says, "What a nice way of putting it." She looks grim, older than I've ever seen her. The corners of her mouth are drooping excessively, as though a child drew them. Her wrinkles, usually mostly horizontal, are today mostly vertical. The tears, which she undoubtedly shed all night, seem to have dug permanent descending lines into her cheeks.

"Don't worry about the agents," I tell her. "They were sort of funny." And I force out a laugh. I decide I'd better blabber something more, because she looks as though she might burst into tears. "I was able to practice my social skills on them," I say.

She gives me the faintest of smiles and appears to be searching for words, but finally she just says, "Well, whatever. Everything seems so trivial now, so sad." She gets up. "I don't want to take up any more of your time. You must be busy." She walks toward the door and turns to me. "Is there anything at all I can do for you?"

"No, thank you. Do you want to go out for coffee or something?"

"I don't want to take up any more of your time," she repeats. "But if you need me in any way, need any favors or anything at all, just tell me. I'll do anything."

"Thank you; that's very nice. Are you sure you don't want to have coffee? You're not taking up my time."

"I know that I am. Anyway, not yet, coffee. It's too soon."

I want to ask her what she means, but I refrain from doing so, because I know exactly what she means. We are just starting to know each other in a new way. We are almost strangers who have just met. We need time to get used to each other.

How sad life is, that a little girl's fatal illness is what it takes to bring my mother to her senses. In a way, I miss her old self, just as, I suppose, she misses my dirty apartment. But I'm sure I should not worry; she'll probably regain her true personality before I know it. At least partly. People don't just change, just like that, permanently.

A week of the Happy Symptom is all it takes for Sara to teach her parrot to say certain things, very distasteful things, which

I'm sure she'll deeply regret having taught him, as soon as the symptom fades.

The parrot now enjoys saying: "We are dying today." "Are we dying today? And today? And now?" "Sara is dying." "Is it time yet? Soon?" "I am a dying person." "Death and dying."

The parrot often asks Sara, or me, or Henrietta: "Are you dying yet?" After we answer "No" or "Yes" or "Shut up," he'll say, "And yet? And yet?"

To this, Sara says, "Isn't it hi*lari*ous? I *love* it!"

Laura asks me to move in with her, so she can take care of me while I take care of them. I accept gratefully. I move in and, to my astonishment, discover that she has bought big gray file cabinets to decorate her living room. These sinister file cabinets are meant to make me feel more at home by creating an environment that is familiar to me.

Sara's pain increases. It reaches such a high level that she cannot go to school. This does not upset her much; she says everyone in school already knows she's dying, and they even started taking the idea for granted, so she's not missing much fun.

Recently I've been thinking a lot about those custom-made jeweled Humpty Dumpties that Sara said she wanted. I wish I could give them to her, but obviously I can't afford them. Not even one of them. Not even one precious eye or earring. Which I suppose is why, one night, I dream that I can, actually, afford one, in a small size, though I did pick the third one, the fanciest one, made of gold and platinum, with diamond eyes, an opal mouth, and sapphire dimples, wearing an emerald earring, a ruby necklace, and a hat of dried flowers, with yellow straw hair sticking out under.

"It's a *lovely* little egg," says Sara, in my dream. "But he was supposed to be sitting in a crystal dish of potpourri."

"Oh, I totally forgot. I'm sorry. You gave me such complicated instructions."

"I'm not *only* interested in the fancy stuff, you know."

"I know. I didn't forget the straw hair, did I?"

I suppose my present has added further happiness to her Happy Symptom, because she starts singing: "I feel pretty-y-y." She skips on one foot on the "y-y-y." "Oh so pretty-y-y," she continues, skipping on the other foot on the "y-y-y." "I feel pretty and witty and gay-ay-ay-ay!" Skip skip skip skip. "La la lee lee, la la lee, la lee la lee, la lou."

"That's bright," I tell her.

"Really, you like it?"

"No, I mean it goes: 'I feel pretty and witty and bright.' "

"Detail. Who's the pretty girl in that mirror there?" she screeches at the top of her voice. "What mirror where?" She is holding the back of her head with one hand, which is something she often does to prevent her brain from dribbling down her back. "Who could that—a pret-ty girl be-e? Which one where who, who, who, who, who? What a pretty girl, what a pretty girl, what a pretty girl."

The parrot whistles along, not daring to compete with his master's voice.

When she finishes her song, I tell her, "I promise you the back of your head is not open, and your brain is not dribbling down your back. You don't need to hold your head that way."

"I *know* the dribbling is supposed to be just a special effect, but it feels so real that I can't help it."

"Don't worry, I'll get you the crystal dish of potpourri."

She seems pleased. She adds my gift to the Humpty Dumpty collection in her room. She says it's the best egg she ever had.

I wake up and realize with sadness that I won't be able to bring her the joy I could offer in my dream. I won't even give her the crystal dish of potpourri, which is the only part of her request I could afford, because she doesn't want it without the Humpty Dumpty.

A week and a half later, the pain and the Happy Symptom have passed, and Sara becomes depressed that she's dying. The other thing that happens is that I am starting to smell the fruit in her.

Notice that I do not make a wish on the white elephant for Sara to live. When it comes to questions of life and death, making a wish on the white elephant is not tempting. (I have a few times in my life been faced with acquaintances' fatal diseases and deaths, and I have never used my white elephant to try to save their lives.) If you don't care quite enough about the person in question, it does not seem wise to ask for the interference of supernatural powers. On the other hand, in the case of a person you love very much and whom you desperately want to live, making a wish seems to trivialize a tragic situation; you feel as though you are performing a disrespectful, frivolous act. It is conceivable that if *I* were the one with a fatal disease, I might use the elephant to try to save my life, though this is by no means certain. As for Sara, I had not, up to now, thought of using the white elephant on her. I suppose that subconsciously it was a mixture of thinking it would be too trivial and not wanting to tamper with this big outside event that did not involve me directly. If destiny wants her to die, then she should die. In addition, if I were to wish for Sara to live and she were then indeed to live somehow, I could never be certain that she was not a living dead of some sort, living against nature.

But the more I think about it, the more I feel I should use the elephant on her: It seems I would be selfish and evil not to. So I take the elephant out of its gray felt pouch and make a wish that Sara will live. When I replace the elephant in its pouch, my conscience is cleared. I did my duty.

Perhaps Sara doesn't wash anymore. Her face is dark, or dusty, or something. It looks as though she has a five o'clock shadow.

Amazing how much that's what it looks like. A five o'clock shadow. I ask her to come closer to me. She acts delighted, probably thinking I am going to kiss her. I scrutinize her face, and I see that it's hair on her face, like the beginnings of a beard. It's very fine hair, like peach fuzz, but slightly too much to be called peach fuzz.

A very cold *thing* runs through me, as though the devil is talking to me, making me aware that he is responsible for this. I am reminded again of *The Exorcist*. I feel that something cruel is going on. I cannot stay in the same room with her anymore. I must leave. And then the five o'clock shadow will end. If I don't see it, it won't exist, I hope. I won't mention it to Lady Henrietta or Sara. If they don't notice, well, then, it doesn't exist.

* * *

The next time I see Sara, she looks fine. There's no five o'clock shadow. I am delighted. I had imagined it.

But when I get closer, I see that it's worse than a five o'clock shadow. It is shaved.

So, Henrietta and Sara did, finally, notice the shadow and decided to shave it off, and they think I never noticed it, and they are not about to tell me about it. I didn't think they would hide something like this from me.

I confront Henrietta when Sara is not there:

"I'm not blind. And I *am* a man. I can see that she's shaving. Were you just not going to tell me?"

"She didn't want you to know."

"What's going on?"

"The doctor said it's an unexpected symptom, that her tumor is now touching a part of her brain that causes it to produce male hormones. But the hormones are only being activated in certain ways: in the ways that grow beards, not the ways that make voices deeper and muscles bigger. Only facial hair."

I have dinner with Laura at Défense d'y Voir. As we are eating, people at the neighboring tables suddenly start to clap at her. She looks at me, amused. She seems used to it.

I lean forward and whisper to her over our desserts. "Why are they clapping?"

"Because I just put sugar in my coffee."

"Why would they clap at that?"

"Because the sugar *disappeared* into the coffee."

"You *must* be joking."

"Not in the least."

* * *

Sara asks me to let my beard grow.

Sara asks me to go buy pet fishes with her. We go. She buys nine tropical fishes. She also buys a fish tank, which I find out later is for the sole purpose of not arousing my suspicion, which she should not have bothered with, because I don't care if she wants to kill her fishes.

She looks like a grieving man, a man in mourning, who hasn't shaved in a few days. She has long stubble, which is darker than the blond, fairy princess hair on her head. In the pet store she wears a scarf over her mouth, like a gangster, like someone with the flu, to hide the sight. As we leave the store, she turns around, faces the customers, and lowers her scarf, smiling, her small red lips peeking through the dark hairs. I look at the people, panic-stricken. Many of them are staring at Sara, some squinting to see better, others looking plainly devastated.

She does the killing by size, starting with the smallest fish. The neon tetra goes in boiling water, the guppy goes in the freezer ("because he's so pretty that I want to preserve him"), the painted glass fish is vacuumed off the carpet. (Before moving on to the next execution, she shouts to me over the noise of the vacuum cleaner, "I think people who are dying have a right to do very crazy things, and that does not mean they're crazy. It means they're dying, and upset. In fact, it means they're sane.") The ram is placed on her mattress and watched while it flaps to death; the dwarf gourami is cut open lengthwise and its skeleton admired; the angelfish is held by its top and bottom fins and pulled in opposite directions (I've always wanted to do that, I think to myself, even though it's not true); the white long-finned tetra is soaked in concentrated blue bath herb essence for three minutes while we talk about whether the color will stick when we take it out, which it does a little, but it was not fatal so she lets the fish flap to death on her bed like the other one. (I tell her, to lighten the atmosphere, that she should have thought of something she hadn't done before, so she offers to eat it, which I prevent her from doing for fear that the blue bath herb essence will make her sicker than she already is, though to her face I just say "sick," not "sicker than you already are.") The baby discus, with its beautiful facial expression, she throws out the window, making me particularly sad; and the last fish, the fat goldfish, she can't think of anything to do with because the last one has to be the best and this high standard is giving her killer's block so *I'm* supposed to think of something which is too much to ask of me because I'm not dying and don't have this need to see what death is like but it finally doesn't matter because she comes up with her own idea. She tries to feed the goldfish to the parrot. He won't eat it. He doesn't like goldfish. Jeremy? No, thank you; I don't eat that kind of fish either. "Okay, then I'll eat it," she says. I cringe. I can't tell her not to, because it has not been soaked in concentrated blue bath herb essence. She licks a fin and stops. She doesn't want to eat it anymore so thinks of something even better. She throws it against the wall. The idea is to throw it until it does not move. She does it again. It is fun and slippery. Sometimes she just throws it in the air and catches it, just to enjoy the fun challengingly slippery feel of it. Finally, it does not move. She goes to the kitchen, comes back with the big kitchen knife, and heads for her parrot. She grabs it around the shoulders and points the tip of the knife at its throat.

I catch my breath. I am shocked. The fishes were one thing, but the ten-thousand-dollar parrot? And it's not at all the price

I'm talking about. It's the animal. It's a big animal, which talks. And as though to prove my thought, "Death and dying," says the parrot, the blade pointed at its sky-blue neck. But after all, a dying little girl is allowed to kill a parrot. She's allowed to kill practically anything.

Sara suddenly drops the knife and charges at me. I look at the knife on the floor again, just to make sure I did not imagine that she dropped it. She punches me, repeatedly, as hard and as quickly as she can, and I welcome it I understand it it should have come sooner it makes me feel better than I've felt in a long time as though purifying me of my crime liberating me from it it is equal I guess to serving a prison sentence and feeling you paid for your wickedness afterward.

But then the parrot joins in, shrieking, and knocks on my head with his beak, like a woodpecker, while Sara continues punching me. He is perched on the side of my face, I'm not sure exactly where, probably on my ear with one foot and on my shoulder with the other. It hurts incredibly, so much that I can't even feel Sara's blows. It bleeds, I can feel, but I don't dare say no, because maybe I deserve this also. And if I said no, she might think I meant her, which I don't. I look down, sort of sadly, but I don't cry because I don't have the right to cry. Then she stops. But the bird does not. "Stop it," she tells it. "Death and dying," it answers, and stops.

I need to wipe off the blood running down my forehead before it reaches my eyes, or I will have trouble blinking. I look around for a tissuelike thing but see nothing, so I remove the parrot from my ear and shoulder and wipe my forehead on its sky-blue and white feathers, enhancing their beauty to red and purple.

"Jeremy?" says Sara.

"What?"

"There's something I want you to do with me."

"What's that?"

"I want to hang glide before I die."

I remember Henrietta telling me that Sara's father died of a hang gliding accident. "That's very dangerous," I say.

"Ha. Ha." She pauses. "I'd really love it."

"I don't know. I don't even know where people do it."

"In the country. An hour away from here."

"You'd have to ask your mother."

"I already did. She said okay."

"Well, then, okay, I'll take you there."

"And you'll fly with me."

"No, I'll just watch. You'll go with an instructor."

"I want to fly with you."

"I don't know how to fly."

"You'll go with an instructor too, but we'll be flying at the same time."

"I don't know. It's very dangerous."

"I'm sure you can't be worried about me. Even if I get crippled for life, it won't be for very long."

"Well, I'm also worried about myself."

"You could do this for me, couldn't you?"

I suddenly become ashamed that I hesitated. Since I can't offer her a jeweled egg, I'll risk my life for her. "Of course I could. We'll do it."

She prances over to me, smiling widely, and kisses me on the mouth. The kiss does not stop. It continues, and it is not a kiss of gratitude anymore. I am again starting to smell the fruit in her. Her fruit is pear. It smells good, sweet. Everyone dying has a fruit in them. The key is to die before the fruit rots. My father's fruit of death had been grapes. I had smelled them. My own fruit, I am certain, I instinctively know, will be lemon, bitter lemon.

The kiss is there still. I am repulsed by her beard. I get little hairs in my mouth, and the mixture of the coarse hairs and the sweet fruity smell makes me feel nauseous, on the verge of throwing up if I'm not careful. It feels good to be repelled by her, because it means I'm more normal than before if I can't be attracted to a little girl.

But no, I'm cheating, it's not true. The only reason I have this feeling of repugnance is the beard, and nothing else, I'm sure. I am monstrous to be repelled by a poor dying little girl who happens to have a beard. I cannot allow myself to feel this way. I mean, really, her beard is one of the *symptoms*, for God's sake, of her *dyingness*. It does not deserve disgust from anyone. Especially not from me, who found her pretty enough to make love with before. Well, I should find her pretty enough to make love with now. I must push away my disgust and try to feel desire for her, despite the beard.

What am I doing? What am I thinking? I'm getting all tangled in these absurd thoughts. I'm losing perspective. The fact that she has a beard is destiny helping me fight this challenge.

I gently push her away.

"I can kill, but I can't have love?" she asks.

"No, not unnatural love. You shouldn't *want* to have it."

"First of all, it's not unnatural love. Second of all, I do want it."

"You promised me that if I remained your friend you wouldn't start this again."

"Things are different now. I'm going to be dead soon. I thought that meant I could do things."

"Yes, a lot of things, but not everything."

"Of course not everything. I can't kill you, but I can kiss you, can't I?"

I don't answer.

She says, "It had to happen, didn't it? At first I thought it might not. I thought I would be noble enough and not take advantage of my dying. But I'm not. Jeremy, I want to make love with you again."

"No. It was probably our lovemaking that caused your disease to begin with."

"You know very well that's not the least bit true."

She's right. I do, most of the time, know that it's not the least bit true, but sometimes I forget.

"Well, then," I say, "the reason you want to do all this love-making in the first place is probably *because* of your disease. It's a symptom of it."

"Well, listen to *this:* 'Do you think that her brain tumor could have caused other symptoms?' my mom asked the doctor. 'Probably not, but like what?' said the doctor. 'Many things. For example, having unusually strong sexual urges for a girl her age?' said my mom, embarrassed. 'Absolutely not,' *said the doctor,*" says Sara, emphasizing "said the doctor" very much.

"How do you know this?" I ask.

"*I was there.*"

"Henrietta asked the doctor in front of you?"

"No, but I was in the other room and heard everything."

"Maybe you misheard."

"No, because my mom repeated the conversation to me afterward. She remembered every word the way I had heard it, and not only that, but *I* also remember every single word exactly the way I heard it both times."

Sara might be lying, which wouldn't make much difference at this point anyway.

"Sara," I say, reasonably, "I am willing to go hang gliding with you. I'll risk my life for you, but I won't sleep with you."

"It's because of my beard, isn't it?"

"No," I say, hoping I am telling the truth.

Sara goes to her room, upset. I sit on the couch and think. I decide to wait for Henrietta, who should be home soon. When she arrives, she is rather surprised to see a fat, pretty, dead goldfish on the floor, and water stains on the wall against which it had been thrown. She is also surprised to see a tiny thing floating around in her saucepan, which I tell her is also a fish. She finds a flat ripped fish in the corner of her living room. Each new fish corpse she finds upsets her more, because it depicts a not very flattering portrait of her daughter's mental state.

"Are you going to do it?" Lady Henrietta asks me.

"Do what?"

"Grant her dying wish."

"I'll go hang gliding with her."

"Not that one. That's not her dying wish. That's merely the wish of a dying girl. I meant the other one."

"She told you about it?"

"Yes."

"Do you want me to?"

"It's up to you."

"I will not grant it. I don't think it would be right."

"Do dying wishes have to be right?"

"No, but they should not be wrong."

"Isn't that the whole point of a dying wish, that for once in your life you can wish for something wrong and people will comply?"

"No," I reply. "There are some things in life that even dying wishes should not ask for."

"Are you doing this for her own good?"

"Yes."

"Why? You think it would harm her to sleep with someone before her death? There certainly could not be any long-term psychological damage."

"No, but I believe she will be more at peace during the last moments of her life if her dying wish is not granted."

"Do you mean she will be more happy?"

"Happiness, at this point, is not the point. It does not matter, it is trivial."

"What *does* matter?"

"Peace and serenity."

"Don't you think she'll get enough of those when she's dead?"

I pause. "Okay, so you want me to fuck your girl?" I hope to shock her into accepting my point of view.

"It's up to you."

"I feel that I should not do it."

"Or rather, you fear that you cannot."

"What do you mean?" I ask, knowing she's alluding to the beard.

"It's the beard, isn't it?" she says.

"No, but if it were, I would thank the beard, because it's making me act the right way."

"You just switched into present tense, which means you just admitted that it is the beard."

"Think what you want."

* * *

People start to clap when we have dinner at other restaurants as well.

Sara has been flipping coins lately, asking Fate if she will live or die.

"Everything in life is a fifty percent chance," she says, to justify her flipping of the coins.

"No, almost nothing is," I tell her.

"Heads means I'll live, tails means I'll die," she says, ignoring my answer. She flips the coin. "It's heads." Indeed it is heads. She flips it again. "It's heads again!" It's heads again. "That means Fate is telling me twice that I'll live. Fate is reconfirming her answer."

"What if you got two tails now, what would that mean?"

"It would mean that I'm bothering Fate too much and she wants me to leave her alone. She's not answering me anymore, and she's leaving the answers up to Randomness."

We go hang gliding. Sara does not shave anymore, so everyone thinks she is a young man. My beard is almost as full as hers. She started letting hers grow before mine.

We fly on separate hang gliders, each of us with an instructor. The parrot follows us. He's big, sky-blue and white. Tears are running out of my eyes, from the wind and from my thoughts. My beard is plastered against my cheeks; hers must be too. Once in a while, I hear parts of the parrot's favorite phrase, "Death and dying." As he circles us, I hear "and dying," or "death and," or even "time yet?" and "soon?"

When we land, Sara says she loves hang gliding and that she

had the best time of her life. It was indeed an unforgettable experience. She suddenly asks me how Laura is doing and how it feels to be living with her. I tell her it feels nice.

"Do you spend lots of time together?" she asks.

"Yes, when she's home. But she often has to leave for a few days to perform in other cities."

"Is she away right now?" asks Sara.

"Yes, actually. She's in California for two days."

The fruit in Sara is starting to smell riper. It is more exquisite than ever, but closer to being less so.

That night, Sara visits me, wearing her dress the color of the sun and her beard. She wants me to shave her beard. She says it's important, meaningful, intimate, sensual, and romantic.

"You won't be able to resist me when you shave me," she says.

We go into the bathroom and I start shaving her beard, and I immediately and uncontrollably begin to cry. Then Sara cries. Our noses run over our mustaches, and our tears run into our beards. After I've shaved half her face, we start to kiss and to hug each other, still crying. Then Sara goes and lies down on my bed. I take out my little white elephant, slide it onto a gold chain, and hook it around Sara's neck. She recognizes it from the story she read in my diary. She thanks me, squeezes the elephant in her palm, and makes a silent wish. I lie next to her and hold her. If at this point she were to ask me again to make love to her, I would not refuse, even though half her beard is still there. But she does not ask. We fall asleep crying.

While we sleep, I dream a strange nightmare, in which Sara wants to handcuff me to the foot of the couch the following morning. At first I refuse, but she insists until I finally agree. She then changes her mind about the location and handcuffs me instead to the bottom drawer of one of the file cabinets Laura bought to make me feel more at home. I see that I will always be a slave to file cabinets. Sara then lowers my pants and sits on me and, still wearing her dress the color of the sun and her half beard, has sex with me. Then, still in the dream, the door to my apartment opens, and my friend Tommy comes in, at which point Sara stops moving and remains sitting on me.

"The door was open, so I came in," he says.

Tommy has a special relationship with doors. They are never closed for him; they simply don't treat him that way. They are always open, unless they're locked. And I have forgotten to lock my door.

"How're you doing, man?" I ask him, trying to sound casual.

"Fine. I was in the neighborhood, so I thought I'd stop by. Are you busy?"

"No, not at all," Sara and I both answer.

"I don't think we've met," he says to Sara, and shakes her hand. He does not comment on her half beard.

They do small talk, which I don't listen to because I'm frantically trying to think of an explanation to give him as to why I'm handcuffed to the file cabinet with Sara sitting on me, in case he asks. But they keep talking, and I'm starting to feel vaguely like a couch: incidental.

"What are you guys doing anyway?" Tommy finally asks.

"We are acting out the famous fairy tale 'The Princess and the Pea,' " I tell him. "I'm playing the mattress."

"And the pea," Sara adds.

"Is he any good?" Tommy asks her.

"Yes, especially as the pea."

"And why the handcuffs?"

"Because I'm an object," I reply, glaring at Sara. "Mattresses and peas are helpless things."

Eventually Tommy leaves, telling us not to get up, he'll let himself out. And that's the end of the dream.

In the morning, I half expect Sara to ask me if she can handcuff me to one of the file cabinets, but she doesn't. She asks me to shave the rest of her beard, which I do, and then she requests me to escort her back home by subway, bec   he wants to be wearing her dress the color of the sun in   ibway. This we do.

When we arrive at Henrietta's apartment, w   her in bed, the blankets up to her nose. Not even her fin   tick out.

"What's wrong?" we ask.

"Nothing. I just have a slight cold." She lo   Sara. "You shaved your beard."

"No. Jeremy shaved me. Don't you think he   good job?"

"Yes. It looks nice."

"He's better at it than we are. You shave me the way you shave your legs and armpits. I shave myself the way I'd shave a doll's head. But Jeremy shaves me the way a real man shaves a real woman's beard."

"Yes," replies Henrietta through the blanket. "You should go tell your parrot a bit about it."

The moment Sara leaves the room, Henrietta whips back the blankets and goes to her dressing table, on which are a bottle of rubbing alcohol, Band-Aids, cotton balls, and a tube of Vaseline.

"What are you doing?" I ask.

"I hurt myself."

"How?"

"I ate all my cuticles and my lips." She turns her face to me and, with bleeding fingers, points to her bleeding lips.

"Why?" I ask.

"I was nervous."

"And your nails too?"

"No, I don't bite my nails. I prefer skin." She presses a Kleenex to her lips. The blood seeps right through, and the Kleenex holds there by itself.

"You don't have a cold?" I ask.

"No; I didn't want Sara to see me bleeding," she answers, the Kleenex flapping in the wind of her breath.

"What brought this on?"

"News." She opens the bottle of alcohol and starts disinfecting her fingers.

I sit on the window seat, sensing it will take a bit of time to get things out of her. "Yeah . . . ?" I say.

"Yeah," she says. Flap flap of the Kleenex. She looks like a flag.

"Is it good news or bad news?"

"That's a good question. And that's the reason I ate myself. I can't decide. Or rather, it's both, perhaps." She wraps Band-Aids around the tips of her fingers.

"What is this news?"

"Wait. Let me put on the last Band-Aid."

I wait in silence. When she is finished with her fingers, she unsticks the Kleenex from her mouth and applies Vaseline to her lips. She then sits motionless and does not speak.

"Can you tell me now?" I ask.

Her pupils turn to me. She springs off her chair, runs to her bed, and dives on it. She buries her face in her pillow, clutching it with clenched fists, her knuckles white. Before I can decide if I should be worried, she slowly gets up, looking much more relaxed now, and comes to sit by me on the window seat. She stares outside.

"Sara's doctor called me," she begins. "He said he spoke to a doctor friend of his, a specialist, about Sara's condition." Her pupils slide from the window to my face and then back, like a puppet's eyes. ". . . a doctor friend of his," she repeats, "who said there may be a cure for Sara." The puppet's eyes slide again to me and back outside. "He needs to test her, to know." The eyes are on me again, full of water now, no longer a puppet's.

I get a bit of my own water in my vision. A smile develops on my face, expressing my joy, but she shakes her head, frowns, and says, "No! That's why I ate my skin. It's because we cannot let ourselves be happy, or it might kill us later."

I take away the smile.

"Jeremy, be careful," she says, mechanically putting one of her fingers in her mouth, to eat its cuticle, and taking it back out instantly when she tastes the Band-Aid. She begins unconsciously to unroll a corner of the Band-Aid. "This news, I'm sure, is just a cruel trick of destiny," she says. "Our hopes will go up, and then they will be crushed when the doctor says, 'Oh, well, I was wrong, there's no hope for Sara, sorry, oops.' "

"Oops," says the parrot, walking into the room like a little person.

The door has been left ajar. Henrietta rushes out, and comes back a minute later, saying, "Sara didn't hear a thing. She's in the kitchen, flipping coins."

Henrietta picks up the parrot and holds him next to her on the windowsill. She strokes his head, and he starts purring loudly (a feat he learned from my cat, Minou, when they met recently).

Henrietta goes on: "I'm afraid I might kill the doctor, or do some such thing, when he says sorry oops."

"Doctors are prepared for that. They have protection," I say.

"You mean like bodyguards."

"Or muscular secretaries."

"You mean nurses."

"Yes."

"Meow," says the parrot.

"I want *you* to take her to the doctor for the test," she tells me.

"Why?"

"Because when the doctor says sorry oops, I will cry. Sara should not see anyone cry about her death. You will not cry."

"I might."

"I don't know if you're saying that because you think it's nice or if you truly believe it. But I know you will not cry. You don't care enough about her."

There are many things I want to answer to that, but as each one enters my mind, I don't utter it. We sit in silence, so the parrot whispers, "Is it time yet?" (He knows how to whisper.)

"Time for what?" asks Henrietta, feigning ignorance.

"Is it time for the death and dying of the yet yet?"

The parrot sometimes startles us with complex sentences.

"It's not funny," says Henrietta to the parrot.

"The yet yet?" says the parrot.

"No, death."

"Death! Death!" shrieks the parrot, flapping his wings, excited at hearing someone other than himself mention his word.

Henrietta squeezes his head with her thumb and forefinger, which always makes him stop. "I want to love him," she says, "but he makes it very difficult."

The parrot calms down and goes back to purring loudly.

"I do care about her," I finally say. "But a lot of things have happened."

"Therefore you will not cry."

"I might not," I concede, but I don't bother trying to convince her that it's not because I don't care about Sara but because I feel as though I have cried out all the tears in my body.

People start to clap when she's walking down the street.

I take Sara to the specialist. She smells rotten. The fruit in her, which previously produced the sweet smell, has rotted. She is past due. The key was to die before the fruit rotted. Poor Sara. I can smell it. It comes out in her breath when she talks.

The doctor tests Sara and then tells us the test was successful, and that therefore there is a possible cure, with a fifty percent chance of success. I look at Sara. She looks at me, her eyes wide. We simultaneously get up from our chairs and hug each other.

"Will my beard go away?" Sara asks the doctor, while we're still hugging.

"Yes," he answers.

"The stubble and everything?"

"Yes. You will be exactly as before."

We talk to the doctor some more. I am frisky, fidgeting, and wagging my tail. Once everything has been said, the cure is given to us in a little bottle, and Sara and I decide to go eat some ice cream in the coffee shop across the street. Walking out of the doctor's office, we talk excitedly to each other, about Sara's possible future, about things she'd like to do if she lives, except that she doesn't say "if," she says *when* she lives.

In the hallway, she flips her coin in the air and catches it, over and over again, absentmindedly, just for fun. "Now I can *really* flip the coin to see if I'll live or die," she says. "It really *is* a fifty percent chance now." But she doesn't look at the coin when it lands.

While we wait for the elevator, she says, "I suddenly have a very strong craving for pear ice cream. Why don't they make pear ice cream?"

Outside, she says, "When I live" (notice the "when") "do you think there's a chance you could ever love me, in a few years?"

"I don't know. We shouldn't think of that now."

"Tell me, Jeremeee," she says, yanking my arm. "Like when I'm seventeen and you're thirty-five, or, if that's still too young, when I'm eighteen and you're thirty-six?"

I don't answer, hoping she'll change the subject.

"So, do you think? Why not, huh?"

I am trying to think of a reply. I must call Lady Henrietta to tell her about the incredible fifty percent news, which will make her ecstatic. I will call her as soon as we get to the coffee shop, which is right across the street we are now crossing.

"Tell *me!*" She yanks my arm on "me."

I laugh, a bit exhausted. We are now crossing it, that street across which the ice cream is and, more important, the phone is also.

"Jeremy, I'm *serious*. Don't you think you could ever be in love with me? I love you." Sara is holding my hand but lagging behind me, making me pull her a bit as she dreams about her fifty percent chance of a future, which is now, suddenly, yanked away from her by the same car that yanks her hand out of mine.

Sara gets hit by a car and dies. That's in other words. Run over by it. Instantly. Without suffering. Her body twitches.

I am screaming. Everybody is screaming and crying. Sara is silent. There is blood everywhere, except on the little white elephant that is gleaming up at me, spotless, from Sara's neck. So familiar. So disconcerting.

The doctor—the specialist—is now in the street, and he pronounces Sara dead.

As I bend down over her, a voice inside me repeats: "Oh really? Oh really, Fate, oh, really?" I am bending down over her, confused. Something went wrong. I don't get it. It's like reading a novel, and something happens, and you weren't paying attention for a moment, and suddenly you don't understand what's going on anymore. I go back over the events I have just lived, to figure out if there's a logical link, you know, cause and effect, or anything similar. The visit to the doctor, the news that she may get well, the happiness and plans for the future, the decision to get ice cream, exiting the building, Sara's question, the crossing of the street, Sara's question again, the yellow car driving right into her. I get it: There's nothing to get.

Sara's fist is clenched. I unclench it. In her palm lies the coin. I take it and dig my fingernail into it, hoping to hurt it, before putting it in my pocket.

Sara's dead eyes are open, aimed at the sky. Although they are not aimed at me, she is looking at me out of the corner of her eye, I know. "I'm serious, Jeremy. So, do you think?" she does not say, but her eyes are still demanding the answer from me. She still wants to know, even now.

"I don't know," I tell her, holding her hand. "When you're eighteen and I'm thirty-six. It's a possibility."

Now the voice in my head is repeating something else: "You didn't even brake. You didn't even brake," over and over again. I go up to the woman of the yellow car, who is crying.

The interrogation:

"You didn't even brake," I tell her. She just stares at me, startled, so I say, "Why did you hit her?"

"It was my fault," she says. "I wasn't looking."

"What were you looking at?" I ask, sensing that this question is tremendously important and that its answer will help me understand everything. "What were you looking at?"

"I don't know. What does it matter?"

"It matters a lot. I *must* know what you were looking at."

She remains silent. Maybe she does not recall, because of the shock of the accident.

"Perhaps if you look back at the street," I suggest, "you might remember what caught your eye."

Finally, she says, "I didn't forget."

"So you know."

But she does not say more.

I try to reassure her: "Don't feel bad about telling me. I know that whatever you were looking at, it was probably a stupid thing to look at. Anything would be stupid when it kills someone."

"I saw a man in a second-floor window."

"And?"

"He was not dressed."

"Not at all?"

"No."

She means he was nude.

She goes on: "He was watching something outside, very intently. I was curious to see what he was looking at, so I looked."

"What was it?"

"Just a bird perched on a lamppost. The man must have been staring at it because it was blue, which is sort of uncommon for Manhattan. I'm sorry."

How relevant to my life. I can imagine that this woman of the yellow car must be ashamed that such a stupid, stupid thing has killed my daughter (I say daughter because that's who the woman must think Sara was). Well, it wasn't *our* parrot who did it. No parrot of mine. No parrot of Sara's. The parrot was part of Sara. Accusing the parrot is like saying she killed herself.

As for the nude man, of course, I would have preferred it if the woman had been looking at a bald man. Then I could hate bald men, not nude men, which would be more tolerable emotionally because I have a lot of hair, whereas I am the type of man who is not almost never naked anymore.

Well, that should certainly please people who think nude men brought on all the misery and insanity in this poor little girl's life, you moralist shits. They even killed her. *Nudity is dangerous*, you're gloating. *I told you so*, you're gloating. *When little girls do naughty things, they get punished. Very good turn of events indeed!*

"Where were you going?" I ask the woman of the yellow car.

"To the veterinarian."

I glance inside her car. There's a dog in a box.

"Is it sick?" I ask.

"Yes."

"Is there a cure?"

"No."

"So why were you going to the doctor?"

"To have him put to sleep."

"I had a dying pet, and I would never have put it to sleep."

"What animal was it?"

A little girl, I realize, is what I'm talking about. I'm about to tell her she should get fishes, but change my mind. Fishes die more easily than anything else in the world.

The ambulance comes. It takes Sara. I ride in it too. And the doctor comes also. He wants to help me in case I don't feel well mentally or emotionally.

In the ambulance, I shout to the doctor, above the screaming siren: "Don't tell her mother there was any hope, okay? Tell her there was no hope."

"I'll do my best."

Now I am screaming, not just because of the noise but out of anger: "No, you must tell her there wasn't any hope. Tell her there was no hope at all and that Sara was going to suffer terribly from her brain tumor, *okay*?"

"I won't call Sara's mother, but if she calls me, I won't lie to her either. She deserves to know the truth."

At the hospital, I call Lady Henrietta.

"That took long" is the first thing she says when she answers the phone. Then, almost breathless, she asks, "Is there any hope?"

"No."

Silence. And then she says, very softly, "You see, I knew it."

"Yes, I know."

I hear her crying. And then she says, "Well, come home. It's getting late."

I am silent now. I want to say "okay." It is on the tip of my tongue. I can hear it in the air, already.

"Okay?" she says. "Can you please bring Sara home now?"

"No."

"Why not?" she asks, annoyed and curious, not at all alarmed, because people who are dying of a disease simply don't die, on top of it, of an accident.

"You should turn on your tape recorder," I tell her.

"It's already on."

"You should come to the hospital. There was an accident. It's Sara."

I tell her that her daughter is already dead.

Not only is there no hope, but your daughter is already dead.

I am appalled by the parrot, who, as soon as we return to the apartment from the hospital, says, "Is it time yet?"

I am surprised that Lady Henrietta, very seriously, answers the parrot: "Yes, it happened. She's dead."

"And yet? And yet?" says the poor dumb parrot, as though mocking her answer. He raves on a bit: "Is it almost time yet? Death and dying?"

The parrot didn't kill Sara. What nonsense. It was the street. Nude men and that street were responsible. No parrot of mine. No parrot of Sara's. I take the parrot's droppings and deposit them on the street where the accident happened, to punish the street.

I feel as though I have been a spectator at a circus, and now the show is over. There was a talking parrot who belonged to a bearded lady who wore a dress the color of the sun, flew through the air on a hang glider, flipped coins, and killed fishes (cruelty to animals). It was a grotesque show with strong smells, blinding colors, and loud noises. Come to think of it, I was not only a spectator, I was also a performer: the elephant master. And I messed up the show. The elephant disobeyed me and trampled on the bearded lady.

One night I have a strange dream, or rather a nightmare. I dream that Lady Henrietta and I are at the doctor's office, and the doctor—Sara's original doctor—is telling us that Sara did not die of an accident.

"Do you mean she was murdered?" I ask, because of movies.

"No. She died of her brain tumor, as was expected," says the doctor in my dream.

"So what was the car accident? Was that her brain tumor?" asks Henrietta sarcastically.

"Exactly," says the doctor. "It was a new symptom: a cancer."

"Cancer of what?"

"Cancer of her space."

"What?"

"Cancer of the space, or place, her body fills in the universe. It is also called cancer of her air, but generally it is called cancer of one's space, place, or air, not her or his space, place, or air. In this case, however, since we are talking about a very specific person whom we knew, we may say her."

"Was it some sort of psychological problem, this 'cancer'?" one of us asks.

"Far from it. Cancer of one's place means that the place one's body occupies in the universe has become cancerous."

"We really don't understand what you're talking about," we say.

"When your place is cancerous, it means it's always at the wrong time. Accidents happen to you."

"Do you mean like being at the wrong place at the wrong time?"

"No. Your place cannot be wrong, but when it is sick or cancerous it becomes at the wrong time, just as a watch can become at the wrong time, except that with your place it's far worse than merely the *wrong* time; it's the *bad* time, the *tragic* time; accidents keep occurring in your place. With Sara, the first accident was the last."

"How do you know all this?"

"I knew it the first day you brought her to me, when I saw the nature of her brain tumor. You may want to sue me; you may hate me for having known and not told you about this symptom: for having known and not told you that it was the last symptom she was going to have and the one that would kill her. I decided to withhold this information from you for your own good."

"Then why are you telling us now, for God's sake? Why not just let us believe she died of a real, down-to-earth accident?"

"I'm not sure why. I suppose it's because I love watching people's surprise. Anyway, honesty is the best policy. Is that a famous quote, or did I just invent it? Even if it comes late. Better late than never. Better safe than sorry."

"So you invented all those lies about her lying down on the sidewalk and closing her eyes?"

"Well, I *did* tell you she would die suddenly, didn't I? And she *was* lying in the street, though I suppose her eyes weren't closed if she was hit by a car. Anyway, I wasn't so far off."

Anger is rising very quickly, to a dangerous, boiling level within me. "I would have prevented the accident!" I cry.

"No," says the doctor. "Only delayed it, which is why I didn't tell you about it. The knowledge would have made your lives hell."

"You murdered her by not telling us!" we scream, with all the rage of our lives.

"You would have kept Sara locked in a little white disinfected room with no furniture, only a floor made of mattress and walls made of mattress. And even then the fatal accident would have occurred eventually."

Brimming with disdain, I spit: "As far as I can remember, there are only four types of deaths in life: disease, accident, murder, and suicide. So far, the only one Sara did *not* die of is the last, but I'm sure that with your help we can squeeze it in somewhere. After all, you've already been so kind as to provide us with murder."

Lady Henrietta and I are able to contain ourselves no longer. We attack the doctor, throwing ourselves at him. We beat him and make him bleed. I knock on his head like a woodpecker. Henrietta punches his chest. "Death and dying," I feel, for some reason, I should say. And then I wake up.

What an asshole of a doctor. I am still full of anger, even though I am relieved that it was just a dream. Sara did, truly, die of an accident, not a "cancer of her place" or "space" or "air." Her accident was not preventable, not foreseeable, not to be expected, and some stupid little doctor in his stupid little office did not know it would happen.

I continue taking the parrot's excrement to that street and dropping it there.

I visit my friend Tommy. I tell him about the accident, I cry, and he tries to be supportive.

He says, "Manhattan is such an unhealthy and repulsive city, not a place for people to live, especially children. There are barely any trees, no animals except pet dogs and pigeons that shit you on the head. Though actually that's not quite true. A few days ago, I was at my girlfriend's apartment, doing my male courtship dance, which she always demands of me before we have sex. The music was blasting, and I was stark naked, when lo and behold, I see a blue bird outside the window. So maybe there is hope left for this mean, repulsive city."

"Was it a parrot?"

"A parrot?"

"Yes."

"I don't know. It wasn't close enough for me to tell."

"I could have you arrested for indecent exposure."

He looks at me a moment, to see if I'm laughing, to see if I'm joking.

Finally, he says, "Hey, lighten up."

"No. It was you that woman was looking at when she ran over Sara. Why the fuck did you have to stand in the window naked? Don't you know that's illegal, and for good reason?"

"What are you talking about? How would you know what she was looking at?"

"Because she *told* me. What address were you at?" I ask, to make sure he was the naked man the woman had seen.

He tells me, and I nod.

He sits down, perfectly white and silent. After a while, he softly says, "Pardon the banality at a time like this, but . . . it's a small world."

"A small circus."

People start to clap at her life.

chapter *ten*

Sara's funeral is attended by dozens of male models.

Lady Henrietta has stopped painting.

"I want to leave," she tells me. "Take me somewhere, Jeremy."

"Where do you want to go?"

"Anywhere. Just away."

"The only place I can think of is my mother's house. Unless you want to spend money on a real trip."

"I don't care at all. I can't think. Your mother went to Disney

World with Sara. I would like to meet her. I want to be with people who have been with Sara when I was not there."

"How long do you want to stay?"

"Don't ask me petty questions at a time like this. I couldn't care less. I have no idea. Maybe one hour, maybe one month, maybe forever, okay? You decide."

Laura understands perfectly and approves of my going to the country with Lady Henrietta to comfort her.

Henrietta and I go to my mother's house. We both sleep in my old room, which has twin beds. The only other bedroom in the house, my mother's, has one big bed, so we have no choice. Henrietta stays in our room most of the time, on her bed, her legs under the blanket, like someone sick. In darkness. She cries incessantly. She gets cold sores under her nose and on her upper lip, from blowing her nose all the time. She lies under a mountain of Kleenex. She vomits once, from crying so much. Her hair is stuck to her face, so I brush it for her and tie it in a ponytail. I wipe her face with cold water. I feed her. She eats absentmindedly. After crying a lot, she gets very cold, and I find her sitting in bed, wearing her winter coat.

Henrietta keeps Sara's braids on her night table, in the long box. Even the little note is still there, on which Sara wrote to me: "Here is a lock, a token of my affection." Henrietta often pets the braids.

My mother is angelic, as I suspected she'd be. She is discreet, sensitive, always there behind the door if she is needed. She wears black. She always whispers. Her face gets bloated, like

Henrietta's, maybe out of sympathy. Perhaps she cries secretly in her room. When she's not behind the door, she sits on the couch in the living room and does nothing. Sometimes she walks around and looks out the window.

It's summer outside. The weather is gorgeous. Not too hot. Very sunny and bright and colorful. The birds chirp. So do the insects. It feels very inappropriate, this chirping. Henrietta keeps the blinds down, but there's a high window in our room, which has no blind. Through it she can see the sky, blue like someone's eyes, and the trees rustling in the breeze.

Henrietta's mourning is a normal mourning. It's very intense, probably as intense as mourning gets, short of suicide, but it is normal—for Henrietta, that is, which means there are still a few pitiful eccentricities here and there, but nothing I couldn't have thought of myself. Actually, that's wrong. I could not have predicted that she would take a liking to spilling water around the house and that she would feel the need to unplug the electrical appliances in whatever room she's in. I cannot figure out the secret meaning of those things.

I take a walk in the woods, the parrot on my shoulder. I give in to some fantasy of life after death. I will utter Sara's name aloud to see if I'll get some sort of response from her. No one is listening, so why not try. It can't hurt.

"Sara," I say, in a normal voice.

The parrot cocks his head and looks me in the eyes. "Sara?" he says.

I walk some more in silence, and then I say again, "Sara."

I get no response from Sara, unless she is communicating to me through the parrot, who repeats, "Sara?"

"Sara," I say.

"Sara," he repeats, not looking at me anymore but staring

ahead in a melancholic way, like a little person. He understands that we're looking for her.

"Sara," I say.

"Sara," he says, his voice becoming deep and mournful.

I look at the trees. I wait for the slightest response to our calling, but there is no variation in the activities of nature. The breeze does not become stronger after we utter Sara's name, not a single branch cracks, no squirrel darts by at that moment, the sky does not become overcast, nor does the sun get brighter.

I start thinking about the afternoon of Sara's death, its bizarre sequence of events. Destiny. I have always craved to control destiny, either through down-to-earth effort or through supernatural means. But she is frighteningly whimsical, Destiny, inexorably so. She will not be controlled by little white elephants. She'll fight them to the death. She does not like to feel pressured, does not like commitment. Only accepts freedom. She's impatient, bored, restless, fidgety, like a little kid who can't sit still at table, with one cheek of her backside off her chair, her legs trembling, waiting, positioned to race away the moment her parents tell her she's dismissed. Except that Destiny does not wait to be dismissed. She races away anytime, all the time. She's capricious, flirtatious, unfaithful, selfish, a clumsy artist, not a true friend but a charming one nevertheless. She's always mischievous, incessantly saying "Oops," then melting into giggles. Always innocent in her evil deeds, never to blame, crowned by a complete and utter lack of sensitivity.

"Sara," I say.

"Sara." The parrot is crying, except that there are no tears.

A plane passes overhead.

* * *

Amanda Filipacchi

Henrietta is losing weight every day. Her face is ravaged. Her eyes are sunken, very red and irritated from the constant crying, and surrounded by dark circles. There are red blotches on her face, and her upper lip is all puffed up, thicker than I've ever seen it. It looks like a boxer's beat-up lip. All this isn't doing much good for my spirits, and I feel she is pulling me down with her.

I try to think of things to make her feel better. I decide to buy her marzipan. I find some in a little bakery in town. I also stop at the supermarket to buy her bottled water, because it's all she drinks. I walk through the aisles. Everything reminds me of Sara, and I realize how deeply her personality has been incorporated into every aspect of my life. My clothes remind me of her, because she used to draw men's clothes. I used to look at pretty women on the street or in the supermarket for the sake of looking at pretty women. Now when I see a pretty woman (especially one with big breasts) I cannot help but think: There goes one of Sara's Barbie dolls. Or is she a Jane doll?

The eggs in the dairy section remind me of Sara's Humpty Dumpties. My facial features float on their surfaces.

My thoughts are suddenly interrupted by the sight of a woman who looks extremely familiar. I slow my gait, trying to remember who she is. I get the feeling she is someone I don't like, though I can't remember why. And then I remember. She is one of my mother's agents. She is the lemon woman, the one who asked me to hand her down the tall kitchen garbage bags.

I stop next to her and say, "Could you please pass me the Ajax on that low shelf. My back hurts."

She stares at me, surprised. She recognizes me. Not saying a word, she bends down and gets me the Ajax.

"I spend my life going back and forth between the supermarket and my home," I tell her. "There are such strange people in the supermarket. People with problems and faults. But I would never pester someone in the supermarket by making subtle references to their fault, even if I got paid to do it. Would you?"

"You're doing it now."

"You started it."

"It was a favor."

"She called you her employee, her agent. Are you offended?"

"No. She paid me for this favor."

"Well, I wouldn't do it as a favor either."

At home, I go to Henrietta's room to give her the marzipan. I stop a few feet away from the door, stunned. I am hearing Sara's voice coming from inside the room. Sara talking to Henrietta.

"Repeat what you just told me," I hear Henrietta say.

"Why?" says Sara.

"Say it in my tape recorder."

"I'm tired of getting all my bad news recorded in your machine."

"Please."

"I got an F in art."

There's a click. I enter the room. Henrietta is sitting on her bed, with her tape recorder on her lap and the box of her daughter's braids next to her. Her hand is in the box, petting the braids and the white ribbons attached to them. Tears are streaming down her face. About fifty crumpled Kleenexes are scattered around her. I sit on the other bed, the box of marzipan on my lap. A brief glance is her only acknowledgment of my presence. She lets the tape recorder run.

"What did you say you wanted to be when you grow up?" asks Henrietta, from the tape recorder.

"A housewife," says Sara.

Again there's a click, signaling the end of one conversation and the beginning of another.

"Can you repeat that," says Henrietta. "Our connection was bad. I didn't hear you quite well."

"Bullshit," says Sara. "You just want to record me. Okay. Dear darling mother, I broke my leg at camp. It hurts terribly much. This is the tenth of August at three forty-three in the afternoon."

Click.

"How many cavities did you have?"

"Three."

Click.

"Is it recording yet?" asks Sara.

"Yes," says Henrietta.

"Melissa said her mother said my mother is perverted, because your house is full of naked men showing off their bodies and trying to be pretty like women."

Click.

"What did you say you wanted to be when you grow up?"

"A hairdresser."

Click.

"So tell me what's wrong," says Henrietta. The sound is muffled.

"You're not gonna record me, are you?"

"No. Tell me."

"I don't know, I'm just sad."

"There must be a reason."

"I wish I had a father who wore clothes."

"What in the world do you mean?"

"I want someone who's dressed most of the time. All the men

who come here are nice, but they're not like normal fathers. All my friends have fathers who are always dressed. My friends have never seen their fathers without their underwear, except one girl, and that was by accident, because none of the bathrooms in her house have locks."

Click.

"No, don't record me."

"Yes, I gotta have this on tape. This is terrible. Repeat what you just said."

"What do you mean, terrible? You always said I should be free in that way."

"I know. I don't mean terrible. I mean incredible. Surprising. Disconcerting. Unsettling. Nerve-racking. Repeat what you said."

"Do I *have* to?"

"Absolutely."

"I'm attracted to Jeremy."

My ears buzz in surprise, but I am careful not to move a muscle, not to show my interest in this new topic of conversation.

"You are?"

"Yes."

"How do you mean, attracted?"

"I want to do it with him."

"Do what?"

"Sleep."

"Do you know what that means?"

"Sex."

"And do you know what *that* means?"

"Yes."

"Are you sure? You didn't learn it from me. You must have learned it from TV or your friends, right?"

"Yes. And books."

"Are you sure you have the right definition?"

"I guarantee you, yes."

"And you're interested in Jeremy."

"Yes."

"Are you planning to do anything about it?"

"Yes. I would like to go to Disney World with him."

"Really."

"Will you let me go?"

"I don't think so."

"You should. Our doorman, on afternoons when you're out hunting for O.I.M.s, would willingly see me in the back room, but he's aggressive and too rough. Otherwise there's my gym teacher in school, a pedophile. He adores me, and we have plenty of free time after class, but I think he might be dangerously insane."

"Don't underestimate my intelligence."

"You know I'm kidding. But it *is* supposed to make you think."
Click.

"What did you say you wanted to be when you grow up?"

"A fact checker."
Click.

"I think I regret it," says Sara. Her voice is muffled. I realize this means the tape recorder is hidden.

"Why?"

"Because he probably won't want to be friends with me now."

"You knew that might happen."

"I know, but I didn't think it would bother me. Now I wish I could keep him as a friend."

"Maybe you'll be able to."

"It's not sure at all."

"I know. You're not in love with him, are you?" asks Henrietta.

"Not that much. Though I wish we could stay lovers. But I'm sure he'd never want to."

"I think you're right."

"He's too influenced by what people think."

Click.

"That took long. Is there any hope?" says Henrietta.

"No." It's my voice.

"You see, I knew it."

"Yes, I know."

She cries. "Well, come home. It's getting late."

Silence.

"Okay?" she says. "Can you please bring Sara home now?"

"No," says my voice.

"Why not?"

"You should turn on your tape recorder."

"It's already on."

"You should come to the hospital. There was an accident. It's Sara."

"Is she all right?"

"No." Pause. "She was hit by a car, and died instantly."

Her scream is long and deep.

The real Henrietta's eyes are closed, but she is not asleep. Her hand is still inside the box, petting the braids. I bury my face in my hands.

An hour later, I am able to persuade her to go out for a walk. We are silent, and we walk slowly. I am also able to persuade her to eat half of a small marzipan mushroom. We don't go far, but an hour elapses before we are back at the house.

We go to our room and find the parrot covered in long golden threads.

"I am a dying person," says the parrot.

I notice a white ribbon on the floor in the corner of the room and realize the parrot has found Sara's braids, destroyed them, and tangled himself in her hair. Henrietta bends over him, touches the threads, and says, "What is this?"

I don't answer, keep looking at the white ribbon.

"Jeremy? What do you think he's covered with?"

I pick up the white ribbon, and I find the box, and I carefully start pulling the hairs off the parrot and putting them in the box.

Henrietta covers her eyes with one hand when she understands, then she comes down on the bird, hitting him hard. She slaps his body and the side of his wing. I'm afraid she will hurt him seriously, so I pull her away.

"He's an asshole!" she shouts at me.

The parrot lies on the floor, motionless. He is trembling, his beak is open, and his black tongue moves in and out slightly, as though he's panting. Some of Sara's hair got in his mouth. His feathers are erect. I touch him lightly. He shivers. He doesn't seem hurt, just shocked.

"You shouldn't vent your anger on him as though he's responsible for her death," I tell Henrietta. "When he saw Sara's braids, he probably thought he had found her."

Later that day, Henrietta tells me, "Someone *is* responsible for her death. I can't live with the idea that the woman who killed my daughter is living out there in the same world I'm living in and that I'm just going to keep on living in the same world as hers without *knowing* her or what kind of person she is. I will feel more complete and satisfied if I know her. I want to meet her."

"Don't get into this," I tell her. "One thing might lead to another."

"I know what you're thinking, but you're wrong, I think."

"You might start hating her and wanting to harm her."

"I knew that's what you were thinking. And you mean harm her as in even kill her."

"It could happen."

"I don't feel it will."

"She might not want to meet with you."

"If the parents of the girl you ran over say they want to meet you in a public place, could you refuse?"

I think for a moment. "Most people would refuse, because it wouldn't be surprising if the parents' only remaining desire in life is to kill the person who ran over their daughter."

Henrietta decides to call Julie Carson anyway, the woman of the yellow car. She sets up her recording equipment. She tells me I can listen on the other phone. A woman answers on the fourth ring. I am startled to recognize her voice so clearly.

"Is this Julie Carson?" says Henrietta.

"Yes."

"I'm the mother of the girl you killed."

(Be direct, why don't you.)

"Oh," says the woman.

"I've been thinking a lot about you, and it would be very helpful to my mourning if I could meet with you. Just to chat and to know you a little bit."

(Helpful to my *mourning?*)

Long silence. "I don't know what to say."

"Please say yes. It would help my grieving."

(It would help my grieving.)

"I don't think I can meet with you," says the woman. "I wish I could help you in every way possible, but I cannot meet with you in person. I'm sure you understand."

"Why? You mean for safety reasons?"

"Yes."

"You think I'd kill you?"

(Be blunt, why not.)

"I don't know."

"Your address is in the phone book. If I want to, I can just wait for you outside your building. So what difference does it make?"

(That's it, bring out all the charm.)

"Is that what you'll do?"

Henrietta waits a moment before answering. "No. I'm just showing you that it makes no sense for you not to meet me in person."

(Such vulnerability is sure to work.)

"I really would rather not. Also, I've been sick since the accident. I can't go out. Please try to understand."

"Perhaps I could come and visit you at home, so you don't have to go out?"

(She couldn't refuse *that*.)

"No."

"You don't care very much about remedying the wrong you've done."

"It was an accident."

"I know that very well. But you don't seem the slightest bit interested in making me feel better. Logically, you should be afraid of making me angry, because *then* you could be in danger."

"Is that the case?"

"I *am* feeling sad and angry, but you're not in danger."

"Please understand."

"I don't want to," says Henrietta.

"But you do, don't you?"

"No. I don't want to."

The woman remains silent.

"Did you end up taking your pet to the vet to kill it?" asks Henrietta. I had told her about that.

"To put him to sleep, yes."

"I'm surprised. I would have thought you might have changed your mind."

"He was suffering."

"Did you do it that day?"

"No, of course not."

"When?"

"The next day. Someone did it for me."

"Who?"

"A friend."

"A man?"

"Yes."

"Your lover?"

The woman hesitates and finally replies, "No, just a friend."

"How old are you?"

"Thirty-eight."

"Older than I am. I'm thirty. What I really want to know is whether you have children, but I won't ask you that, because if you *do* have children, you'll say you don't. Do you have children?"

"No."

"I might need to talk to you again sometime. Also, I might

come and see you outside your building. But I won't hurt you. I would be very surprised if I hurt you. Goodbye."

Henrietta waits for the woman to say goodbye, but it doesn't happen. The woman hangs up silently. "Jeremy?" says Henrietta on the phone.

"What?" I answer in my receiver.

"So what do you think?"

"I think you should paint."

Henrietta goes back to bed, and I watch TV.

"**H**ow does it feel to be clapped at, everywhere you go?" a famous interviewer asks her on TV.

"It's funny. It's cheerful," she replies. "I like it. I wonder when people will get tired of it."

"I predict never. Fifty years from now, people will still be clapping at you, some without even remembering why. They will simply know: She is the person one claps at. But the question I want to ask is, Will *you* ever get tired of it?"

"I predict not as long as I live."

Two days later, Henrietta is still in bed. She's lying on her side, motionless and silent. I walk around the bed to look at her eyes. They are open and unblinking. She could be dead.

"Henrietta?" I say.

Her pupils move to my face.

"Are you feeling okay?" I ask.

"Yes," she groans.

"I was wondering if you'd like to go for a walk."

"No."

"A drive?"

"No."

"Would you like to paint?"

"No." She closes her eyes.

"I think it might make you feel much better to paint."

She doesn't answer.

"I'll even pose for you if you want."

She sighs.

"I'll even pose naked for you if you want."

She snorts, and I'm not sure if it's a sob or a laugh.

"I have some painting stuff you could use, from when I was a kid. I even have some oil paints. I can bring them in here."

Henrietta does not answer, which is better than a refusal, so my mother and I carry all the paints and brushes and canvases to Henrietta's room. We sit her at a desk, in front of a canvas. I ask my mother to leave because I don't want to pose nude in front of her. I take off my clothes and, remembering Sara's rule, I lie on the bed in the most comfortable position I can find.

I talk to Lady Henrietta about light subjects, like how pretty the weather is, how pleasant it is to walk outside, how nice my mother is. To amuse her, I tell her about the agent I caught in the supermarket. I see her making a few brush strokes on the canvas. Good. She answers my comments briefly, sadly. Her brush strokes look different than usual. The movements of her arm look broad and negligent. And then suddenly they stop. She does not move anymore. She just sits there staring at me.

"What's wrong?" I ask.

"I'm sorry Jeremy, but I can't paint you. I've painted you once already. I'm just not interested in doing it again."

I get up and look at her canvas. On it there is a stick figure of me, lying on a stick-figure bed.

"Oh yes," I say. "I can see you're not inspired."

She goes back to her bed and plops down.

"I know just how to fix the problem," I continue. "I will find you a very inspiring model."

"Don't bother, Jeremy."

"I want to bother. I just need to know one thing: Do you want a beautiful man or an Optical Illusion Man?"

"I don't know and I don't care."

"Please, Henrietta. I'm sure it'll make you feel so much better to get involved in your painting, even for just one hour."

"O.I.M." I hear her mumble.

My mother and I go to a bookstore. In the psychology section, we see a man checking out all the books. We wait to see what he will do. He might be a good O.I.M., depending on what he'll do, how he'll move.

I decided to bring my mother along because if I'm going to start picking up people, her presence gives me more courage, and makes me seem safer. In addition, two people give off an air of greater authority and credibility than one does.

The man finally takes down a book entitled *How to Break Your Addiction to a Person.*

My mother nudges me, her eyes wide open, and her mouth in the shape of an *O. O* as in "Oh! Look at what he's reading." Not *O* as in "O.I.M.," for I haven't told her about that, about what kind of man we're looking for.

I instantly decide that he's a very good Optical Illusion Man. What an unlikely type of man to be addicted to a person. What type of person is she or he? Does she or he know?

He's about forty. He looks like he works in an office. He must have stopped at the bookstore after his job, to see if he could get some help in overcoming his infatuation with that woman, or man, perhaps.

"Excuse me," I say.

The man turns around. He seems very self-conscious about the book he's holding, the way he's so aggressively not looking at it, but maybe I'm just projecting onto him the way I would feel in his place.

"We were wondering if you'd be interested in posing for a painter."

The man licks his lips in confusion. He puckers his mouth, about to say something, but seems unsure of what to say. "I'm sorry?" he finally says.

"We need a model, to pose for a painter, and we were wondering if you'd be interested. It's just for an hour or two, today or tomorrow. And there's a salary of fifty dollars an hour."

He asks us questions, which we answer. Then he says, "No, sorry."

He wanted to get as much information as possible, as many goodies of our weirdness, though knowing from the very beginning that he was going to say no. He wanted to hear all the juicy details, so that he'd have a wonderful story to tell his adored person, and maybe she or he would like him back after he told about so great an experience in such a clever, witty way, and how he looked down upon that weird man who pissed the hell out of him when he caught him reading *How to Break Your Addiction to a Person.*

I would never have the guts to pick up such a book in public. And anyway, I don't *have* an addiction to a person, thank God. I have had in the past, but at this point in my life I'm free.

It's not so hard to find O.I.M.s, I realize. Almost everyone is an Optical Illusion Person. Isn't everyone almost a certain way, but not quite?

We go to hardware stores. Big men with blond mustaches tell us no. Sometimes they don't even speak, they droop their eyelids halfway down their eyes and slowly shake their heads. Sometimes they say "*Hell* no!"

In bakeries, men say "Naah," very nasally, while they are buying their pastries.

In shoe stores, men try to be nicer. They're more educated and more polite. They are elegant and seated. They are heads of families, those men, with wives and small children at home, in houses with chimneys that smoke only on rare occasions. Their socks smell like flowers, and after they tell us no, they tell the salesman, "Ouch, they're a bit tight."

In the pet stores, the men are more surprised than anywhere else, I wonder why. And they express their surprise verbally, no mere lifts of the eyebrows. "Well, that's mighty unusual," they say. "I've never heard of this before. It's original. Wowee. Well, well. But I'm sorry, pal"—slap on my arm—"I'd love to, but I'm very busy. Good luck, though."

"**I** don't know if we'll ever find an O.I.M. who's interested," I mutter, walking down the street.

"What's an oim?" asks my mother. "I didn't know we were looking for an oim."

"Not *oim*. O.I.M. Optical Illusion Man. A man who is almost a certain way but not quite." I don't feel like getting into it deeper than that. Only one of us needs to know what we're looking for.

We enter a coffee shop.

My mother points to a man sitting at a little table near the window. He's alone, eating a chocolate crepe. I must admit she's right. She is absolutely and completely right. She has an amazing talent for finding the best O.I.M. A great eye for it. It must be beginner's luck.

O.I.M.ness emanates from every shred of his person. He is even more extreme than I am. Exquisite choice. Superb specimen. He eats slowly and quickly at the same time; it's hard to tell which. Two chews, swallow. One chew, swallow. Slow chews, but few chews. Even though the chews are slow, there are so few of them that the crepe disappears quickly. His eyes and mouth droop, but his wrinkles smile, giving, one moment, the impression of happiness, cheerfulness, verge of laughter, sense of humor, and, the next moment, deep despair, sadness, must comfort him, want to ask him what's wrong. He has big, dark, young eyes, a young, plump mouth, but wrinkled skin. The wrinkles are deep but somehow young. They are not dry, not thin. They are deeper folds. Fat, juicy wrinkles. Fresh folds of flesh.

We sit in front of him, and I say, "We were wondering if you'd be interested in posing for a painter."

"Is he femooss?" he asks, in a voice that is not only heavily accented, probably from French, but also slimy, weak, and drawn out, creating an overwhelming combination.

"It's a woman," I tell him. "A little famous. Are you interested? You have a good mouth."

"Sank yooo. Eats just the face, then?" Soft voice. It envelops you and touches you in private places with too much familiarity.

"No, she paints the body also." I try to make my own voice like a whip, to counteract his. "Nude," I add.

"Noood! Zat's good. I'm flattered, but ma mouse is not a very good representation ov ma neckud bowdy."

He's rubbing his body against mine, merely with his voice, and I am relieved when he addresses my mother in the same way.

"When is eat?" he asks her softly, intimately.

"Today or tomorrow."

"Zat's good," he tells me, with much breath in his voice. "Eat sounds interesting."

"It's not." Whip-whip. "You go there, you pose, and you're done," I tell him.

My mother looks squarely at me. Her face is open and illuminated, as though she has seen a new side of me. Yes, I can be strong too, Mom.

"I don't know eef I shood," he says. "On top of eat, I have a girlfriend."

"This has nothing to do with having a girlfriend. It's professional. Nothing else."

"*Ah, oui? Mon oeil!*" he says, which is about the only thing I know in French and which means, literally, "my eye," which means "my foot." I am exasperated.

"All we need is a simple yes or no," I tell him. "We don't have all day."

"Eats yes."

I didn't even mention money.

The Frenchman says he's available immediately, so we all drive home. He undresses and lies down on Henrietta's bed. I sit on my bed. I don't want to be hovering over Henrietta, putting too much pressure on her. I make light conversation.

The Frenchman seems to think that all this is very perverted. He giggles nervously and leers at us incessantly. He seems to enjoy all the attention bestowed on his flabby white body. He

thinks that we think it's beautiful. Henrietta works for about
ten minutes, then stops. The painting she has made of him is
scarcely better than the stick figure she made of me.

"I don't want to paint, Jeremy," she says.

"He's not good enough?"

The Frenchman glares at me.

"He's fine," she answers. "I just don't want to paint anything.
I'm sorry."

Before putting his clothes back on, the Frenchman insists on
seeing what Henrietta painted. His eyes open wide in surprise,
and he looks at Henrietta. She stares back at him, completely
uncaring. He looks at the painting again. I can tell he is dying
to say something—"You should take lessons," or "You are a
bad painter"—but all he does is look at her again, raise his
eyebrows slightly, look at me, frown, turn away, and bob his
head forward once, like a hen, before disappearing into the
bathroom to put on his clothes. If only he could see one of
Henrietta's old paintings, he would admire her skills.

We pay him and drive him back to town.

You may have sensed that my mother is a bit subdued these
days. I haven't been telling any extravagant tales about her
behavior. That's because there haven't been any such tales to
tell; she still hasn't returned to her old self, her Disney World
self. But I must admit I don't mind much. Her new self is quite
pleasant. For now at least. Appropriate.

Henrietta insists on dressing up in men's clothes every day now.
With a jacket and pants and shirt, and a very formal, tight tie,
and men's shoes, and sock garters.

"Men's clothes meant a lot to her," she explains.

"They only meant a lot to her because you omitted them from your paintings," I tell her.

"That doesn't make any difference. She drew them and loved them, and that's all that matters."

Henrietta often doesn't cry now but just sits motionless, as though deep in thought. I ask her what she's doing. She says, "I'm trying to figure out why Sara died. I'm sure there's an explanation."

"What sort of explanation are you talking about? Do you mean spiritual?"

"Maybe not."

"Do you mean supernatural, or magical, or astrological?"

"No, not that at all."

"Do you mean scientific?"

"Probably."

"But we know the scientific reason."

"No, that was the medical reason."

"Well then, what sort of scientific are you talking about?"

"Unknown scientific."

"Like what?"

"I don't know. It's unknown."

"But I mean what area of science?"

"It could be any area, though I would think it's probably space, and life, and the mind."

"Life as in 'life on other planets'?" I say, trying to be funny.

She looks at me, not amused, but not hurt, as I was afraid she might be. "No, not that at all," she says serenely.

* * *

Henrietta wants to go back home, says she's not feeling better at my mother's. I don't think she should give up so soon. It's only been a week. I feel terrible, totally powerless. If anything could have helped her, it would have been to paint. That was the best chance she had. As soon as this thought enters my mind, I realize I'm lying. I haven't done quite enough for her.

A tiny idea germinates in my mind. It remains very little and almost subconscious, because I suppress it. But it's there, nagging at me: I could offer myself to her. That might be the most helpful thing I could do. She probably wouldn't accept, but it's the gesture that counts. But then I tell myself: Jeremy, your body is not a cake. You don't offer it to be polite. You are not a cigarette either, and should not expect her to say, "No thanks, I don't smoke," or "Yes, thanks a lot."

I just feel it's my duty to do this. I love my girlfriend, Laura, but I feel as though I'm not a true friend to Lady Henrietta if I don't offer myself completely. I know this reasoning sounds demented. It does to me too, but the idea is planted in my brain, and I can't get rid of it, no matter how hard I try.

That afternoon, she tells me, "Before she died, I was wondering how it would be for me once she was gone. I knew it would be horrible, that I would be in terrible pain, but I thought I would be strong enough to get through it. I even imagined that, a day or two after her death, I would sort of turn to stone and be very unemotional, especially outwardly. But that's not what happened. I can't stop crying, and I feel as though I'll never be able to stop."

I hug her and stroke her hair, and yet I think that now is not the right time to offer myself. Tonight would be better. I'm very nervous about the idea, but I feel I should at least try, knowing that I would later be ashamed if I hadn't.

That night, she is lying on her bed, her back to me. I lie down next to her and wrap one arm around her. She hugs my arm, and I feel the tears on her cheeks.

"Don't cry. Turn around," I tell her.

She snivels but doesn't move.

"Turn around. I want to tell you something." I gently pull her shoulder toward me. She turns and looks at me. She looks like a child. Grief has swollen her face, giving the impression of baby fat. She seems vulnerable and helpless.

Now that she is facing me, I don't know what to say, so I just kiss her. She does not push me away. I hug her and kiss her, and nothing is said. It seems as though nothing is thought either. For some strange reason, everything feels very right and appropriate, as if this will solve all our problems, will take away our sadness. But then I realize it's not true, it can't be true. Pain doesn't go away just like that.

Maybe it does. The next morning Lady Henrietta smiles at me for the first time in a long time. She says, "We can go back home now. Would you mind if we left tomorrow?"

"Don't you think you should stay here a little longer, to get through this hard period?"

"I'm okay now. I feel much better and at peace, as though something has been resolved and things are the way they're supposed to be."

She puts the lid on the box of tangled hair and says, "What happened between us last night made me feel as though we were in touch with Sara. It brought us closer to her. I think it was right."

A moment later, she adds, "You did not betray your girlfriend. You were not unfaithful to her."

chapter *eleven*

I decide not to call Laura before going back to New York, because I want to open our apartment door unexpectedly and catch her off guard. This might not seem very nice, but ever since two nights ago, when I betrayed her with Henrietta, I have been overcome by doubts about her faithfulness and love for me. I've even started doubting the supposed greatness of her personality. Is she really as wonderful as I thought? Could she be hiding something dreadful, like an evil character trait, a man in her bed, or contempt for me? Part of me is nevertheless looking forward to being with her and being consoled by her, but I just can't shake off this nagging fear that I might be disappointed, which is why I haven't called her.

I'm in the elevator, going up to our floor. My heart beats quickly, and I take deep breaths. I try to imagine what she'll be doing when I enter the apartment. The worst possibility I can think of is finding her in bed with a man. The best possibility is finding her sitting at her piano, composing a piece just for me, with Minou lying on top of the instrument, listening rapturously.

But then again, she could be doing much more ordinary things, like running errands or drinking orange juice in the kitchen.

When I arrive at the door, instead of ringing or knocking, I quietly use my keys. Since part of me strongly suspects that she's too good to be true and is betraying me behind my back, even hating me perhaps, I suddenly get a vision of her sitting at her piano and holding a little voodoo doll of me, sticking pins into it and setting its hair on fire. And then, when I come in, she would quickly hide the doll inside the piano, not even caring that the ash of the burnt hair gets all over the little felt hammers of her piano and ruins them.

I open the door and look straight at the piano. My heart sinks a little when I see that she is not sitting there composing a piece for me. I am about to head for the bedroom, because the possibility that she might be in bed with a man does not seem too unrealistic. But suddenly, a movement in the corner of the living room catches my eye. It's her. She's sitting on her piano bench, but not at the piano; she's at the file cabinets, the ones she gave me when I first moved in, to make me feel more at home. I never touched them, or used them, and I wasn't aware that she had filled them. But obviously she had, because one of the drawers is open and her delicate fingers are flipping through the manila folders. I am suddenly jealous of those ghostly gray file cabinets, which have haunted my life in various reincarnations and which are now stealing my girlfriend, or at least placidly receiving her caresses. I have always found them sinister, menacing, sneaky, depraved, heinous, bureaucratic, their cold metal bodies lurking in the shadows of the living room like sinful thoughts. Minou, who is lying on top of them, is watching me approach, but Laura is not yet aware of my presence.

"Hello, Laura," I say.

She turns around and exclaims, "Jeremy!" in complete joy. She gets up and hugs me. "I *missed* you," she says.

She is wearing my raincoat and boots. I open the coat a little, because I see a piece of breast and wonder if she's completely naked underneath. No, she's wearing my Jockey shorts.

She smiles and partially explains her attire: "At first I was only wearing your underwear, but then I got cold, so I put on your coat."

"And boots?" I offer.

"Yeah."

I hug her and put my hands on her backside out of curiosity. Just as I suspected, she is wearing nothing under my Jockey shorts, which, come to think of it, is normal.

She looks extremely beautiful, even without makeup, though she is wearing the diamond earring I gave her, the one I found on the sidewalk one evening. But she always wears it, so that's nothing special.

"What are you doing with the file cabinets?" I ask her.

"I open them sometimes, when you're not here. They make me feel as though I'm in touch with your soul, your mind, and your essence."

I'm touched and insulted at the same time. I'm not sure I

should be flattered to remind her of a file cabinet, or rather to have a file cabinet remind her of me.

I noticed but didn't really register the fact that there is a mattress on the floor, next to the file cabinets. Now I register it.

"You've been sleeping here?" I ask, concerned.

"Yeah; it just made me feel closer to you. Don't worry, it's no big deal," she says, waving at the mattress dismissively.

In a way, I *have* been betrayed. She did not sleep with a man, but she did sleep with a file cabinet. And she petted a file cabinet very affectionately and even erotically and sensuously, staring at it lovingly, flipping through its files.

I wonder what she's filled the files with. Probably ordinary dull stuff. Bills. But then, as I'm standing there, I start fantasizing. It wouldn't be so bad to remind her of a file cabinet if she's filled it with very interesting files. That would make me feel good, in fact. Maybe the files are empty but labeled with elements of our future life together, like "Car," "House," "Son," "School." How charming that would be. It would show her devotion to me, her love for and near obsession with me.

Or each file could be labeled with a quality of mine.

Or maybe she labeled them with parts of our past, things we did together, and each file might be full of souvenirs from a particular evening, or restaurant. For example, maybe in one file she keeps my dirty Kleenexes from when I cried.

She's obsessed with me, I think to myself, flattered. This beautiful creature, even more beautiful than Lady Henrietta, whom most men would kill for, is obsessed with me. But then again, maybe the cabinets are full of files of her male conquests, with pictures and complete reports of their sexual prowess, and I'm just one of the files. . . .

I must see what is in the files, because then I'll know what she thinks of me.

I glance at them, not wanting to seem indiscreet, but I don't see anything written on the folders, so I bend down and look closer. They are not labeled, so I open one, and then another. They're empty. I look at her, bewildered, and doubly insulted, and worried about her sanity.

"So," I say, "not only am I a file cabinet, which is bad enough, but I'm an *empty* file cabinet?" Is that what she thinks of my mind? That I'm very stupid and have nothing in my head? I ask her as much.

"No; on the contrary," she says. "You have plenty of things in your head, but they are mysterious and intriguing things, which no one can know but you."

We kiss and lie down on the mattress.

"I'm so glad you're back. I missed you infinitely," she whispers, her eyes closed as she kisses my neck.

I feel great desire for her at this moment. I love her. But I know that before we go too far, there is something I must tell her.

"How has your show been going?" I ask, to delay having to tell her what I have to tell her.

"It's going great."

"Are you tired of the clapping yet?"

"I predict not as long as I live."

"I know, I heard you say that on TV."

"Then why are you asking?" she whispers, kissing me.

"To delay having to tell you what I must tell you."

"Oh?"

We are entwined in each other's arms, and I am wondering if I should bother telling her this thing at all. I know I must, so I reluctantly disentangle myself from her.

"Before we go further, there's something I must tell you."

"Yes, you said that already, poor Jeremy, poor Mr. Acidophilus," she says jokingly, stroking my hair.

I take her hand out of my hair and clasp it in my palms. I must not be distracted. "When I was in the country with Henrietta, she was very depressed," I begin. "I thought she would never recover. I tried to distract her and ease her pain in every way I could think of. Nothing worked. I felt so helpless that I finally decided to comfort her in a more personal, intimate way."

Laura is lying on her back, motionless, staring at me with unblinking eyes. Has she understood, or do I need to elaborate? I find the silence very uncomfortable, so I decide to kill it again.

"I made love with her, out of total desperation and sadness. I wasn't sure it would help her, but it did. The next day she seemed less sad. She said she felt she had been in touch with Sara. And she also told me that I had not been unfaithful to you."

As each word comes out of my mouth, I feel it is vicious and bad. I guess I have just ended my relationship with Laura. But even now, if I could go back a few minutes in time, I would not withhold the confession from her. I've done enough wrong in the past. I don't want to commit the additional, though comparatively pathetically minor, fault of being false.

I look at her, and there are tears in her eyes. My heart constricts.

Finally, she speaks: "I don't know you as well as I thought I did. I never thought you could do something like this. I don't know anyone else who could. You're noble and generous."

Does she mean I'm noble to have confessed, or is she being sarcastic?

She moves closer to me and rests her head on my chest. "I

love you so much," she says. "I'm glad you were able to help Henrietta."

For a moment I am surprised, but then I realize that it makes sense. Her response fits with her extraordinary, angelic personality. It's the side of her that's more human than any human I know, and therefore not quite human. I hold her delicately, respectfully, as though I'm holding a sacred object, or a saint. But then our awe becomes more sensual, our tenderness more violent: our behavior sinks into the more mundane pattern of making love.

Just as we finish, the phone rings. Laura answers it.

"Hello? . . . Oh hi, Henrietta," she says, looking at me significantly. "I'm fine, and you? . . . Was it nice in the country? . . . You must be exhausted after the drive. . . . Yes, he's right here." She hands me the phone.

"Hi. How are you feeling?" I ask Henrietta.

"Pretty good, actually. What about you, are you tired?"

"A bit."

"Oh well," she says, "I suddenly got this craving to paint, and I was wondering which model I felt like calling over, and it turned out to be you."

"I'm flattered, but are you sure? When you tried painting me at my mother's, you seemed totally uninspired."

"It had nothing to do with you. I just didn't feel like painting at the time. But now I'm dying to."

"I'd love to pose for you," I tell her, glad to hear that she has regained her taste for painting and eager to help in any way I can.

"Really?" she says. "Like even now?"

"You mean today?"

"If you could, I'd love it."

"Hang on a second." I cover the mouthpiece with my hand and say to Laura, "She wants me to pose for her, but I wanted to spend the evening with you. I don't know what to do."

"Go pose for her. She sounds like she's in pretty good spirits, so you should help her keep them up."

I take my hand off the mouthpiece. "How about in a couple of hours?"

"Thank you. Be hungry," Henrietta says, and hangs up.

She greets me at the door, wearing some sort of dressing gown or kimono. A goldish kimono.

In the middle of the room is set up the largest canvas I have ever seen her use. It is square, as tall as me. She says she will do a vertical, life-size portrait of me. She wants me to pose standing up.

I feel strange just standing there, stark naked, without even leaning against anything, without the slightest thread of satin to decorate me, to hide me, to pull one's attention away from my nakedness. Next to me, Henrietta has placed a stool, on which is a tray of canapés. There is also a glass of champagne and the inevitable marzipan, which today is in the shape of little pink elephants. She has an identical tray next to her easel.

She tells me I'm allowed to move my right arm and my jaw, to eat the food. I eat a pâté canapé, lick my fingers, and say, "I'm glad you feel like painting again," just to make conversation. "Are you now going to concentrate more on your serious art than on your commercial art?"

"Don't talk," she says. "Let's just appreciate the food and the sensual pleasure of creation."

So we pose and paint and eat in silence for a few minutes.

Then she starts talking. Light, pleasant, amusing, unmemorable, insignificant conversation. I feel good, even though I've been standing virtually motionless now for about half an hour. I feel I could stand here many more hours, as long as there's a steady supply of canapés, champagne, marzipan elephants, and unmemorable conversation.

She gets up once in a while, to change my position slightly. One inch to the right, feet closer together, one step back— Wait! I don't want to get too far from my stool of marzipan elephants and insignificant conversation. We'll bring the stool closer, she says. Yes, closer, I sigh, comforted, as I bite off the trunk of a little pink elephant.

She goes back to her seat but soon puts down her paintbrush again. "Your position is still not quite right," she says, and adds pitifully, "Sara would have known right away what was wrong."

I am moved by the sadness and truth of that statement. I want to wrap my arms around Henrietta, I want us to cry into each other's necks, the poor mother. But I don't dare leave my carefully frozen position, for fear of displeasing her.

She gets up to fix my stance again. She walks behind me, and I wait with curiosity to see what adjustment she will think of this time. For a moment I hear nothing. Then I feel two warm, soft bumps of flesh against my back. I could swear there's no kimono cloth between my back and those fleshy bumps, but maybe I'm wrong, though I doubt it, but maybe I am, but no, but maybe.

Henrietta could not possibly be trying to seduce me. One does not stand behind someone, with one's breasts pressed against their back, when one is trying to seduce them. She must be doing something else.

"What are you doing?" I ask casually. My voice is not betraying my eyes, which are open wide in surprise.

"Changing your position," she answers.

That's what I thought she must be doing. I am reassured and relieved. But the next instant I feel her whole naked body against my back. Definitely no kimono cloth in between.

"You're changing my position?" I ask, just to make sure I'm not misinterpreting what I'm feeling.

"In a sense," I hear her say softly.

"Would you care to elaborate?"

She kisses the back of my neck and then my shoulders. Her hands slink around my waist and move up toward my chest, not wanting to be too daring at first, I suppose. She slides her fingers through my hair, grabs a handful, pulls my head back and to the side, and kisses my lips. She can do that because she's tall.

"I meant verbally," I say, my voice sounding peculiar, because my head is cocked back so far and twisted so unnaturally. I am looking into her eyes at a strange angle.

"No words," she says, and kisses me again.

"I don't know if we should do this," I say, certain that I must look like a chicken with its neck broken.

"You have no choice," she says.

"Really?" And because of movies, I instinctively look down to see if she's holding a gun. I am puzzled that she's not.

"Then why do I have no choice?" I ask.

" 'Then'? Why do you say 'then'?"

"I mean 'then' as in, 'Since you're not pointing a gun at me, *then* why do I have no choice?' "

"That's not quite grammatical, I don't think."

"Neither is that."

"I know," she says.

"Well, mine made sense with my train of thought."

She kisses me.

I tell her, "I don't know if we should do this. As I was saying."

She does not repeat that I have no choice. She demonstrates it.

It was because I was not prepared. I was caught off guard and wanted to help a friend. Twice, it doesn't mean anything; it's not a pattern, not a mistress. Three times, it would mean something; it would be a pattern and a mistress. The question is, what am I going to do with this one? Am I going to tell it or not? Would it be overdoing it to tell it?

Yes. I've thought about it, and I think it would be overdoing it. I mean, what's the point? Laura said it was okay. She didn't specify "twice," but it was probably included.

I change my mind. I decide that it was probably not included.

"It's good, but maybe you shouldn't do it a third time," says Laura, after I tell her about the second time.

"That's what I was thinking," I say.

To my great surprise, Lady Henrietta calls me again a few days later. She wants me to pose for her again. This is a joke, I think to myself. She could at least be honest with me. At first I object, but she assures me she just wants to paint me and nothing else. I yield, because I still want to help her.

I go to her apartment. She paints me for about half an hour and tries to seduce me once more. Well, I don't give in this time, because three times, it's a mistress. I leave her apartment.

I don't hear from her until a few days later, when she calls me again, asking me to pose for her. I cannot believe my ears. "No," I say, "no."

"I swear to God I won't try anything," she says. "I just want to finish the painting. I just need you to pose once more. If I try anything, you can just leave. I mean, I can't *rape* you."

I'm not so sure. I heard that women can, somehow, rape men. But I agree. I go and pose for her. She does not try anything. She paints. And then she says she's finished and tells me I can see the painting.

I look at it, and a hurricane of chills courses through my body. I have felt this way only one other time in my life, that time long ago when I made my first wish on the little white elephant and found the coin.

The painting I am staring at is of me and Sara, combined in one person. Our "being" is naked but has no sexual organ; just smooth flesh, like a doll. I cannot determine whether the face is mostly mine with Sara's soul shining through, or the other way around. The hair is unspecific, blurry. Henrietta was able to capture Sara's innocence and mischievousness and combine it with my dullness, insecurity, and frailty. The effect is so subtle and seamless that I cannot help but question my own sanity. Could I be hallucinating? Could I be imagining a resemblance to both of us when in fact it is just me, or just Sara? I look away, close my eyes, and look back. The resemblance to us both strikes me more forcefully than before. I cannot take my eyes off this creature, ourself, which, despite its mischievous air, looks sad. Our past is contained in its expression; it knows everything. I am suddenly reminded of the monstrous, diabolical painting in *The Picture of Dorian Gray*. This seems as supernatural, though perhaps not as malefic or demonic. It is the most superb optical illusion Henrietta has ever created. Unquestionably a masterpiece. But one that I hate. The portrait frightens me, as does its creator. I cannot help but feel that Henrietta is trying to control me, trying to cast a hypnotic, imprisoning spell over me through her painting. I am deeply disturbed and feel faint. I must leave her apartment immediately, or rather escape, before all trace of willpower is drained from me.

"Goodbye, Lady Henrietta." I haven't called her by her full fake name in a long time. I am shaking and my hearing is numb as I walk to the elevator, so I barely hear all the things I suppose she must be saying. "Goodbye. Goodbye," I say a few times more, not very loud, not looking at her, mostly to myself.

I think I should not see Lady Henrietta for a long while. She's insane, and I guess she has become obsessed with me, so it would do her good not to see me for a while. Therefore, I am going to France with Laura. We are going to spend two weeks with some of her friends, on their boat in the Mediterranean.

My mother has agreed to cat-sit Minou while I'm gone. As I'm packing her in her box, Minou says: Did you tell your mother to give me heavy cream at least once a day?

I never agreed to that. Three times a week at the most, I answer.

Stingy. Well, did you tell her?

Three times a week; yes.

And did you tell her that I don't like baths? Last time, she gave me a bath simply to amuse herself.

I'll tell her.

And also that I'm not particularly interested in meeting other cats. If she knows one who is dying to meet me, then I don't mind sitting with him or her for ten minutes, but she must not arrange a second visit without my approval.

How will you give her your approval?

If I like the cat, I'll touch him or her at some point during the initial visit.

I suddenly stop what I'm doing, perplexed. My cat is talking to me. I stare at her, in search of that wonderful dumb look she has given me these past few months, but it's not there. She's overflowing with intelligence and knowing. I try not to wonder what this signifies about my life.

Okay, I'll tell her, I answer.

On the friends' boat, Laura and I share a cabin. When we unpack our bags, I carefully remove the Mickey Mouse mask that I brought along as a souvenir of Sara. I nail it to the wall.

The first two days of the trip are predictably pleasant and relaxing. On the third day, I receive a disagreeable shock. I'm alone in our cabin, dressing for dinner, when I put my hand in the pocket of my jacket and find a photograph of Henrietta's latest painting of me, the one that horrified me so much. I also find a long blond hair, which I almost don't notice. Henrietta must have slipped these things in my pocket the last time I saw her, doubtless in a feeble, pathetic attempt to trouble me. And it works. I am troubled and frightened. A photo and a hair. Makes me think of black magic, voodoo. But I won't let myself stay upset. When I leave this cabin in five minutes to go to dinner, I will be fine. I put the photo and the hair in a drawer.

As I should have expected, I am not fine a moment later. Nor hours later. In fact, I become haunted, not by the photograph, as one would think, but by the hair. I start having nightmares every night about long blond hair. I dream of Rumpelstiltskin, and my having to weave hair into straw and then into gold; I dream of the Scarecrow in the Wizard of Oz, made of hair instead of straw; I dream of Rapunzel; and I dream of quicksand, of slowly, inexorably sinking in a lake of soft, warm, silky, fatal yellow hair, and suffocating.

People clap at her overseas. In Corsica. In Sardinia. In fancy restaurants. They've heard about that funny, quirky, intriguing, amusing little New York *thing*, these rich Europeans—that little New York whim, that little New York indulgence, of clapping at almost nothing, of clapping at almost no one, at a nobody whom one simply . . . claps at. The few who haven't traveled and seen it themselves have at least heard about it, seen her photograph in magazines and newspapers, seen her on TV. And so they clap, to contribute to the movement, to propagate the trend all over the world. Every little clap counts.

Apart from those very good reasons for clapping at Laura, there is the far more important, far more significant, intrinsic reason, which is that to not clap, or, worse yet, to not recognize her, or, worse yet, to ask people why they are clapping, is, as always, deadly. Therefore, cultured people, rich people, and socialites secretly study her photograph and memorize her face in the privacy of their homes, to prevent a disaster from occurring. Or so the media say.

Laura tells me she has a fantasy of running through a crowd of people who are clapping at her. Their clapter would be like wind in her hair. The crowd would part for her like the sea parting for that guy in the Bible, but only slightly; the crowd would still be close to her, lightly touching her as she runs through it. She would run as fast and as powerfully as possible, until she would enter her audience in a deep, advanced, and "beyondish" way.

"Beyondish as in 'beyond,'" Laura explains to me, "as in 'another dimension.'"

One day the media upset her. She comes running to me. She has just spoken to a friend of hers in New York, who has told her she's made the front page of the *National Enquirer*. The headline goes: "Laura's show will go on, even in death." And the article says: "Laura has stated in her will that when she dies she wants her entire fortune to be spent on having someone stand at her grave at all times and clap forever, or until her money runs out. Shifts are allowed."

"I am outraged!" Laura fumes. "How egomaniacal do they think I am? They're mocking me."

Laura starts having strange dreams. In the morning she calls down to me from her top bunk:

"Jeremy?"

"Yes."

"I dreamed that I started loving my audience too much and wanted to make love to them. In the street, when they clapped at me, I took off my clothes and wanted to make love to the world. Then I got arrested."

"Really?" I tell her. "I dreamed of Rumpelstiltskin." We dream about what's on our minds.

* * *

Another morning she calls down:

"Jeremy?"

"Yes."

"I had a terrible nightmare that people couldn't talk to me anymore. No one. All they were able to say to me was 'Clap clap clap clap.' Even you."

"Really?" I tell her. "I dreamed of the Scarecrow."

"Jeremy?"

"Yes."

"I had a terrible nightmare that people's hands were like mouths that were snapping open and shut. They wanted to devour me, all those hand-mouths, like a thousand piranhas. Like: clap clap clap, yum yum yum."

"Really?" I tell her. "I dreamed of Rapunzel."

"Jeremy?"

"Yes."

"I had the worst nightmare that people started clapping me. They clapped me."

"You mean they clapped at you?"

"No. They clapped *me*. They clapped *on* me. They *slapped* me."

"Oh."

"Yes. Beating me. And then killing me. They clapped me to death."

"Hmm. I dreamed that I was sinking in a lake of hair."

[279]

* * *

"Jeremy?"

"Yes."

"I dreamed that I shot the clappers. Not all of them, but many. And no one arrested me, and it made sense. I mean, could you imagine them arresting me for shooting the clappers?"

"Yes. Why can't *you*?"

"Because in a sense, you know, Jeremy, I own the clappers and can therefore do whatever I want with them. They give themselves to me. Clapping is a gift of their entire being. Do you realize that everyone, anyone, would willingly have me over for dinner at any time?"

"Hmm." She doesn't realize that all my dreams have hair in common.

One day I look at myself in the mirror and I am paralyzed with horror. I am virtually certain that I see a dreadful change in my face. I look more like the creature in the painting than I used to. I look more like Sara. I rush to the drawer in our cabin and take out the photograph. I compare my face in the mirror to the face of the creature. There is less of a difference than there used to be, I'm sure of it.

No, I must be imagining it. I must be going a little insane, that's all. It's temporary. Tomorrow my mind will be back to normal, and so will my face.

The following day, my face is not back to normal; it may even be a bit worse: I look younger, prettier, more feminine. Shitness. At breakfast I examine everyone to see if they notice a change in my face. No one seems to.

Later that day, Laura pulls me aside and says, "Jeremy, I've been thinking about something."

Here it comes; she'll make a polite, discreet inquiry concerning the change in my face.

But she doesn't. She says, "I think I'd like to modify my will."

"In what way?"

"Well, I decided that finally it *would* be a good idea to have someone stand at my grave and clap forever or until my money runs out. Shifts allowed."

"Why?"

"I should have thought of it myself: It would make me feel better. When I'm dead I probably won't care, but *now* it makes me feel better to think that there will always be someone standing there clapping at me. I want to state that in my will. I won't feel well until I do. I must do it now."

"I think you can wait until we get back to New York."

"But what if something happens to me before then?"

"It's highly unlikely."

The following morning, my face is changed even more. I can bear it no longer. In the galley, I pull Laura aside, show her the photo of Henrietta's painting, and ask if she doesn't think it looks mighty much like me.

"It's a painting of Sara," she says. "How could it look like you?"

"First of all, it is not a painting of Sara, because *I* posed for it. It is a painting of me *and* Sara. But don't you think it looks a lot like me right now? Look at my face." I hold the photo next to my cheek.

Laura looks at my face and at the photo. "No. It looks like

Sara," she says. And her eyes remain fixed on mine awhile. I'm sure she's lying.

I cut myself a piece of cake, put it on a plate, grab a fork, and go to our cabin to eat it and think about my problem. I sit on my bed and slowly, thoughtfully, eat the cake. I look at the Mickey Mouse mask nailed to the wall, but it doesn't inspire me with any helpful thoughts. It looks demonic. Suddenly, I am reminded of something. I will do what Dorian Gray did to his demonic painting, and if I die in the process, as he did, so be it. I place a pillow on my lap, put the photograph on the pillow, grab my cake fork, and stab the creature in the chest. The fork prongs pierce the photo, but I don't feel any stabbing pain in my chest, which is just as well. However, the spell might be broken now and my face be back to normal. I go to the bathroom and look in the mirror. I'm not back to normal.

I leave the cabin in search of our host. When I find him, I show him the photo of Henrietta's painting and ask, "Don't you think this painting looks exactly like me?"

He looks at me with surprise and then smiles. But I am not smiling at him. I am looking at him earnestly, so he sobers up and says, good-naturedly, "She's a pretty young girl. Is she a relative of yours? Paintings can be deceiving. I don't see much resemblance here, but in real life you two probably look more alike. It's a shame the picture has this strange injury," he says, sliding his finger over the fork holes.

Perhaps he's telling the truth. Perhaps I'm making it up, the resemblance.

But at dinner they are definitely looking at me strangely, Laura and the host. They are having trouble hiding their shock at the metamorphosis in my face. I catch them gazing at me, and as soon as I look at them, they avert their eyes politely. I'm nervous. I'm panicked.

The next morning there is no longer any difference between my face in the mirror and the face in the photo. I look fifty percent like Sara. My mouth has shrunk, and my lips have become smooth and delicate, like rose petals. My nose is finer, my eyes are more clearly defined, and all my wrinkles are gone. My stubble is gone. I don't need to shave. I have no more facial hair; no more beard.

Now Sara is in me. Henrietta has imprisoned me. I have become her creature, her creation, her child. There is no escape, and I don't want an escape anymore because I feel I am suddenly so vulnerable in the real world that I can function only in her warped reality. I must decide what to do. I need time.

In any case, I can no longer go out in public looking this way. I can't even let Laura see me. So I unhook the Mickey Mouse mask from our cabin wall and put it on my face. At first it fits comfortably, but after a while I feel hot and humid. That's a small sacrifice, to conceal the black magic going on underneath the mask.

I wear the Mickey Mouse mask: at breakfast, at lunch, at dinner, and in between, because it's only strange, whereas the transformation in my face is supernatural, worse than strange.

When I eat, I lift the mask up slightly, just enough to uncover my mouth, so I can put food in it. I lower the mask when I chew.

How do people react to the mask? They are amazed, amused, annoyed, impatient, condescending, contemptuous, and finally indifferent, all of which is normal, healthy, fine with me, and much better than the covert glances I was getting yesterday when they could see the change in my face as plain as day.

Under the mask, I think about what I should do. After much thinking, certain things become clear. For instance, I'm responsible for Sara's death. If I hadn't entered her life, she would probably still be alive. She would not have crossed the street at the particular instant when that yellow car was there to hit her. Now I owe Henrietta my life. We are bound to each other by our unhappiness. I won't feel at peace until I do the right thing. I belong with her, I belong *to* her; I must return.

And when I return I will tell her the truth about Sara, about her fifty percent chance of recovery. I realize I will be contemptible not to spare her the agony of knowing how tragic Sara's accident really was, but I can no longer bear the pain all by myself. If we are to have a close relationship, we should both know the truth. I will then comfort her and stay with her always.

I must get rid of Laura so that I am free to go back to Henrietta. I try to think of how to accomplish this. Behind the mask, I am plotting. I finally make my decision. I will drown her.

I will do it now, right now. It's a nice afternoon. I will take her for a walk—we're in port today—and I will drown her. I ask her if she'd like to go for a walk; she acts delighted. Before we leave, I hand her a pen and a piece of paper.

"Take these," I say, "and write your will the way you want it: the clapper at your grave forever, if that's still what you want." Because after all, I think she should be allowed to write her will before she drowns. It's just common courtesy.

She looks at me with surprise and says, "Why now?"

"Because it has to be written and signed by you. I don't think they'd believe me if I just told them, without your signature."

"But why *now?*"

"Because you were right. It's best not to wait," I tell her through the mask. "You'll feel more at peace if you get it off your chest. You'll be more relaxed, our promenade will be more carefree."

So she writes whatever she wants on the piece of paper and hands it to me. It says: "I want my fortune to be spent on everything that was written in the *National Enquirer:* clapper at my grave forever or until money runs out, shifts allowed, etc." Her signature is at the bottom.

I fold the paper, tuck it in my pocket, and we go on our walk. I must find a place to drown her. A place with lots of people. Some sort of event. An event that attracts large crowds. A concert would be perfect.

Eventually we come upon an outdoor circus. That will do. It's very crowded. The people are standing, watching, and clapping at the show. I bring Laura to the edge of the clapping crowd, and I watch her sink, becoming engulfed in the sea of clapter. She looks at me with confusion, but the people soon close in on her. She tries to hang on to me, to my clothes, but I don't help her. The crowd is clapping at the circus, not at her. She sinks into a sea of anonymous clapter. She is submerged in someone else's success. I gaze at her through the eyes of the Mickey Mouse mask, and I am comforted that she cannot see the blank expression on my face as I watch her sink.

On the way back to New York, I feel much better and saner. My mind is cleared.

I know I'm going to have to face people when I get back. I dread having to face them. They will still clap at Laura. They will clap at her death. They will ask me, "How did she do that death trick? Is there any chance you might ever reveal how she did that death trick? How subtle. Ah! The naïveté of it, the deceptive simplicity of it! The vocabulary is rich, and the language, my goodness, the language is sublime. She is a genius, her choice of tricks is superb, exquisite. I *love* the way she deaths! I mean, the way she dies."

When the plane lands, I go to Lady Henrietta's apartment. She is ecstatic to see me, as I knew she would be.

She says, "When you were away, I realized why it was so important for me to be with you. The memory of Sara can be preserved more vividly between us. I can't be with anyone else, or it would be like abandoning Sara. But between us, she will live."

I hug her.

"Where's Laura?" she asks.

"They loved her to death. She drowned in success." I avoid specifying that it wasn't her own success.

I tell Henrietta I want to take her out to dinner. She says she needs a minute to change and goes into her room.

While I wait, I spot on a low table by the couch a magazine with a totally black cover and a white title: *Suicide*. Under the title: "The Cheer-up Magazine for Every Man or Woman Who's Ever Thought of Committing It."

I open the magazine and read an advertisement at random:

Do you come out of Disneyland feeling depressed?
Wanting to jump off the roller coaster?
Or to kick the giant mouse in the balls?
Having trouble enjoying even the simplest pleasures in life?
You need to put your life in perspective. We can do it for you. Come visit us at DEATHLAND, where we offer high-quality suffering. Your petty problems will evaporate in seconds. Your bigger problems will disappear in hours. The death of a loved one will be forgotten in a day.

(We guarantee that our simulations are as effective as the real thing, or your money back!)

To receive your free brochure and sample meal kit, simply call:

   1–800–570–HELL

CALL NOW! WE'LL PUT YOUR LIFE IN PERSPECTIVE

The world isn't as I thought it was.

As I keep waiting for Henrietta to get ready, I absentmindedly glance around the room, and I am astonished to see in a corner, next to the hateful painting of me and Sara, a large painting of Tommy, nude.

When Henrietta comes back out and sees me staring at the painting, she says, "Oh, yes. Tommy got in touch with me through your mother, because he was so upset to have been the indirect cause of Sara's death. He wanted to talk to me and offer help if I needed it."

"Why did you paint him?" I ask.

She takes the suicide magazine from my hands, flips through it, and says, "Because I read an article in here that said that to get over a tragedy, it can be helpful to make a picture of the person who is responsible and then tear it up, or cross it out, or burn it, or stab it, or harm it somehow. I wanted to try, so Tommy agreed to pose for me." She hands me the magazine, opened to a page with an article entitled: "A Healthy Mixture of Voodoo and Art Therapy Will Kill Those Suicide Blues."

I look at the painting of Tommy. It is not damaged in any way, but there *is* a big kitchen knife lying next to it on the floor.

"When are you going to damage it?" I ask.

"I don't know. I've lost interest. It now seems pointless and trite. I doubt it would make me feel better, especially since there was no hope of Sara recovering from her illness. She was going to die anyway, so the car accident didn't make much difference, did it?"

I pick up the knife and hesitate a moment before placing it in her hand. I close her fingers over the handle.

"There was hope."

FOR THE BEST IN PAPERBACKS, LOOK FOR THE

In every corner of the world, on every subject under the sun, Penguin represents quality and variety—the very best in publishing today.

For complete information about books available from Penguin—including Pelicans, Puffins, Peregrines, and Penguin Classics—and how to order them, write to us at the appropriate address below. Please note that for copyright reasons the selection of books varies from country to country.

In the United Kingdom: For a complete list of books available from Penguin in the U.K., please write to *Dept E.P., Penguin Books Ltd, Harmondsworth, Middlesex, UB7 0DA*.

In the United States: For a complete list of books available from Penguin in the U.S., please write to *Consumer Sales, Penguin USA, P.O. Box 999— Dept. 17109, Bergenfield, New Jersey 07621-0120*. Visa and MasterCard holders call 1-800-253-6476 to order all Penguin titles.

In Canada: For a complete list of books available from Penguin in Canada, please write to *Penguin Books Canada Ltd, 10 Alcorn Avenue, Suite 300, Toronto, Ontario, Canada M4V 3B2*.

In Australia: For a complete list of books available from Penguin in Australia, please write to the *Marketing Department, Penguin Books Ltd, P.O. Box 257, Ringwood, Victoria 3134*.

In New Zealand: For a complete list of books available from Penguin in New Zealand, please write to the *Marketing Department, Penguin Books (NZ) Ltd, Private Bag, Takapuna, Auckland 9*.

In India: For a complete list of books available from Penguin, please write to *Penguin Overseas Ltd, 706 Eros Apartments, 56 Nehru Place, New Delhi, 110019*.

In Holland: For a complete list of books available from Penguin in Holland, please write to *Penguin Books Nederland B.V., Postbus 195, NL-1380AD Weesp, Netherlands*.

In Germany: For a complete list of books available from Penguin, please write to *Penguin Books Ltd, Friedrichstrasse 10-12, D-6000 Frankfurt Main I, Federal Republic of Germany*.

In Spain: For a complete list of books available from Penguin in Spain, please write to *Longman, Penguin España, Calle San Nicolas 15, E-28013 Madrid, Spain*.

In Japan: For a complete list of books available from Penguin in Japan, please write to *Longman Penguin Japan Co Ltd, Yamaguchi Building, 2-12-9 Kanda Jimbocho, Chiyoda-Ku, Tokyo 101, Japan*.